Book 2 in the Amber Ridge Series

unraveled

NYSSA KATHRYN

❀ Created with Vellum

He's her neighbor...her enemy...so why has she told everyone he's her boyfriend?

Sky Williams has a neighbor from hell. Every day, Becket finds a new way to torture her. Sometimes it involves cutting trees on her property line; other days—most days—it includes using an annoying nickname he knows she hates. It's safe to say she can't stand the guy. So why then, when her parents persistently try to set her up with one of their church friends, does she find herself blurting out that she's dating Becket?

Retired Navy SEAL Becket Hayes has a great life. His family is amazing, he's the fire chief of Amber Ridge—a job he loves. And more recently, he's found unexpected joy in fighting with his cute but easily riled neighbor. She seems to take offense at his very existence. So when she publicly declares Becket her boyfriend, he's intrigued enough to play along. It's just meant to be for show, but the longer they "date", the less fake it feels.

When a string of seemingly unconnected incidents occur, putting Sky's life in danger, Becket suddenly has even more reason to remain close. It appears there are parts of her past that refuse to be left behind. And someone determined to ensure Sky has no future—with or without Becket.

ACKNOWLEDGMENTS

To my incredible team—thank you. Kelli, you are my book doctor and fill all my plot holes. Jessica, you make sure my story sounds professional. And Amanda and Jen, thank you for taking out those pesky errors. A special thank you also to my amazing cover designers at Deranged Doctor Designs and the cover photographer Sarah Hall—this cover is everything.

Thank you to my beautiful ARC team for reading, reviewing and filling me with confidence before I send my book baby into the world.

And thank you to my beautiful husband and two amazing daughters—every day I am reminded of how lucky I am to have you.

CHAPTER 1

Something wasn't right. What? The playlist? Were the songs too slow?

Sky Williams leaned her hip against her dining room table, studying the printed plans in front of her.

No. That wasn't it. It was a fundraiser ball. She'd chosen the perfect mid-tempo playlist to get people out on the dance floor.

Maybe it was the food. She didn't have enough variety. Too much sweet and not enough savory.

No. That wasn't it either. She had at least a dozen savory options and half a dozen sweet. That was plenty.

So, what was it?

Argh. Maybe it was nothing. Maybe she was just overthinking the entire dang thing and the fundraiser would be a perfect success, just like every other fundraiser she'd organized.

Ha. The last fundraiser had been a trivia night, and Rosemary Symes and Ivory Hanks had gotten into an argument about whose dog was better behaved. Then Mr. Bruno, who'd had one too many drinks, had jumped in and claimed it didn't matter whose dog was better behaved, because they both looked like monkeys' asses.

Now, if it had been her, she would have laughed the ridiculous, drunken joke away, but Rosemary and Ivory were very sensitive about their dogs, and Ivory had ended up throwing her drink into Mr. Bruno's face.

Her phone rang and Sky picked it up, already knowing who it was without even looking at the screen. "Ivory's going to throw her drink on Mr. Bruno again."

Her mother chuckled. "No one's throwing a drink on anyone, Skylar."

"You can't guarantee that." She pursed her lips, still studying the millions of pieces of paper scattered over the table. Plans and receipts. Ideas scribbled on sticky notes. "Something's wrong with the fundraiser."

"What's wrong?"

"I don't know. I'm looking at the plans and I can't figure it out."

"Then how do you know something's wrong?"

"It's just…a feeling." Not the most scientific method to know a problem existed, but she was right.

"Honey, you're overthinking this. Despite some oversensitive dog owners, your last fundraiser was a success, and this one will be, too."

Sky nibbled her bottom lip. The last one *had* been a success. They'd raised a ton of money for the dog charity, and she was hoping they'd raise a lot for this one too.

"Are we still handing out fliers on Wednesday?" her mother asked.

"They're printed and ready to go. Thank you for helping."

"Of course. Anything to spend time with my only daughter. Now, I called to talk to you about Tony."

The groan tried to slip from her throat, but she swallowed it.

Her mother may want to talk about Tony, but *she* did not. She'd known Tony since they were kids, and the day his family moved away she'd been happy, because even as a ten-year-old, she'd found him annoying. And smelly. How a kid could maintain their stink into adulthood, she wasn't sure, but he had. A disgusting onion odor that could be detected a mile away.

She'd actually nicknamed him Stinky Tony. Well, not to his face. But in her head, it was basically his legal name.

"He's still staying with your father and me."

"I know that, Mother. You told me he'll be with you for a couple of months the other night, when you showed up with him at Indigo."

Not only had her parents shown up with him, they'd then left the table to "get a drink from the bar" and hadn't returned for *thirty minutes*. It was the most obvious date setup she'd ever endured.

She was thirty-two dang years old and her *parents* had set her up on a date.

"Well." Her mother cleared her throat. "We were actually talking this morning, and he mentioned that he'd love to have another meal with you."

"No." The word was out before her mother had finished speaking, and probably with a tad too much aggression, but no way was she sitting through another meal with Stinky Tony, trying not to gag while being bored to death with his insurance talk.

"No?" her mother asked, for some reason sounding shocked.

"I'm not interested in him."

"Oh, Skylar, why not? He's lovely."

Lovely? Every time he spoke, she wanted to take her fork and drive it into her skull. He'd gone on and on about insurance policies and how his company could get her the deal of her life. "You only think he's lovely because his family used to be members of your church."

Her parents were big churchgoers, and her father in particular liked to harp on about how she needed to marry someone from the church with good values and ethics...blah, blah, blah.

Like he thought anyone who didn't attend the church couldn't have good values. Which would include her, then.

"That's not true," her mother argued. "I like him because he has a good head on his shoulders, he has a successful insurance business, and he's funny."

"Name one funny thing he's said."

"Well…I can't off the top of my head."

She moved to the window, watching the clouds race over the gray sky. "He's been living with you for a week, Mom. If he's funny, something should spring to mind."

"Really, Skylar, I don't know why you're being like this. When I was your age—"

"You were married to Dad and already had me. I know. You've told me." About fifty *gazillion* times.

"Well, it's true. And your father and I just want you to have a man who can…"

Sky's back straightened and she didn't hear whatever her mother said next, because her entire focus turned to her neighbor, who was walking across his lawn. Her very annoying, obnoxious and rude neighbor. In fact, she was pretty sure he stayed up at night plotting new ways to torture her. A month ago, it was blocking her fence from going up because of a city ordinance technicality. And before that, it was installing external cameras that filmed her front yard, as well as his own.

And right now, he was holding a chainsaw and wearing earmuffs.

No…he couldn't be walking toward the tree. *Her* tree, which he'd already cut without her permission earlier that year.

"Mom, I've got to go."

"But—"

"I'll call you later." She hung up and ran toward the front door. She wasn't wearing shoes or a sweater, but there was no time. Her psychotic neighbor could probably have her entire tree down before she could blink.

She sprinted across her front lawn, the cool chill of the morning slapping her in the face. She reached the tree seconds before he did and planted herself in front of it. "Don't even think about it."

The words didn't have quite the impact she'd intended, mostly because she was winded. Man, she really needed to start working out.

A corner of his full lips lifted and he pulled off the earmuffs. "Hey, Peaches. You look angry. Did you ever take up that meditation I suggested? It could do you wonders."

"For the fiftieth damn time, my name is *Sky*. And I don't need meditation. I need you to move away. Far, far away. And not just from my tree."

The other side of his mouth lifted now, like he enjoyed her anger. "Ah, but then we'd lose sweet moments like this."

"Sweet?"

"Wrong word? What about fun? Joyful. No, I know—exciting."

"I'd agree with you, but then we'd both be delusional."

He chuckled and lowered the chainsaw, the muscles in his bronzed arms flexing.

Do not look, Sky. The man might be pretty on the outside, but he's the devil incarnate on the inside.

"Your tree's blocking my street view. It's a safety thing."

A safety thing? For him or her? "It's my tree and I say it stays how it is."

He looked at his watch. "Look, Peaches, I have to head to work in an hour, so if we can speed this along, that would be great."

"Speed *what* along?"

"You call me all the unladylike names in your vocabulary, I stand here, unaffected and charming. You go back inside, and I give this tree a little trim."

Her jaw dropped. She was going to murder him. There was going to be a warrant out for her arrest because he'd be dead.

"First of all, you are about as charming as a frog. Second, the last time you gave my tree *a little trim*, you butchered it. Key word, *my* tree."

"Come on. It's hanging over my property. If it means so much to you, I'll save you the branches."

"You put a stick in my hand, and you'll know what it feels like to be a piñata."

He threw his head back and laughed.

That wasn't meant to be funny. It was an accurate account of what would happen if he so much as touched her tree. Okay, maybe hitting this man with a stick wasn't the smartest idea. He was a million feet tall, and word around town was that he was a former Navy SEAL. But anger could do crazy things to a woman, including give her superstrength.

"Look," he said, finally sobering. "Let's make a deal. I trim the tree, and you stand right there and supervise. If I get too excited, I give you permission to pick up a stick and hit me with it."

"How about we make a different deal? We wait until my fence permit arrives and you can trim any limbs hanging over it."

"That's not gonna happen."

"Yeah, because you know the tree's not on your property."

"No. The fence isn't happening."

Her eyes narrowed. She'd already bought the fence but had made a silly mistake and applied for the wrong permit, something her *kind* neighbor here had been all too quick to point out.

"There's nothing you can do," she said, straightening. "The application's in and once it's approved, the fence is going up."

"Why are you so fixated on me not seeing your front yard? Got something to hide?"

"No. Got something to block…*you*."

The corners of his eyes creased. "Do you know, this lovely old lady, Mrs. Ferrington, lived in that house before you. She used to bake me cobbler and get my mail when I was away. I wonder what happened to her?"

"She probably got the hell away from you so she could live her last few years in peace."

"I miss her."

Sky slammed her fists onto her hips. "Go away and take your chainsaw with you."

"Just as soon as I've trimmed this tree."

God. He was *infuriating.* "If you don't go back into your house right now, I'm going to…" *Shit.* What was she going to do?

He lifted a brow. "Call the sheriff's office? You could, but I'm not sure having my brother drive out here worked so well for you last time. Or you could try my sister, but she'll just tell you I'm as stubborn as I look and you should let me trim the tree."

It was actually unbelievable that the egotistical jackass had a brother who was the town sheriff. You'd think if God was going to make her live next door to Becket Hayes, he'd at least give her a town sheriff who hated him as much as she did.

She folded her arms. "I'm not moving. You'll have to physically remove me to get to the tree."

"Honey, if that's your way of asking me to touch you—"

"Oh my God, I keep thinking I'm dealing with an adult, and then you speak."

He laughed. He actually laughed at her.

She was plotting ways to murder him when his phone rang.

He glanced at his cell. "You're lucky. Duty calls. Should we pick this back up tomorrow? Noon, maybe?"

He was a firefighter—fire chief, actually. And she absolutely would not be admitting how sexy he looked every time he stepped outside his house in uniform.

"You go anywhere near my tree and I'll murder you in your sleep," she said.

That damn smile widened. Then he leaned closer, the black specks shining in his brown eyes. "A visit from you in my bed late at night? Doesn't sound so bad."

CHAPTER 2

*B*ecket Hayes stared at the screen in front of him. One of the guys had called in sick, so he'd come in early to call in a replacement. Fortunately, Becket loved his job. Hell, he lived and breathed his position as fire chief.

And the call couldn't have come at a better time. He'd needed an escape from his fiery neighbor, with her cute hazel eyes and button nose. At some point, arguing with her had become a highlight of his week. The insults she threw his way never failed to make him smile.

Not that that was why he'd gone out there. That tree *did* need a trim. It blocked his external cameras from catching some of their street. And that was a problem.

He didn't just have the cameras because the former SEAL in him took safety seriously. There'd been a string of break-ins here in Amber Ridge in the last few months. Three, to be exact. Something his brother had told him even before it was reported in the local news.

Whoever the perp was, they were good at picking locks, taking everything they could find that was worth anything, then getting out without leaving a trace.

Jesse had put more deputies on patrol, but for Becket, that wasn't enough.

So, yeah, he wanted a good view of his street, and if his pretty neighbor wasn't happy that those cameras covered her front yard, well…that was too damn bad.

He rose from his chair and moved out into the long hall. He passed the training room, the bathrooms and dorms, and a couple more offices. At the end of the hall was the gym, but he turned left into the kitchen and dining area.

Teddy and Moose sat at the table. Teddy was one of the younger firefighters, while Moose, an older African American, was probably their longest-serving firefighter at the station.

"I'm not kidding, she was *hot*."

Moose frowned at Teddy. "A woman you met in a retirement village parking lot while you were visiting your grandmother was hot?"

"Why do you ask like that?" Teddy looked up at Becket. "Beck, back me up here, man. Women who visit grandparents at nursing homes *can* be hot, right?"

Becket stopped at the coffee machine. "I can confirm, women with grandmothers can be hot."

But why the hell, when he thought of hot women, did Sky come to mind?

Because her curves had looked damn good in those tight jeans this morning? Because her ample chest had pushed against the thin material of her white shirt?

Fuck, he needed to get her out of his head.

"See." Teddy shoved Moose in the shoulder.

"Shove me again, kid, and you'll be going on that date with a limp."

Becket smirked. The two of them fought a lot. But to be fair, Teddy could be a cocky ass. He'd only joined their station a couple months ago, and yeah, he was good, but he also knew it.

Teddy scoffed before looking at Becket. "Hey, did you replace Mac?"

"Yeah, Irene's here." Irene was another older firefighter at the station, and his second in charge.

Moose shook his head. "Too many kids calling in sick. Back when I started, we'd pull double shifts and still get on with our business."

"Not sure that's good either," Teddy said, lifting his coffee. "You need sleep in this line of work."

Moose straightened. "Hey, when I was young, I didn't need much sleep to survive."

It was true. How many nights had Becket gone without sleep when he was a SEAL? Too fucking many.

"Beck, how's your brother and his woman?" Teddy asked.

Becket's fingers tightened around the mug. Jesse's partner, Aspen, had been kidnapped, and just when he'd gotten her back and thought she was safe, she'd been put in danger a second time by someone no one had ever suspected.

Just like Becket, Jesse was former special operations, but when someone you loved was in danger, that training didn't take away the fear.

"They're both just trying to move on." Jesse had taken a month off work and had only just gone back. It had taken him a long time to feel safe enough to leave Aspen.

Moose shook his head. "There are some real sickos around these days."

"There've always been sickos around," Becket said quietly. He'd run into his fair share during his time in the military.

The move from SEAL to firefighter had been a pretty easy one. He was still putting his life on the line to help others. A common misconception was that firefighters only fought fires—they didn't. They performed rescues and attended medical calls. They had to be prepared for incidents like vehicle extractions and the release of hazardous materials.

The job was full-on, which was why training was hard and not everyone made it.

Suddenly, the alarm rang through the station, then the radios sounded.

"Station 8, there's a vegetation fire on some land at five-thirteen Maple Terrace, Amber Ridge," the dispatcher said.

Becket cursed and took one last sip of coffee before tipping the rest down the drain.

Moose and Teddy were already on their feet, and they all ran to the apparatus bay. Footsteps sounded around him as other firefighters moved to the engines. Everyone pulled on their jackets and helmets before Becket got into an engine cab with Irene, while Moose and Teddy climbed into the back.

He pressed his foot to the floor as Irene tapped the address into the GPS. The house was less than five minutes away. They'd make it there in three.

Irene turned to look at him. "What was that big-ass smile on your face when you got to work today?"

"Is it a crime to be happy?" he asked.

"No, but there's usually a reason behind it."

"Nope, just happy." It was a damn lie. Anytime he saw Sky in the morning, he couldn't wipe the damn smile from his face.

"Why do I not believe you?"

Because you're perceptive. "Would I lie to you?"

She scoffed. "Yes. You lied to me yesterday about eating my donut."

"That was Moose."

"Hey!" Moose jumped in. "Don't bring my name into this."

"It was Moose," Teddy confirmed. "I saw him."

Moose slapped Teddy in the back of the head.

"Ow." Teddy rubbed his scalp. "Beck's the one who said it."

Irene turned to look at the guys. "Everyone needs to stay away from my donuts."

Becket bit back a grin. Irene loved her donuts, but unfortunately for her, so did others at the station, and not everyone was above thievery.

He'd worked at the station for five years and been the chief for two. Moose and Irene had been there for a hell of a lot longer, so this donut shit wasn't new.

They pulled into a long dirt driveway and saw the fire, right in front of the house.

"Damn," Teddy said. "That's a big yard fire."

"And it's close to the house," Moose added.

It was. It was also getting dangerously close to the forest around it.

He stopped the engine and they all got out, the truck behind them doing the same.

Becket pulled out his radio. "Battalion 1428 on scene. We've got a one-fifty by one-fifty spot fire, moderate rate of spread, but growing closer to the forest. A single-structure home close by at threat."

His team pulled out the hoses as the door to the house opened and an older lady came out. She looked to be in her mid-sixties and held a dog in her arms. If the fire wasn't their focus, he might have stopped and questioned what the hell kind of dog it was. The thing was almost bald, with random bits of hair sticking out. Becket wasn't a dog person in general, but that one was damn ugly.

He crossed over to her. "Ma'am? My name's Becket Hayes. I'm the fire chief. Did you call this fire in?"

"Yes, I did. Oh my, it's gotten big."

"What's your name?"

"Rosemary Symes. And this is Bella. I made a little fire to burn off some of our old items, but it just grew out of control."

How the hell she had thought starting an uncontained fire on land surrounded by forest was a good idea, he had no idea. He'd talk to her later. "My team's taking care of it. Please stay back."

The woman nodded, and Becket returned to the crew.

Everyone worked in threes, with one person holding one end of the hose and another holding the body, then the third controlling the tap.

"Ready water," Moose called.

The water was turned on, and Becket watched as his team worked hard to put out the blaze.

When embers flew through the air, Becket cursed and pointed. "Spot fire." He rushed to grab another hose, flatten it out and connect it. Irene came behind him to hold the line, then he sprayed water onto the smaller spot fires.

It took them about twenty minutes, but finally, his crew put out the flames.

Damn, he loved his job. He loved the rush of adrenaline. The way his crew worked together as a team. And he loved knowing he was making a difference.

When he returned to Rosemary, she placed a hand over her chest. "Oh, thank you all so much!"

"You can't start another fire, Rosemary. Not here. If the wind had changed, the entire mountain could have gone up."

"I'm sorry. I haven't been living in this house for too long. I didn't realize."

It seemed more like common sense to him. "Now you do."

Half an hour later, they were packed up and back in the engine.

Becket leaned his head back as Irene drove.

"It feels good to help people, doesn't it?" Irene said, almost to herself.

"Hell yes, it does," Teddy confirmed from the back seat.

It was why Becket had become a firefighter after leaving the military. He wasn't built to sit behind a desk. He needed to be in the middle of the action. He needed the hit of adrenaline. The knowledge that he was saving people from the front line.

He felt Irene's eyes on him without even looking. He shot a glance her way. "What?"

"Just wondering if you're gonna tell us what had you in such a good mood this morning yet."

Jesus. She wasn't going to let it go. "I wanted to trim a tree outside my house."

"And..." Teddy pushed, when Becket didn't give any more.

"And...my neighbor had a problem with that."

"Why would she have a problem with you trimming a tree in your yard?" Moose asked suspiciously.

"*Her* yard. But it overhangs into mine."

Irene chuckled. "Okay. Now I'm getting it. You tried to chop her tree down, she said no, and you wouldn't let up because you're a pushy bastard."

"I prefer to think of myself as persistent," Becket corrected. "And why are you on her side?"

"Because she's right."

He grabbed his chest, feigning hurt. "Five years working together and this is the loyalty I get?"

Irene snorted. "Telling you when you're wrong *is* loyal. Now, you want my advice?"

"No."

"Leave her and her tree alone."

The corners of Becket's lips lifted, because unfortunately for Sky, that wouldn't be happening. Not until Jesse caught this thief and Becket knew they were both safe.

CHAPTER 3

"How's that beautiful neighbor of yours?"

Sky barely stifled a groan as she stopped at the front desk of her doggy daycare. She *did not* want to talk about Becket. So far, she hadn't seen him today. Which made it a good day.

"He's not beautiful." Okay, maybe he was a little bit beautiful, but that was completely offset whenever he opened his mouth. "He wanted to cut down my tree on Monday. I wouldn't be surprised if I got home today and all I had left was a stump."

She rifled through the filing cabinet a bit more aggressively.

Dolly, the older receptionist at the center, turned from the front desk. Her brows were raised and her big blond curls looked extra bright in contrast to her red-rimmed glasses. "What do you mean, he tried to cut down your tree?"

"He's unhinged. I think his time in the military destroyed his capacity for social interaction."

What the heck kind of person enjoyed filming other people's front yards and cutting down trees and telling her she couldn't have a boundary fence? The fence would go up though, and the day it did, she would smile at his misery.

"Doesn't make him less beautiful," Dolly sang.

Sky wrinkled her nose. But it wasn't just Dolly who liked to sing Becket's praises. Everyone in this small freaking town talked about their *sexy fire chief* like the sun shone out his ass. But those people didn't have to live next door to him.

She looked up from the filing cabinet. "Do you know where Garfield's file is? I need to double check his medication."

"Oh yes, I took it out this morning to add some notes. I think I left it in the office. One sec."

As Dolly moved into the office behind the desk, Sky's gaze ran over the large sign on the wall.

Sky's Doggy Daycare.

She still had to pinch herself that she'd opened this place. Back in Cheyenne, she'd owned a pet-friendly café. But this was different. This was exactly the kind of business she'd always dreamed of opening.

And it was doing well. Apparently, there was a big demand for a doggy daycare here in Amber Ridge. Some people used it while they worked. But a surprising number of elderly used it, as they put it, to socialize their dogs and help them make friends.

Worked for her.

She was just closing the drawer of the filing cabinet when the ding of the front door sounded.

She looked up to see their newest employee, Kristina. Well, new employee as of today, but they'd met before today at the interview. "Kristina. Hey. Sorry, is it eleven already? I'm afraid I lost track of time."

Kristina pushed a lock of short brown hair off her face. "That's okay. You must be busy."

"Yeah, busy thinking about a certain sexy firefighter," Dolly muttered, as she walked back into the room and handed over Garfield's file.

Sky gave the other woman a withering stare before looking

back to Kristina. "Come on. You can leave your bag in the staff room and I'll show you around."

Kristina put her bag into a storage cube, and they headed back through the foyer and then down the hall. "I know I've already given you a small tour, but I'll just show you around again to refresh your memory."

"That would be great. I'm afraid I have the memory of Dory."

"I love that movie." She paused at the first room. "To the left we have the bathroom. Then a couple of indoor playrooms—one for the big dogs and one for small."

"Do they use them often?" Kristina asked.

"Oh yeah, especially if it gets too cold outside or it's raining." She kept moving.

"Sounds smart."

"Are you still enjoying Amber Ridge?" The other woman had only moved here a few months ago. Apparently, she moved around a lot but was hoping to settle here.

"I'm loving it," Kristina said. "I thought it might feel too small for me, but it really doesn't."

"Really? There are days this town feels the size of a shoebox to me."

Kristina laughed, but Sky couldn't be more serious. Everyone knew everyone and that meant everyone knew everyone's business.

Sky stopped midway down the hall at the door leading outside. "Farther down the hall is a big wet area where we wash the dogs, and at the very end is the kitchen, which is filled with about ninety percent dog food and a couple of human muffins."

Kristina laughed. "I'll have to be careful I don't mistake dog food for human food."

"The cookies are particularly deceiving." She wrapped her fingers around the door handle. "Are you ready?"

"For what?"

Sky just grinned as she stepped outside.

Immediately, half a dozen dogs ran up to her. Some jumped up, some just licked her. She knelt and laughed as she patted them. Bella squeezed between the larger dogs and lay her head on Sky's lap. She gave her an extra-tight cuddle. Bella was here a lot, so they'd formed a special bond. Rosemary had even asked Sky to look after Bella overnight a couple of times.

More dogs licked her face, and her smile widened.

This was her form of therapy.

Kristina laughed as she crouched to pet them. "Oh my gosh, they're gorgeous."

"They really are. They all have their names on their collars, but most of them are regulars, so you'll get to know them pretty quickly."

They got everything here. Labrador Retrievers, German Shepherds, Border Collies. Even a few Boxers.

She was just rising when her walkie-talkie went off.

"Sky?"

She pulled it off her hip. "Yes, Dolly?"

"We just got a call asking if we could temporarily house a lost Dachshund puppy until the owners are found."

"What about the Humane Society?"

"They're dealing with an outbreak of kennel cough, and they can't take any new animals until it's under control."

Damn. "He's not microchipped?"

"Apparently not. Some owners just aren't responsible."

"Okay. Of course we'll house him." She pushed her walkie back onto her waistband as Pearl, a middle-aged woman who'd been with Sky since she opened, walked up to them.

"Pearl, this is Kristina. She's new. Do you mind if she shadows you today?"

"Not at all. Come...learn from the master."

Sky chuckled as she went back inside. She swore she never

smiled as much as she did while at work. It was her happy place. The business she'd built not just to service the community but for *her*.

She'd never thought she'd come back here. But her parents were getting older, and after everything that had happened in Cheyenne, she needed the familiarity. The safety that had started to elude her in Wyoming.

A small shudder ran down her spine as she reached the front desk area.

Dolly was grinning ear to ear.

Sky frowned. "Why are you smiling like that, and why does it make me nervous?"

"I'm just happy."

"I don't buy it. The last time I saw you smiling this big, you'd done something dirty with old man Jacobs." Sky gasped. "Did you do something dirty again?"

"In the five minutes since you've been gone? Honey, this body deserves to be loved and that takes time."

Sky chuckled. "Okay. So what is it?"

"I'm just excited to see who's going to walk through that door in a second."

Sky glanced at the door, then back at Dolly. "Well, is it the person bringing in the Dachshund?" A funny feeling began to swirl in her belly. She'd never actually asked who made the request, just assumed it was a deputy or maybe the sheriff. "Who was it who found the dog?"

Dolly's eyes lit up. "Well, technically, he didn't find it. Janice on Tenth did, in her yard, and the cranky old woman was too scared to touch it, so she called—"

The door opened and Sky's jaw dropped.

No…

Becket Hayes.

He wore his work uniform. It cut across his shoulders in just the right way. That, in combination with his day-old stubble, already made him look too freaking good. But today, he also held a Dachshund puppy.

He could be on the cover of a freaking calendar—he was so picture perfect.

An older African-American man stood behind him, but damn her and her inability to take her gaze off Becket.

One corner of his mouth lifted. "Hey, Peaches."

She straightened her spine. "Becket."

The guy beside him shifted his gaze between them. "You two know each other?"

"Yeah, Sky here's my neighbor," Becket said.

The guy's brows lifted. "Your *neighbor?*"

Why did he say it like that? Like he knew something about her? What had Becket told him?

Dolly cleared her throat. "I'm Dolly."

Becket glanced at Dolly for a second. "Becket. It's nice to meet you, ma'am."

Oh, don't you pretend you're a gentleman, buddy.

The second firefighter stepped forward. "I'm Moose, and this little guy is Bear."

"He has a collar?" Sky asked.

"No, I named him," Becket said, focused on her once again. "I'm not really a dog person, but I thought it suited him."

Not a dog person? Why was she not surprised? He probably hated kittens and thought babies weren't cute either.

She cleared her throat. "Well, I'll take him, and he can play with the other dogs."

She reached out, but Becket shook his head. "He's heavy. I'll carry him out."

"He's a puppy. I think I'll be fine." She reached for him, but Becket shook his head again.

"I insist."

So this man was as annoying and domineering in his work life as he was in his personal.

"Fine. This way." She turned, not bothering to see if he followed.

"I'll just…wait here," Moose said slowly, like he wanted to be as far away from them as possible.

She didn't blame him. It must be hard to work with Mr. I-Know-Better-Than-Ever-Other-Human-In-The-Universe
all day.

* * *

BECKET'S LIPS twitched at the way Sky stormed off in front of him. And the way her hips swayed in those jeans. How this woman made jeans look so good, he had no fucking clue.

"Stop staring at my ass."

The twitch of his lips turned into a full-fledged smile. "How do you know I'm staring at your ass?"

"Because I know what kind of person you are."

"The kind who saves dogs and puts out fires? Some women would find that hot."

"No, the kind of person who does what he wants with no regard for others."

"Are you still mad about the tree, Peaches?"

She spun. "*Stop* calling me Peaches!"

"I thought you liked the nickname."

"What I *like* is a day free from my pompous ass of a neighbor."

"So I'm a pompous ass who does whatever he wants and stares at women's asses. Man, I really suck."

"Sorry if my brutal honesty is inconveniencing your ego." She turned and started walking again.

He gave Bear a pat. "Ignore her. She has rage blackouts."

"Only when you're around."

He followed her outside and stopped dead as half a dozen dogs ran up to them. Some were big, some small. But shit, there were a lot of them. Even if he had been a dog person, this was a fucking circus full.

"This is what you do for work?" he asked in disbelief.

"Yep." She lowered to her haunches, embracing them. She even allowed them to lick her face.

Christ, he couldn't think of anything worse. But they clearly made her happy. "How the hell are you such an angry person if you love what you do so much?"

She threw a glare his way. "Look in the mirror and you might figure it out."

Then she looked back at the dogs, and her scowl turned into a smile. It was so wide and uninhibited that his chest suddenly felt too fucking tight, and he couldn't drag his gaze away if he tried.

Shit, she was gorgeous.

An older woman stepped up to them. "And who do we have here?"

Sky rose. "Pearl, this is Becket, the town fire chief. His team found this little guy, and he's going to have a stay with us until his owners are found."

"The Humane Society's working on it," Becket added.

The woman nodded, then looked at Sky. "Okay. So, separate him until we know he plays nice?"

Sky nodded. "Thanks."

Pearl took the dog from him, and Sky went back inside without even sparing a glance his way.

He followed her. "This is a nice place you work at."

"That's kind, coming from a dog hater. And I own it."

Wow. Impressive. But he should have figured that the neighbor who'd made it her life mission to hate him would start a business around the one animal he disliked.

"I don't hate dogs. I just don't—" He stopped and frowned. "Do you smell that?"

"The only thing I smell is the stink of your oversized ego."

He grabbed her arm. "Sky—"

She spun. "Hey, what are you—"

"Smoke. Do you smell it?"

Her frown dropped and her eyes widened as her gaze flew behind him. Then she took off toward the end of the hall.

That's when he saw it—a kitchen. And the damn oven was on fire. Flames roared behind the window in the closed door.

Becket cursed and jogged after her.

Sky turned off the oven and went to open the door, but he grabbed her wrist. "No. You'll just feed oxygen to the flames."

"So what do we do?"

He scanned the room, spotting the small, rectangular box mounted to the wall. Circuit breaker. He ran over to it, opened the metal door and flicked off the switch labelled oven.

"We wait," he said as he moved back to Sky. "With no power or air, it'll die out."

"Should I open a window?"

"Wait for it to completely go out first, just as a precaution."

She nodded.

It didn't take long. A couple minutes, tops.

When it was finally out, Becket opened the window closest to the stove.

"Irene must have left some food in there," Sky whispered, almost to herself. "She's done it before."

He turned to look at her. She was pale. Too pale.

He stepped close. "Are you okay?"

She looked up at him, and for the first time, there was no animosity in her eyes. No anger. Just...fear?

He gripped her upper arms, scared she was going to pass out. "Hey. It's out. You're safe."

She nodded quickly. "I know, I just...I don't like fires."

"Have you had a bad experience?"

Her eyes flared, her lips parting. But then she blinked and sidled away. "Sorry. I'm being silly. I'll see you out."

Becket didn't move right away. Because he'd seen that look in other people before. People who'd been touched by fire. People who'd felt the violence of the flames.

CHAPTER 4

"$\mathcal{T}$ony mentioned you this morning."

Sky almost rolled her eyes. There were so many ways she could respond to her dad's comment. But her coffee was good, The Tea House was busy—there was no reason to start an argument with either of her parents. "And what did he say?"

"That he was looking forward to the next date."

Her fingers tightened around her mug.

Sometimes she needed to remind herself that her father meant well. He loved his church, and in his mind, if she ended up with someone who shared the same faith as him, she was in good hands.

What he failed to realize was that she was a grown-ass woman who could make her own decisions. Granted, not all those decisions were good ones, but they were hers.

She sipped her coffee, taking a second to find some calm. "And did you tell him there won't be another date?"

She knew she was setting herself up for disappointment. She shouldn't be disappointed. Because she also knew what was coming.

Her mother quietly sipped her coffee while her father leaned forward, his bushy white brows creasing. "I told him that you were thinking about it, because that would be the smart thing for you to do."

Smart? Had her father used that word just to push her buttons? "I am quite capable of making my own *smart* decisions. Thank you, Dad."

Her father opened his mouth to respond, but her mom touched his arm and got in first. "Darling, we just love Tony."

"I know that."

"And we think you could love Tony, too, if you gave him a chance."

"I *have* given him a chance. I'm not interested."

Her father's frown deepened while her mother kept pushing. "But, honey—"

"Mom…Dad. I came to have coffee with you both. I know that Tony is staying with you, but I would prefer to talk about how *you're* doing. We can talk about food or health or how your fishing trip went yesterday, Dad. I could tell you what I'm wearing to the fundraiser, and you can tell me why I should wear something else."

"Skylar—"

Her mother grabbed her dad's hand to once again silence him before she spoke. "We're doing well. Your father caught three brown trout yesterday. We're glad you invited us here. We love the coffee and the company, although it's still odd to me that we come to a tea house for coffee and pie."

Sky had thought the same. But word had gotten around town about how good both the food and drinks were, and Lord, oh Lord, they were right. The coffee. The sweet tea and the pie. Even the turkey sandwiches were to die for.

"Now, what are you wearing to your fundraiser?" her mom asked.

Her father still looked unhappy, but that was Roger Williams.

He liked to talk about what *he* liked to talk about, and it wasn't what he was wearing to her fundraiser.

"Well, seeing as you asked." Sky cleared her throat. "I have this floor-length red dress—"

"I thought you'd wear yellow," her mother interrupted. "Yellow suits you."

Lord, give her patience. "I rented a—"

"You rented your dress?" Her father interrupted this time. "Skylar, if you're struggling with money—"

"I'm not struggling with money. I just don't need to buy a ball gown for one event when I can rent one."

Her mother shook her head. "Sky—"

"You're going to love it." And if they didn't, she didn't really care. The event was about raising money for a dog charity, not pleasing her parents…which seemed to be an impossible task anyway. "What are you both wearing?"

Her mother straightened. "Oh, I have this gorgeous knee-length brown dress. It's got tulle and lace and it's just beautiful."

"I'm excited to see it." She looked at her father. "What about you, Dad?"

"I wanted to wear my black suit, but your mother—"

"Thinks we should match," her mother finished. "So he's wearing his brown suit."

She laughed. At least it wasn't just *her* that her parents were trying to control—they did it to each other too.

"I think your photos will look lovely whatever you both wear," she said, receiving a smile from her mother and a *humph* from her father.

Then the corners of her mother's lips turned down.

Sky frowned. "What is it?"

"I was just wondering who *you'll* take photos with."

Oh, man. Not this again. "Mom—"

"Just hear me out. I want you to be happy. All I've ever wanted is for you to be happy."

"I *am* happy."

"You're not lonely when you get home to an empty house? You don't hate that you have to go to functions by yourself?"

Okay, she needed a break from this. "I'm going to ask Mrs. Gerald if I can leave these fliers on the counter."

She left the table before either of them could stop her.

She tried to tell herself it wasn't their fault. They'd both been raised to believe that every woman needed a man to take care of them. They'd met at church over forty years ago and never looked back. They wanted that for her, as well, but often forgot that she was her own person.

Honestly, some days she wondered why she'd moved back home.

Mrs. Gerald, the owner of The Tea House, stood at the front counter. "Hi, Sky. Is your coffee okay?"

"My coffee is great. Phenomenal, actually. I was wondering if it would be okay for me to leave some fliers on your counter for a fundraiser ball I'm organizing."

Mrs. Gerald's brows rose. "What are you raising money for?"

"The Humane Society of Western Montana. They do a whole host of great things, like provide shelter for pets and rehome animals. They have a pet food pantry and provide animal education. The ball I'm organizing is almost sold out, but I'd love to get the last few tickets sold in the next week."

"It sounds wonderful. Of course. Leave them wherever you'd like."

"Thank you."

Mrs. Gerald turned, and Sky was just setting the fliers onto the counter when a large hand slipped around her and took one from the top of the pile.

"Join us for an unforgettable evening of elegance at our charity fundraiser."

Sky's head whipped up and she looked into a set of deep chocolate eyes.

Becket.

He wore a white T-shirt that made his suntanned skin look even darker, and man, oh, man, his biceps stretched the material.

"Give it back."

"Aren't these for people to take?"

"Yes, but—"

"Well, Peaches, I'm people." His gaze returned to the flier. "Dress in your finest formal wear and enjoy live music and cocktail food. The ticket price will help to raise money for The Humane Society of Western Montana." His gaze rose. "I didn't know you were such a do-gooder."

Her eyes narrowed. "Guess you don't know me very well."

"We should change that. I think I'll attend."

"You're not going."

"Are there still tickets available?"

"Well, yes, but—"

"Then I'm there. Contrary to your beliefs, I do like to support good causes when I can."

"You're not serious?"

"I am. I love doing good."

She shook her head. "No. You're not actually going, are you?"

"I absolutely am. We'll drink a margarita together and discuss that tree that's coming down. Maybe even talk about what to do with the fence you've already bought that's not going up."

Then he nudged her shoulder and headed across the café to a booth.

She had never in her life met anyone who made her so furious.

* * *

BECKET WAS STILL SMILING as he slid into a booth. He glanced down at the flier in his hand. He wasn't a ball kind of guy.

Anything that involved dressing in a suit or any form of formal attire was usually a hard no.

But a fundraiser run by Sky? Yeah, he could fit that in. And the fact that she told him he couldn't go was just an added perk to attending.

The door to The Tea House opened, and he looked up to see his sister walk inside.

"So, I can confirm my new roommate does not want to be my friend," Clara huffed as she dropped into the booth opposite him. "This morning, I made her chocolate chip waffles. *Chocolate chip waffles*. And do you know what she said? No, you don't. And you won't even believe it when I tell you. She said, 'Thank you, but I don't like chocolate chips,' then she *walked out*.

"First, who the heck doesn't like chocolate chips? Second, who walks out of the room when someone makes them waffles without even trying one?" She glanced down at the piece of paper in his hand. "What's that?"

Becket lifted a brow. His sister rarely required much in the form of a response when she got on a rant about something, so he wasn't surprised she'd moved on so quickly. "It's a flier."

"For what? And why are you smiling like that?"

"Like what?"

"Like you did something to piss someone off and it made you happy."

He chuckled. Damn, his sister knew him well.

She yanked the flier from his fingers. "Oh. I'm going to this."

"You are?"

"Yeah, with Indie. We've got our tickets and bought our dresses yesterday. I think Jesse and Aspen are going too."

His sister, cousin, brother and brother's partner were all going, and he didn't even know about it? "Why didn't anyone tell me?"

"Because you have to wear a suit, and you'd hate it, and it's run by Sky, who you also hate."

"I don't hate her. She hates me."

"I'd hate you too if I bought a fence and you blocked it going up."

"She got the wrong permit. I was doing her a favor."

She scoffed. "Well, don't do me any favors." She eyed the flier again. "Wait, are you just wanting to go because she's organizing it?"

"Maybe."

"Beck, don't ruin her night. Please."

"Why would I want to ruin her night?"

"Because getting a rise out of Sky seems to be your new favorite hobby."

It wasn't new. They'd been neighbors for an entire year, and it had started on the day she moved in.

His gaze went to Sky, and as if she felt his eyes on her, she looked his way and immediately rolled her eyes and looked away.

Clara followed her gaze. "She's here. Oh, man."

"Why oh, man?"

She looked back at him. "That explains the I-did-something-bad smile you had on your face."

"I didn't do anything bad. I just told her I was going to her fundraiser."

"Yeah, I'm sure she took that well." Clara rose from the booth. "I'm going to say hi. Order me a coffee."

When his sister walked away, he read over the flier again.

Twenty seconds later, his brother Jesse slid into the booth. "I'm going to that."

"So I heard. Didn't want to tell me about it?"

"Why would I tell you about a formal event that's being organized by a person you don't like and where you have to wear a suit?"

"Why does everyone think I don't like her? *She* doesn't like *me*."

Jesse lifted a brow at him.

Becket leaned back in his seat. He needed a change in subject from his siblings' low opinions. "How's Aspen doing after everything?"

There was a small tightening of Jesse's jaw. "She's doing okay. She's resilient. More so than me. She keeps asking if *I'm* okay."

"*Are* you okay?"

"No. I'm a fucking mess. Every time I'm not around her, I feel this crippling need to be back by her side. This morning, she basically kicked me out of the house, claiming the only way for me to be okay being away from her would be to actually leave."

"But you've been leaving her now that you're back at work, right?"

"Yeah, but only because she won't come with me."

"I think she's right. You need to spend time away from her so you can realize she's safe without you."

He scrubbed a hand over his face. "I know. I just don't like it."

"How's Holden?"

Jesse and Holden, his brother's best friend, had become tight when they were assigned to the same Ghost Ops team. "Yeah, he's good. Settling into town and getting lots of woodworking jobs."

"That's good."

Clara slid back into the booth beside Jesse. "I saw Mrs. Gerald didn't come over here, so I ordered us three coffees. Double shot for you, Becket."

"Thanks." His gaze shifted to Sky, who was leaning over the table talking to her parents. She always seemed kind of frustrated when she was with them. "How was Sky?"

Clara lifted a brow. "You really want to know?"

"Yeah."

"She's good." Clara lifted a shoulder. "She's excited for her fundraiser."

"Did you know she owns a doggy daycare?"

His sister grinned. "Yeah. That must kill you, with your hatred for dogs."

"I don't hate dogs any more than I hate Sky. I'm just not a dog person."

Who the hell wanted to wake up to dog breath in their face? Hell, who wanted to go for a walk and have to pick up dog shit? Fuck no.

"Do you know much about her past?" Becket asked before he could stop himself, remembering the fire in her building.

Clara frowned. "Her past?"

"Where was she before she came to Amber Ridge? And why did she come back?"

"She's an acupuncture client of mine, and a friend, so I can't really share anything."

Becket nodded. "Client-patient confidentiality. Got it."

"Why do you want to know?" Jesse asked.

"No reason." That was a damn lie. His mind flicked back to the expression on her face after the oven fire. Most people wouldn't have been so affected. Her face had lost all color.

He also found it interesting that she owned a daycare for dogs and ran fundraisers for animal shelters, yet, as far as he knew, didn't have a pet of her own.

One thing he *did* know was that she intrigued him. He wanted to know more about her. He wanted to know her story.

CHAPTER 5

He'd done it. He'd butchered her tree. He'd *butchered* her *freaking* tree.

Argh. She was going to kill him.

Pure, unadulterated rage burned through her veins as she glared at Becket's house. A part of her wanted to march right on over there and strangle him now. But she was late. And even though the need to murder him was strong, her need to get ready for the ball was stronger.

Damn him. He knew she'd be busy tonight.

Sky stomped inside and slammed the door closed. Tonight was supposed to be fun. A celebration. And she was not going to let her no-good neighbor ruin that.

She jogged upstairs and jumped into the shower.

Maybe she'd throw a drink on him tonight. No, better yet, she'd call Jesse tomorrow and get him to arrest his own brother.

Ha. That probably wouldn't happen.

He thought he'd won this one. But the joke was on him—because today, her building permit for the fence had finally come through. The fence was going up, and there was nothing her deranged, yard-mutilating neighbor could do about it.

A small smile returned to her face as she got out of the shower and dried off.

Sky could just picture the scowl on his face when he saw the fence up, and it brought her far too much joy.

She should be thinking about the million and one things she had to check once she got to the venue. The food. The drinks. The music. It should all be on her mind. It wasn't. Becket was.

She dressed quickly, applied her makeup and did her hair before pulling on her dress. The dress was formal but also with a hint of sexy.

She stepped away from the mirror and glanced out the window, her heart giving a sad kick at the sight of her naked tree. The worst part was, there'd been no reason for him to do it. Yes, he'd said it was a safety thing. And yes, she was well aware of the town thief that had been in the paper. But if *her* tree blocked *his* view, that wasn't her problem. He still had plenty of street view with the branches fully intact.

She hated him. It didn't matter how pretty his face was, she did not like Becket Hayes.

Her phone buzzed from her dresser, and she lifted it to see it was her mother.

"Hey, Mom. Are you and Dad ready to go?"

"We're all dressed, but I need you to tell your father there'll be food at the fundraiser. He's insisting on stopping for dinner on the way." There was a shuffling noise. "Roger, take the phone."

"Who is it?"

Sky chuckled at her father's confused tone.

"Who do you think? It's Skylar. Take the phone."

There was another shuffling sound, then her dad's voice again. "Skylar?"

"Hi, Dad. There's food at the fundraiser."

"But you said we don't have set seats or individual plates."

She put the cell on speaker and set it onto the dresser to put on her left earring. "That's right. It's cocktail food."

"Cocktail food?"

What century was her father from? "Food will be brought around by servers on trays, and you can take what you want. There'll be plenty."

"Oh. I don't think I'll like that."

"Roger, stop being a stick in the mud," her mother scolded. "It'll be great. Give me the phone."

Sky's grin widened as she switched ears.

"Your father's being difficult," her mother said. "But what's new? See you soon."

"I'll see you soon, Mom."

She hung up and turned to her mirror, inspecting the dress, then her makeup and hair. She'd put up her hair to show off the twisted spaghetti straps at the back.

Good. She looked good.

Good enough for Becket to take a second look?

The thought came out of nowhere, making her nose wrinkle. God, why would she care if that dog-hating, tree-butchering neighbor took a second look at her?

She didn't. She absolutely did not. And even if he did take a second look, she wouldn't know, because she wouldn't be looking at *him*. Unless it was to plan his impending death.

After throwing her lip gloss and phone into her purse, she locked her house and headed toward her car.

She told herself not to look at the tree again, but damn if her gaze didn't go straight to it.

It looked so bare.

Damn Becket.

She'd worked a half day today at the doggy daycare, and being a Saturday, it hadn't been busy. Although…there'd been one new dog. A Border Terrier named Marty. Her fingers tightened around the steering wheel as she drove, thinking back to that morning. The second he'd trotted into the daycare, her entire body had frozen—because he'd looked so much like her Charlie. His strong jaw. His short, shiny coat.

A familiar ache twisted inside her chest.

Some days, she almost forgot he was gone. Some days, she still woke up expecting to see him next to her. Or hear him barking when she got home.

Tears pushed at her eyes, but she forced them back.

This is for you, Charlie.

And it was true. Every fundraiser lifted some of that unbearably heavy weight on her chest, like she was somehow making up for what had happened to him. And even though she wasn't sure she'd ever feel ready to have another dog, running the doggy daycare allowed her to still get her daily fill.

The parking lot at the events center was almost empty. Good. Guests hadn't started arriving yet.

Inside, there was a wide grand foyer with a huge staircase in the center, but she headed for a function room to the left.

When Sky stepped into the room, she couldn't hold back her gasp. Beautiful. The lights were dimmed, making the chandelier sparkle above the large dance floor. There was a bar at the back and a band setting up at the front. Cocktail tables were scattered around the space, covered with black cloths and decorative glass animal centerpieces.

She smiled at the balloon arrangement with "The Humane Society" lit up in the center.

"Perfect," she whispered.

"It really is."

She spun to find Clara Hayes beside her. She wore a floor-length sky-blue dress and stood with a woman who had the most dazzling emerald-green eyes.

They'd actually gone to the same high school, but because Clara had been younger than her, they'd never spoken. Now she saw Clara regularly for acupuncture, and they'd become fast friends.

"Hi, you're early!" Like half an hour early.

Clara cringed. "Sorry. A bad habit of mine. I hate to be late so sometimes get to places absurdly early." She turned to the woman beside her. "This is my cousin, Indie."

Sky smiled at the woman. "Hi, Indie. I'm Sky Williams. It's nice to meet you."

Indie dipped her head. "You too. This place looks great."

"Thank you. Now I just hope it goes well."

"I know it will," Clara said, gently touching her arm. "All your fundraisers have been perfect."

"Thank you." Clara had such a calming energy about her. It was just one of the reasons Sky loved seeing her for acupuncture.

Clara inched closer. "Hey, I'm not sure if you're aware, but Becket's coming tonight."

All the fine hairs stood on end at the mention of his name. Then she remembered her tree. Could she strangle him here? No. It was a formal fundraiser. Maybe tomorrow.

She forced a smile to her lips. "He told me."

"Sorry. Hopefully he's on his best behavior."

His best behavior? Ha. She didn't even think he knew what that was.

"He doesn't bother me." *Lie.* "He's oil and I'm water. Everything he says and does rolls right off me." *Big...gigantic...lie.*

As if the universe needed to prove that point, the doors opened and two men walked in, both tall, both broad—one of them Becket.

Good God. Did people not know how to arrive at events on time? And why did he have to look so hot in formal wear? Like *really* hot?

The suit cut across his broad shoulders too freaking perfectly, and when his gaze hit hers before running over her body, it felt like he was undressing her with his eyes.

She kind of liked it.

No. No, you don't like it. You don't like him. Remember the tree, Sky. And the fence. And every other thing he's done to you.

Her hands fisted. "I've, um, got to go talk to some people." She turned and took off in the opposite direction, almost running from the neighbor who she absolutely needed to avoid at all costs tonight. Because part of her wanted to kill him.

But another part of her wanted to do something she absolutely would never admit out loud.

* * *

RED SILK ROLLED over Sky's thighs as she moved, and Becket couldn't fucking look away. He'd been watching her all night. The imprint of her nipples against that dress. Her sexy back and shoulders. How a *back* could be sexy, he had no fucking clue, but hers was.

"You should talk to her."

Becket forced his focus to shift from her to Holden, who came to stand beside him. "She's been doing everything she can to stay as far away from me as possible."

In fact, as the ballroom had filled up, she'd conveniently always been on the *opposite* side of the room as him. He wasn't going to lie, he was kind of surprised. He'd expected the woman to rage at him the second she saw him.

"Why would she do that?" Holden asked, even though he knew their history.

"I trimmed her tree this morning."

"Trimmed?"

Okay, maybe it was a bit more than a trim. "It was blocking my view of the street."

"Ah, the town thief." Holden's fingers tightened around his glass. "Have you told her that's why you did it?"

"Yep. I told her it was a safety thing. She didn't seem to care."

"Did you tell her it was for her safety too?"

"I assumed she'd know that."

Holden shook his head. "With your history? Probably not. Talk to her."

He sipped his beer. Holden was right. It would still probably end up in an argument though. Every conversation with Sky did.

Holden frowned at something across the room. "Your sister was looking tired when I spoke to her."

Becket followed Holden's gaze to Clara. Five years ago, she'd been diagnosed with stage four Hodgkin's Lymphoma. She'd gone through chemo and had responded well to it, going into remission before the end of treatment. Since then, there'd been no cancer found in her body, but she still suffered from chronic fatigue, and everyone, especially family, worried about her.

"Maybe I should get Mom to talk to her about not pushing herself too hard," Becket said quietly.

Since her diagnosis, Clara had changed. There was rarely an experience she said no to, and if anyone questioned her on her decisions, they always got the same response—that life was too short. So far, she'd jumped out of planes, taken a million different courses, and completely changed her profession from lawyer to acupuncturist.

Whenever he or Jesse tried to have a conversation with her about slowing down, she got defensive.

"I might go over there and make sure she's okay," Holden said.

Becket nodded, appreciating that the man was looking out for Clara. Even though Holden had only just moved to town, he'd been part of their family a lot longer. His own mother had died when Holden was a teenager, and she'd been the only family he'd had. Once he and Jesse started getting closer as friends, he'd started joining *their* family for holidays, slotting right in.

Becket was just lifting his beer when Sky walked past, heading toward the bar. He should leave her the hell alone, he knew that, but damn if he wasn't a sucker.

He set his beer onto a table and crossed over to stand beside her. The scent of lilacs surrounded him—her scent. One that he'd grown to really like since meeting her.

"Nice fundraiser you've organized."

She jumped and turned, eyes widening as she looked up at him. "Becket."

She said his name like a warning, and he almost laughed.

"In the flesh." He cocked his head. "You look nice."

"Really? You know what *doesn't* look nice? My tree." She leaned closer, a bite behind each word. "I don't know whether to kill you myself or call the sheriff on you."

"Why not both? Call the sheriff and then kill me. It will make discovering my remains a bit quicker."

Her eyes narrowed. "Is this funny to you?"

"Don't be mad. I told you I did it for safety reasons. Your safety too." As suspected, that didn't seem to appease her at all. "Come on, this is a fundraiser. Smile and tell me I look nice too. I know you're thinking it."

"You want to know what I'm thinking when I look at you? Two billion years of evolution for *this*?"

He threw his head back and laughed. He'd never been insulted as much as he had in the last year, having this woman as his neighbor, and he fucking loved it.

The bartender stopped in front of them. "Hi, what can I get you two?"

"We're not together," Sky said, as if the very idea repulsed her. "I'll have a piña colada."

"Beer, thanks." He looked down at her. "You're a bit frosty to a donor."

"I'm frosty because I got home to my tree no longer looking like a tree."

"Okay, maybe I went a bit crazy with the trimming."

"A bit?" If looks could kill, hers would be murdering him on the spot. "There's no tree left."

"Sure, there is. There are branches."

"Two. You left *two* branches."

"Now you don't need to pay anyone to trim it." Her glare grew darker, and he almost laughed. "I'll buy you a new potted plant."

"I don't want a potted plant, I want my tree back."

"Here you go."

Sky huffed as she turned back toward the bartender. When the woman held out the credit card machine, he paid before Sky could.

She turned toward him. "Why did you do that?"

"Penance for the tree."

She rolled her eyes. "Like that could make up for it. And by the way, I got the permit for the fence. It's booked for next week."

"Not happening."

"It is."

"It's not."

She inched closer and jabbed a finger into his chest. "You can't bully your way out of this one, Becket. The fence is going up and that's that."

"No, it's not."

"You're impossible. And you're also wrong." She lifted her glass. "You enjoy Delusion Island over here. I'm going to have fun."

He chuckled, because she didn't look like she was having fun. He, on the other hand, never had more fun than when he was around her.

CHAPTER 6

God. Did Becket think he was funny? Because he wasn't. He was about as far from funny as you could get.

Arrogant? Yes. An asshole? Absolutely.

"Skylar."

She stopped as her mother appeared in front of her. Not just her mother, but her father too. Shit. She'd been so deep in her "I hate Becket" trance, she hadn't even seen them coming. "Hi, Mom and Dad. Sorry I haven't had much time to chat tonight."

"Oh, you're the organizer, honey." Her mother patted her hand. "We understand."

Her father glanced around the ballroom. "You've done a magnificent job, Skylar. Well done."

"Thank you." She took a big gulp of her drink, hoping it would cool the anger.

Nope. Anger was still burning hot.

"Are you okay?" her mother asked with a frown.

Not even a little bit. "I'm great. Just busy. Are you two having fun?"

"We are." Her mother glanced over her shoulder before looking back at her nervously.

Wait—Sky knew that look. It was her "I'm nervous because you're not going to like this" look. And yes, Sky *could* read all of that from one expression. "Is everything okay?"

Her father cleared his throat. "Yes. Everything's wonderful. We, um, actually invited someone here tonight."

Her belly dipped. "Dad…you didn't."

"Well, darling, he's living with us," her mother interrupted, obviously trying to keep the peace. "And you should see him in his suit. He looks spectacular!"

"Mom—"

Her father gestured someone over.

Tony walked up beside her father. He was six feet tall with shaggy brown hair that fell into his brown eyes. Some might think he was cute. She didn't.

"Sky. It's so good to see you again." He leaned forward and kissed her cheek, and she held her breath too late, getting a big breath of onion.

Yuck.

He pulled back. "I was wondering what happened to you, since you haven't responded to my texts."

His texts asking for a second date? She'd responded to the first one, saying "no" as kindly and gently as possible. "I've been busy."

She turned to her parents, sending an "I can't believe you did this" glare their way. Her mother, at least, had the good sense to look guilty…while her father looked happy. Far too damn happy.

Sky gave everyone a tight smile. "I need to get back to my rounds."

"Tony can join you," her father piped in.

Tony stepped forward, but she retreated, the onion smell hitting her nose far too hard—again. And she could still feel his sloppy kiss on her cheek. "No."

Her father frowned. "Skylar, don't be rude. He's here for you."

Oh, the things she could say to her father right now.

"I don't mind helping," Tony added. "I have a background in project management. I'm sure I'd be able to assist."

"I'm dating someone." The words shot out of her mouth like a freight train. But once they were out, she couldn't take them back.

Her father rolled his eyes. He actually *rolled his eyes*. "Skylar—"

"I am," she pushed.

"You don't need to lie," her mother said gently.

"I'm not lying."

"If you were dating someone," her father said, frowning, "then wouldn't he be here tonight?"

"He is." Man, the lies were just rolling off her tongue now. But she refused to spend one more second with bad-breath, sloppy-kisser Tony, and if anything could stop both him *and* her parents, it was a fictitious boyfriend.

Her father raised a brow. "Okay, where is he?"

At that exact moment, like the heavens and Earth aligned—or did her the biggest disservice in the universe—Becket walked toward them.

She yanked his arm and jerked him to her side, hard.

He frowned slightly. "Uh, are you going through something, Peaches? An episode maybe?"

She smiled at him, the warmest smile she'd ever sent his way. "Hi, honey."

He looked at her like she'd lost her mind. And yeah, she'd lost it somewhere between the gross cheek kiss and the grabbing of Becket's arm.

She turned to her parents and Tony. "Mom, Dad…Tony. This is my boyfriend, Becket."

The instant silence that descended between the five of them was almost comical.

Becket cleared his throat. "Uh, *honey*, I think we need to talk."

"Sure. But I need a big hug first." She pulled him close and put her mouth next to his ear, then shout-whispered. "Do this for me and I won't put up a fence."

"I don't—"

"Don't do it and the fence goes up Monday."

There was a small pause. "And you don't mention the tree or the cameras again."

Her back teeth ground together. She didn't want to agree.

"Guess I'll—"

"Fine," she groaned before straightening.

A cocky grin stretched Becket's mouth, and it made her want to slug him. He slipped an arm around her waist and tugged her flush against him, making her side feel all tingly.

"Hi." He stretched out a hand in the direction of her parents. "I'm Becket Hayes. And I'm dating your daughter."

She swallowed the acid in her mouth.

For a moment, no one took his hand. In fact, everyone's stillness was so awkward, she squirmed.

Eventually, her mother took his hand. "Um, hi. I'm Esther."

"It's nice to meet you, ma'am."

Her mother nudged her father. "Roger. Shake his hand."

He mumbled something under his breath before shaking Becket's hand. "Roger. Skylar never mentioned she was dating anyone."

"Skylar's choice." He looked down at her, warmth and maybe some humor in his eyes. "She tends to like her privacy. Don't you, Peaches?"

She offered him a tight smile.

"Peaches?" Tony asked, a look of almost disgust on his face.

"It's my nickname for her," Becket answered before she could. "I used it once and she just loved it so much that it stuck."

Good God.

"Sorry. I haven't met you," Becket said, holding a hand out to Tony.

"Tony."

They shook hands, and Tony winced, presumably at Becket's grip. He pulled his hand back and scowled before muttering, "I'm getting a drink."

Mission accomplished.

"Did I just see you two fighting at the bar?" her mother asked suspiciously. "And at The Tea House last week. You two were arguing at the counter."

"That's what we do," Becket said. "We argue, but we always make up when she realizes who's right."

Too close. He was too freaking close.

She tried to shove a bit of space between them with her elbow, but he just hauled her closer, his arm like steel.

"Yes, honey," she said to Becket through gritted teeth. "I *do* realize who's right. And it always comes as a surprise to *you*."

"I'm not sure that's accurate."

"I am." She smiled at her parents.

Her father just glared at them, while her mother's frown deepened.

"I still wish you'd told us, Skylar," her mom said.

"It's probably partially because Skylar is a bit self-conscious about dating the town fire chief," Becket answered, his thumb grazing her side.

She barely bit back the scoff. "Yeah, he's kind of a big deal. Just ask him."

"Do you attend church?" her father asked.

"No, sir. But I can assure you, I have great values and ethics."

Yeah, because it was so *ethical* to cut down someone's tree.

Sky cleared her throat. "We should get back to the ball."

Her mother looked at Becket. "Will you be joining us for dinner at Skylar's house on Friday night?"

Sky opened her mouth to tell her parents no and make up some "he has to work" excuse, but Becket got in first.

"Definitely. Six thirty, right?"

What the heck was he doing?

"Six," her mother corrected.

"I'm looking forward to it."

Interesting…because he wasn't coming.

Her mother glanced at the dance floor. "You two should dance."

"Oh, we don't—"

"We absolutely do," Becket cut her off. His hand slid down, his strong fingers tangling with hers. "Come on, Peaches. Let's dance."

One second she was in front of her parents, and the next she was on the dance floor, pulled flush against Becket's chest. And unlike Tony, he smelled good. Really good.

What had she done?

* * *

THE SILKY MATERIAL of Sky's dress was so thin, he felt like he was touching her bare waist. And fuck, but her floral scent toyed with him.

She hadn't looked up at him once since they'd stepped onto the dance floor. In fact, her blue eyes had remained fixed on his chest like it was the most fascinating thing she'd ever seen.

His lips twitched. She pulled a stunt like that and thought she could go silent on him?

"So, we're dating?"

"No." She shook her head. "I mean, yes, but not really."

He spun her, and when she returned to him, he reeled her in so close that her entire front pressed to his. "Is this because of that douchebag wearing the fake Armani?"

"How do you know he's a douchebag?"

Becket could have laughed. "Other than the fact I've never met anyone wearing fake Armani who I liked…he was looking straight at your chest."

"He was?"

How had she not seen?

She sighed. "Tony was a neighbor and part of my parents' church growing up, and they love him. He's back in town for a few months, and my father's fixated on the idea of us dating."

"And you don't want that?"

She scoffed. "Do I want to date someone who smells like onions and whose favorite topic of conversation is insurance? No."

Becket hadn't smelled any onions, but then, Sky had been flush against his side, so all he'd smelled was her. "He sounds like a catch."

"He makes *you* look like a million bucks."

Becket chuckled. He did that a lot around her. "You really know how to make a man feel special."

"Don't pretend you like this any more than me."

"Depends. How much are you liking this?"

She squirmed in his arms. "The only reason you're dancing with me is because I told you I wouldn't put up the fence."

It was definitely one perk. Not the only one though.

He swiped the back of her hand with his thumb and swore he felt a shudder roll down her spine. "Okay, if we're dating, we need to get some facts straight."

"Why? This is just a one-night thing."

"No. I'm coming to your dinner Friday night."

"No, you're not."

"Yes, I am. I was invited."

"No. You were asked if you were coming."

"Same thing."

"It is not the same thing. I'll tell them you're sick."

"What if your parents come up to me after this dance and want to talk about us?"

Her frown deepened, like she knew that was a possibility. "What facts do we need to get straight?"

"How many times a week do we have sex?"

She spluttered and tried to pull away, but he gripped her waist so tightly she didn't get an inch of space.

"My parents would *not* ask you about our sex life," she gasped.

"No, but Horndog Tony might."

He got a twitch of her lips from that one. "Fine. Three times a week."

His brows rose.

"What?" she asked.

"You really think you could resist me four nights a week?"

She rolled her eyes. "Here I was thinking three was too many."

He could have laughed again. Instead, he slowly dipped his head, his lips almost brushing her ear. "I have a feeling, one night together and neither of us would be able to wait very long for the next."

There was a sharp intake of breath. "You really think a lot of yourself, don't you?"

"It's nothing you haven't thought yourself, Peaches." He spun her again. "Who made the first move?"

"Obviously you."

"Why obviously?"

"Because of that big ego of yours. It wasn't even a thought in your mind that I might say no. Next question."

"Where'd we go on our first date?"

"Burt's Pizzeria."

He barely held in the snort. "I would never take a woman there, first date or fiftieth date."

Burt had the worst pizza in Montana. Hell, probably America. But people in the small town kept him in business because they liked him. And yeah, Becket ate his fair share of bad pizzas to keep the guy going, but never on a date.

She frowned. "Really? I thought cheap and easy was your thing."

He growled softly and tugged her closer. "For our first date, I took you to Blackbird Kitchen in Bozeman. You ordered the mostarda pizza, I ordered a salsiccia and we shared."

There was a small gasp from her lips. "How did you know I order the mostarda from Blackbird?"

"I've seen the boxes in your trash can and took a guess on the mostarda. That's a big drive for pizza."

She pulled back and looked at him closely, but this time, it was like she was trying to work him out. "I've gotten to know the owners. Now we choose a halfway point, so their delivery guy drives halfway to me and I drive halfway to them."

"That's still quite an effort for pizza."

"I like pizza. Especially theirs."

"As your boyfriend, that's good to know. I'll add it to the list."

"List?"

"Pizza. Dogs. Organizing fundraiser events. Those sweet teas that Mrs. Gerald makes."

"You know that I like sweet tea?"

"You drink it at The Tea House. So does Clara. No idea why, the stuff tastes like sugar water."

She was still frowning, almost looking as if she was seeing him for the first time.

"One more question," he said quietly. "Why don't you have a dog?"

The change in her was immediate. Her body stiffened and her cheeks paled. But it was her eyes that *really* changed. Any humor or happiness left them, and they almost grew sad.

Suddenly she took a big step back, tugging out of his arms. "Thank you for saving me tonight. Like I said, it was *just* for tonight…but I'll keep up my end of the deal. I should go talk to some people from work."

Then she turned and walked off the dance floor, her spine too rigid.

Why would a question about a dog incite that kind of reaction?

He left the dance floor and joined his brother, who was watching Clara and Aspen dance.

Jesse looked at Becket as he approached. "Tell me there's something wrong with my eyes and you weren't just dancing with Sky Williams."

"Nothing wrong with your eyes, brother. Sky and I have turned a corner."

"You're kidding?"

"Nope." He watched Sky as she spoke to a couple of people across the room. Her head turned, and their gazes locked. Her eyes did that widening thing, which told him one thing—she felt it too.

What exactly "it" was, he had no idea. All he knew was that he liked being around her...probably too much.

CHAPTER 7

No. No, no, no.

Sky lifted her phone, looking at the text again, still not believing what she was reading.

Mom: Your father didn't want to leave Tony home alone, so he's invited him to dinner tonight. I hope that's okay.

No, it was not okay. And both her parents knew that. She'd made her thoughts on Tony pretty freaking clear. And it was interesting that they'd only invited him *after* she'd told them that Becket was sick.

Her fingers moved quickly over her cell, typing out a text that could only be described as furious. Then of course, the second she read it back, she deleted it. She couldn't send that to her mother. It had two curses and a semi-curse in it.

Besides, it was more her father's doing than her mother's, and an angry text wouldn't change things. Even if she wanted them to uninvite him, they wouldn't. And it was too late to cancel or change plans.

God, her parents infuriated her. Her father inviting Tony and her mother only dropping it on her ten minutes before they came was so calculated and...just unkind.

She finally wrote out her reply.

Sky: I wish he hadn't.

She hit send and dropped her phone to the kitchen counter before slicing the cucumber with a bit more aggression.

To make matters worse, she hadn't seen Becket since the ball…and was actually disappointed about it. Gah. Why she was disappointed to not see a neighbor she didn't even like, she had no idea. It wasn't because his arms had felt good around her. And it certainly wasn't because when he'd spoken to her on the dance floor, the velvet tone of his voice had slid over her body and made her feel all sensitive and tingly.

She didn't like it. Any of it.

But it would be fine. Becket wouldn't be there tonight—something she should be happy about—and even though Onion Breath Tony was coming, he still thought she had a boyfriend. So there should be no more talk of dates.

She'd just finished the salad and added a fourth place setting to the table when her doorbell rang.

Her gaze flew up to the clock. Her parents were five minutes early. They were never early. In fact, they got everywhere at almost the exact time, to the minute, that they were told. It was something she'd always found annoying but never understood why.

She moved to the door.

"Hey, you guys are—" She stopped, the words dying on her lips. Not her parents. Not even close. "Becket."

"Hi." He held a tray covered in foil and a bottle of wine.

"What are you doing here?"

"Six, right? I know, I'm early—a terrible habit of mine."

"That wasn't…" She shook her head. "I told my parents you're sick."

"Well, lucky for you, *girlfriend*, I am feeling like rainbows and sunshine." Then he kissed her on the cheek as if he'd done it a million times and walked into her house. "What is that delicious smell? Pot roast?"

What was going on? Was she living in a twilight zone?

She closed the door and spun toward him. "I told you, you only needed to play along for one night." Although, now that Tony was coming, maybe it was better that he was here.

No. How could having her sexy-as-sin neighbor here, pretending to be her boyfriend, be better? It wasn't. This wasn't a huge, crowded ballroom. This was her *home.* He'd be here all night. Smelling far too good and sitting far too close.

Becket frowned at the table. "It's set with four places."

"Good counting."

"But if you thought I wasn't coming..." Understanding crossed his face. "Oh. You tell your parents I'm sick, and they invite Tony, a guy they're still trying to set you up with even though you've made your feelings clear about him."

It sounded even worse when he said it. "Becket, why are you here?"

He lifted her glass of wine and sipped. "They know I live next door. Even if I was sick, it would be weird for me not to stop in and say hi. Besides, what exactly did you plan to tell them at every future get-together?"

"Well, I was going to wait until Tony left town and then tell them our sad but simple breakup story."

"Was I going to come off the asshole in this story? I was, wasn't I?"

She rolled her eyes and moved into the kitchen, where she grabbed a fifth place setting. "It doesn't matter. They're not your parents."

"It *does* matter. I have a reputation to uphold in this town."

"Good God, it's a wonder you have the energy to get out of bed with that big head on your shoulders."

"I've been carrying this big head my entire life. I'm used to it."

Her lips twitched, and she hated that she found him funny. He wasn't. Not even a little bit.

Once the fifth place was set, she turned—only to freeze. Becket was adding olives to her salad. And he looked far too comfortable working in her little kitchen.

She opened her mouth to tell him she couldn't do this. That asking him to pretend to be her boyfriend in the first place had been a gigantic mistake…but the doorbell rang.

Too late now.

She sucked in a shaky breath before turning and heading to the door. She pulled it open and forced a smile to her lips. "Mom. Dad…Tony." Okay, Tony's name didn't just slide off the tongue.

She gave each of them a kiss as they came inside, making sure to hold her breath when she greeted Tony.

"Becket," her father said, sounding shocked.

Sky took her time closing the door before turning.

Becket didn't look fazed at all.

"Hi." Becket dried his hands on a dish towel before crossing the room. He kissed her mother on the cheek, then shook her father's hand. When he shook Tony's hand, just like at the ball, the other man cringed.

How hard was Becket shaking the guy's hand?

"We thought you were sick," her mother said.

"Fortunately, I started feeling better just in time." He slid an arm around her waist as she moved to stand beside him.

Why on earth did she have the sudden urge to lean into him? Her body was betraying her, dammit.

Her father's eyes narrowed on Becket, while her mother looked intrigued, and Tony just kind of looked angry. At least that was one positive to having Becket around.

When the awkward silence stretched, Sky cleared her throat. "I'll slice the roast, then we can sit down to eat."

"I'll do that," Becket offered. Then he freaking kissed her on the cheek *again*, this time also squeezing her waist.

She told herself she didn't like it, but her pulse picked up speed.

The next ten minutes were a mess of her and her mother trying to make small talk, her father and Tony sulking, and Becket acting like everything was normal and he'd been in her kitchen a million times before.

She felt like she was on a freaking sitcom. What had happened to her quiet dinner with her parents?

Testosterone…that's what happened.

She'd just set the last of the food onto the table and they were about to sit when that onion stench grew stronger.

"Sky." Ugh. There he was. "Is it okay if I use your bathroom?"

She forced her lips to stretch into a smile as she turned to look at Tony. "Of course. It's just down the hall." She led him into her hall and opened a door. "Here you go."

"Thanks." He didn't go inside. Instead, he stepped closer to her, eliminating some of the space between them. "I have to admit, I've been struggling with this a bit."

"This?" she asked.

"You and…*him*. I really enjoyed our date, and—"

"It was hardly a date, Tony. It was dinner with my parents."

"Regardless of what it was, I had a good time with you. And I thought you had a good time too."

How on earth had he thought she'd had a good time? She had to have yawned at least half a dozen times, and they hadn't even finished eating when she'd made a pathetic excuse to leave. Something about needing to feed her fish. She didn't have a fish!

"I wasn't planning on dating Becket. It just happened." Understatement of the century.

Tony stepped forward *again*, almost touching her. "It's just hard to let go of the idea of you and me when your father's spoken so much about what a good match we'd be."

Well, let it go, man. "Tony—"

"Everything okay here?" Becket asked as he entered the hall, tall and broad…and angry. He stopped beside her and tugged her close. And even though this thing between them wasn't real, it was a relief to be closer to him than Tony.

Safe. That's what she felt when she was near Becket.

Tony's eyes narrowed and he moved back.

Okay, her hallway was feeling far too small right now. "It's fine," she said, looking up at Becket. "I was just showing Tony to the bathroom."

Tony straightened. And…was he pushing his chest out? "Strange that Roger didn't even know you existed a week ago, especially because you live next door."

"Just because someone doesn't know I exist doesn't mean I'm not here."

Tony scowled and opened his mouth, but Sky put a hand to Becket's chest. "Come on, we should get back to my parents." She pushed, but he didn't move.

"I'll see you out there," Tony said, staring at Sky.

"*We* will see you out there," Becket corrected. Then he led her out of the hall, her heart beating far too fast. Because Becket was fighting for her like he *was* actually her boyfriend, and it felt far too real.

CHAPTER 8

*B*ecket leaned back in his seat, half listening as Esther Williams spoke. She'd been the one doing most of the talking all evening.

His plate was empty and his stomach full. The food had been good. Another new thing he'd now learned about Sky—she was a hell of a cook. Although, even the good food couldn't make up for the cold tension Tony and her father were putting off.

What the hell was wrong with her dad? Inviting a guy Sky clearly didn't like, because he thought her boyfriend wasn't coming. Did he not care about what *she* wanted?

"And she sleepwalked right out into the backyard, let the stray dog inside, and went back to bed," Esther continued.

Becket glanced at Sky. "You sleepwalk?"

She shook her head. "I don't—"

"She does," her mother interrupted.

Tony leaned forward, suspicion on his face. "Even I know she's a chronic sleepwalker. Shouldn't that be something her *boyfriend* knows?"

Becket flashed a smile, knowing it would just make him

angrier. "Did she sleepwalk away from you, Tony? Were you a bit too close?"

Rage flared in the man's eyes.

Bingo. But why the hell was this idiot anywhere near her while she was sleeping?

"Tony would stay over sometimes," Esther said, breaking the silence.

"After church," her father added, the single sentence one of the only things he'd said all night.

"How long have you been part of the church, Roger?" Becket asked.

The older man's brows lifted, as if surprised by the question. "My entire life."

"I can see why it would mean a lot to you."

"It does," he answered, voice a bit softer.

"It's how we met," Esther said affectionately. She looked at Sky, her expression clouding with something like sadness. "We'd hoped our Skylar would be a lifelong part of the church."

Sky took a gulp of wine. "Unfortunately, that wasn't the case."

A few seconds of silence passed before Becket spoke. "My mom tried to get us to church once."

"She did?" Esther asked, clearly intrigued.

"Yeah. I have a lot of respect for people who have your kind of faith." He looked at Sky. "And for people who choose their own paths and beliefs."

Sky frowned, but Becket couldn't tell if it was at him or his mention of faith.

When Tony's eyes lingered on Sky a bit too long, Becket draped an arm over her shoulders. "Well, this has been lovely." Tony rolled his eyes, while Sky gave a quiet scoff. "Do you do this regularly?"

"At least a couple of times a month," Esther answered.

He looked at Sky. "You never told me, Peaches."

She smiled at him, but it didn't quite reach her eyes. "I haven't told you lots of things, honey. We only just started dating."

"What about before that?" Tony asked. "Friends? Enemies?"

"Mortal enemies," Becket said, once again smiling at Tony. "She even wanted a fence between our properties so she didn't have to look at me every day. I think it was because even then, she was attracted to me but too shy to ask out the fire chief."

She stomped on his foot under the table, and he bit back a laugh.

"Yeah, that's exactly it." She looked over at her family. "We didn't quite hate each other, but if he'd been drowning, I probably would have given him a high five."

Esther's brows shot up.

"I mean, even a high five would have been a stretch," Becket added. "I picture you with popcorn and a folding chair."

"It would've been good entertainment."

Tony scowled at them as Sky took another sip of her wine.

"So you fought about a fence?" her father asked.

Becket leaned forward. "And my security cameras—"

"Which covered—and still cover—my front yard," Sky cut in.

"About me trimming her tree—"

"*Butchering* my tree."

"But look at us now."

"Look at us now." Humor actually sparkled in Sky's eyes before she rose to her feet. "I'm going to clear the table."

"I'll help." Becket stood.

Esther helped as well, and the three of them moved around the kitchen while Roger and Tony discussed the last church sermon at the table.

"So," Esther started, "your family's been in Amber Ridge for quite a while, haven't they?"

"Yes, ma'am. My siblings and I were all born here, and my mother still lives in the same house."

"And your father?"

"He passed away when I was young. A stroke."

Sky's gaze flashed to him, and Esther gently rested a hand on his shoulder. "I'm sorry."

"It's okay. It was a long time ago. My mom's pretty great. And she'd never leave Amber Ridge."

"People don't tend to leave here," Esther murmured.

Becket looked at Sky. "Why'd *you* leave?"

Sky paused, her hand still on the dish she was rinsing. "I wanted to live somewhere else for a while, where no one knew me." Her gaze flickered briefly to her mother before returning to the dishes.

Ah, it wasn't just about the town. It was about getting space from her parents and their expectations. She didn't have to explain further for him to get it. She loved them, but they were clearly a lot, both assuming they knew what was best for her.

"She deserted us for a while," Esther chided. "But we're glad she's home. It's been hard for our Skylar to leave what happened in Cheyenne back in Cheyenne."

Sky's head whipped around. "*Mom!*"

"What? I'm sure you've told him about the fires."

Becket frowned, his attention fixed on Sky. "Fires?"

She gave her mother what could only be described as a warning glare. "Mom, *stop*. Not tonight."

"But, honey—"

"I'm going to take out the trash." She grabbed the bag, which wasn't even half full, from the trash can and quickly left through the back door.

Esther came to stand beside him and lowered her voice. "I think I should tell you something that I'm sure Sky hasn't told you. Skylar thinks she's…well, she thinks she's cursed."

Becket frowned and tracked Sky through the window as she crossed the yard toward the big trash can.

"A lot happened in Cheyenne, and if you can convince her that the universe *isn't* out to get her, then we'd be grateful."

What the hell was she talking about?

"What happened in Cheyenne?" It was probably low of him to ask her mother and not Sky, but he was sure if he asked her, she wouldn't give him the entire story. Hell, she probably wouldn't give him anything.

"There was a—"

"Esther," Roger called from across the room, "what are you whispering about?"

Esther turned back to the food containers she was packing. "Nothing."

Becket's gaze returned to the window. He straightened. There was a broken slat of wood in the fence between Sky's yard and her other neighbor…and he could've sworn a shadow moved past just as he looked up.

Without a word, he lowered the plates he was holding and went outside. Sky obviously didn't hear him coming, because when he reached her right as she turned, she cried out before pressing a hand to her chest.

"Good God, Becket, you scared me to death!"

"How long has that been broken?" he asked, nodding at the fence.

"Um, maybe a few months. It happened after a storm."

"Who lives there?"

"Just an older woman. She's a bit of a recluse. I don't see her very often. I think she may have dementia. And the few times I've knocked on her door, she didn't seem to care for the company. Why?"

He moved over to the fence and stuck his head through. The yard was overgrown, with big bushes and trees, but no sign of anyone.

"Becket." She touched his shoulder, and he straightened. "What's going on?"

"I saw a shadow when I was inside."

Her brows rose. "On the other side of the fence? No. She

wouldn't be out this late. It's too dark and cold."

His thoughts too.

A cool breeze rolled through the air, as if to prove her point, and Sky visibly shivered.

He needed to get her inside. He slid an arm around her waist and nudged her toward the door. "Come on."

They took three steps before she stopped and turned toward him. "Wait, I need to ask you something."

"Can this wait until we get inside?"

She shook her head. "No. My parents and Tony are in there."

"I know."

"They think we're together."

"I know that too."

"Tonight, Mom hasn't brought up me dying alone once, Dad didn't make me sit next to Tony, and Tony hasn't touched or hit on me…well, apart from whatever that thing was in the hall."

Jesus, the guy was an asshole.

She shuffled her feet, wrapping her arms around her waist as goose bumps pebbled her skin. "So, I was wondering…can we do this for a bit longer?"

He lifted his brows. "*This?*"

"Date. No, not date…pretend to date. Just until Tony leaves town."

"Yes."

Her eyes widened. "Yes? Just like that?"

"Yeah."

He had no fucking idea why he was doing this. Because the woman made him smile regardless of whether they were fighting or not? Because he liked being around *her* more than he liked being alone?

"Thank you." She glanced furtively at the kitchen window, and one side of her mouth lifted. "Mom *and* Tony are watching us."

"Really?"

"Yeah. Dad will probably join them soon. We're officially animals in a zoo."

"Then should we give them something to look at?"

She frowned. "What do you mean?"

"Well, if we want to make this look real…" He stepped closer and curled an arm around her waist.

Her mouth opened in an O, but she didn't pull away.

Slowly—so damn slowly that she had all the time in the world to move back—he lowered his head.

She didn't move back.

He kissed her.

Her lips were soft, and her floral scent so fucking strong it surrounded him. He swept his mouth against hers, his other hand lifting and cupping her cheek.

At first she was stiff in his embrace. But that only lasted a second before she melted against him, her fingers grabbing his shirt, scrunching the material.

Shit, she felt good in his arms.

He pulled her closer and she moaned, the sound so fucking sweet he committed it to memory.

When her lips parted, he slid his tongue past them, and this time she hummed as he tasted her. She was a mixture of red wine and something infinitely feminine.

Her fingers trailed up his neck, and he had an urge to lift her. Drag her entire body against his.

Another groan slipped into the air, and this time he wasn't sure if it was her or him.

He was losing himself when she pushed lightly at his chest. He wanted to growl in protest, and it took too much self-restraint to step back. But he did it.

Her eyes were slightly glazed as she whispered, "I think they'll believe this is real."

Hell yes, they would. Because for a moment, he'd been so lost in the kiss, even *he'd* thought it was real.

CHAPTER 9

Sky looked up as Kristina came outside with a very wet Arlo. Sky was currently working on project "don't think about that kiss with Becket." She'd been working on it for three days, and so far it had been going well, but only because the doggy daycare was such a good distraction.

Sky scratched Bella's head, the Chinese Crested Dog never far from her side. "How'd you do with your first solo wash?" she asked.

Arlo shook his wet fur, and Kristina scrunched her eyes as water splattered all over her.

Sky laughed. Arlo was a very large, very happy German Shepherd. He'd been attending the doggy daycare since Sky had opened the place and usually had a wash twice a week.

Kristina looked down at her damp clothes. "Well, I'm not sure who got wetter, him or me."

"Even with the gown, it can be hard to avoid getting soaked."

"I realized that pretty quickly. He's lucky he's cute."

They were all cute. She swept her gaze over the dozen dogs in the outdoor play area.

Bella snuggled her head into Sky's lap, and she grinned down at the dog.

"How does a doggy daycare compare to your previous office job?" Sky asked.

"I get a lot more wet kisses."

She laughed. "I would hope so."

"This move has been good for me. I needed a change."

"I know that feeling."

Kristina looked up, curiosity lightening her eyes. "I thought you grew up here?"

"I did. But then I moved away. It was great until it wasn't anymore." She swallowed the lump in her throat. It took her a moment to get more words out. "So I came back here because I needed some familiarity."

Kristina's brows furrowed, and she seemed to debate her next words. "Glad to be back?"

"Some days." The days when her parents weren't completely overbearing.

"Well, at least you have people here who care about you. I've been finding it hard to make friends. I went to the bar the other night but left after an hour because it felt weird drinking alone."

Sky's heart squeezed. "I'll go with you next time."

"You don't have to do that."

"I know. I want to."

There was a small pause before Kristina responded. "Um. Okay. Yeah, that would be fun."

"Great. How about tonight? They do half-price jugs of cock-tail at CJ's on Wednesdays."

"Jugs of cocktail?"

"Yep. It's as great as it sounds." Her watch beeped, alerting her that she had somewhere to be. "I need to run off to an acupuncture appointment, but I'll text you the details."

"Sounds good."

Sky smiled before heading inside. She was actually looking

forward to CJ's. She needed a night out. Since returning to Amber Ridge, she hadn't exactly been a socialite. In fact, the only person she really hung out with was her mother.

That was kind of sad, wasn't it?

Dolly looked up from the front desk. "What's put that smile on your face?"

"I'm getting some half-price cocktails at CJ's tonight." She grabbed her bag from the office.

"Damn, woman, and here I was thinking you'd gotten laid."

Dolly's words dragged her mind right back to Becket's kiss. It was far from sex, but the way his lips had moved against hers, the strength in his arm as he'd wrapped it around her—it had felt like more.

She shook her head. *Stop thinking about it, Sky. It was all for show.*

She rounded the desk and pulled open the door. "Nope. I'll see you tomorrow, Dolly."

"There's still time," the older woman called as the door swung shut.

Jesus. Did that woman ever get her mind out of the gutter?

On her way to Clara's home acupuncture studio, Sky cracked her car window open…only to frown.

Smoke. The smell wasn't strong, but it was there, lightly lingering in the wind. And it immediately made her chest feel so tight that it became hard to breathe.

Memories tried to swamp her. Memories she worked so hard to keep deep inside.

She quickly rolled her window back up, but the subtle scent of smoke was still there, pulling her back to when she'd lost Charlie.

A lump formed in her throat, but she swallowed it. Sometimes just thinking about him made her want to fall apart. Not everyone understood. Her parents certainly didn't. You had to have had a pet, loved a pet like family, and then lost them far too early, to get it.

When she reached Clara's, she took a moment in her car to just breathe. But even when she knocked on the door to the garage Clara had converted into an acupuncture space, she still didn't feel okay.

Clara opened the door and smiled. "Sky. Hi. Right on time. Come in."

"Hey. Thanks."

She hadn't even gotten inside when Clara touched her arm. "Is everything okay?"

Crap. Did she not *look* okay? Or was this just Clara being Clara? The other woman had this freaky way of reading people.

"I'm fine. I just...I smelled smoke on the way here and got worried."

"Yeah, I smelled it too, but I'm sure Becket and his crew have it handled." Clara sat at her desk, while Sky took a seat beside her. "There's something else though, isn't there?"

Sky glanced down at her hands, which were clasped tightly in her lap. And the words just fell out of her. "I lost someone in Cheyenne due to a fire. My dog. It might sound silly, but—"

"It doesn't sound silly. He was your family."

She blinked back tears. "He was."

Clara reached out and took her hands. "I'm *so* sorry."

This time, she couldn't stop the tears from rolling down her cheeks. "Thank you."

To her parents, Charlie had just been a dog. Sky had felt so alone in her grief. It was one of the reasons she'd opened up the doggy daycare. And it was why she ran so many fundraisers. Forever trying to make amends for being the reason Charlie lost his life.

She scrubbed the tears from her face. "I think this appointment couldn't have come at a better time." She'd been getting acupuncture for most of her adult life because it always made her feel good. Especially at stressful times.

Clara pushed her chair back. "Why don't you hop up on the bed? I know just what points to do today."

"Sounds great." She slipped off her shoes and got comfortable on the bed.

Clara reached for Sky's arm and touched her pulse. Clara always started sessions this way. All acupuncturists did. Sky had asked Clara about it once, and she'd said something about Qi and blood and organs...it had all gone over her head. She also checked her tongue sometimes, but she had no idea why she did that.

Clara turned and prepared the needles. "How's everything else in your life going?"

Sky could have laughed. Between her parents and Tony and Becket, her life was somewhere between a comedy and a tragedy. But she hadn't told Clara about Becket pretending to be her boyfriend because, one, she hadn't seen her, and two, what was she supposed to say? *Your brother has agreed to pretend to date me so my parents won't set me up with a guy who smells like onions?*

"It's okay," Sky finally answered. "I'm going to CJ's tonight with someone from work, so I'm hoping some cocktails will fix everything."

Clara turned back with a tray of needles. "Oh, I'm going to CJ's too, with Indie."

"What a coincidence." Although, not entirely. CJ's cocktails were popular in this town. "I'll see you there."

"You definitely will."

Clara stared at her feet, and the moment the first needle went in, she felt the first bit of tension ease from her body. She had no idea how this worked, but it did. It was magic.

* * *

FLAMES BURNED in front of Becket's eyes. Bright yellow flames that covered the ground around him.

He held the hose over his shoulder, pointing the water at the fire as Teddy held the body of the hose behind him. His crew was working with another station. They'd been out here for an hour, not only putting out the original fire but also all the spot fires. The damn wind wasn't helping.

By the end, his crew was on the scene for another hour before the last of the flames were finally extinguished.

Thank God.

He pulled off his helmet and turned to Teddy. "You okay?"

Teddy nodded. "That was a big one."

No shit. The biggest they'd seen in a while. The question was, what had started it?

They headed back to the road to see Wayne, the chief of Station 62, standing by one of his engines with his guys. They'd called Wayne's station for backup when it was clear the blaze was bigger than expected.

When Wayne saw Becket and Teddy, he strode toward them. "Investigators are on their way, but I know the cause of the fire."

By the tone of Wayne's voice, Becket knew he wasn't going to like the answer. "Tell me."

"Arson. Just off Highway 58, someone doused trees and vegetation in gasoline, then set them alight."

Becket's muscles contracted. They hadn't had an arsonist in town since he'd become chief. "I'll let our sheriff know. Thanks for the backup."

Wayne dipped his head.

Becket moved back toward his truck, his muscles tight, anger heating his blood.

"Shit," Teddy cursed under his breath. "Someone set the mountain on fire."

"I don't know how people can be so sick in the head that they'd intentionally start a fire." Fires were aggressive, and they didn't show mercy. Give them oxygen, and they'd burn right through anything. They'd take lives. Homes. Everything in their path.

"Sick in the head is correct," Teddy said quietly.

When they reached the engine, Becket climbed in and lifted his radio. "Everyone okay out there?"

He waited until he got confirmations from each of his crew members before calling his brother.

Jesse answered on the third ring. "Becket. How'd it go with the fire?"

"We took care of it, and my crew's starting to clear out."

"Good. The investigator there?"

"Not yet. But the chief from Station 62 believes it was arson. Gasoline was used to set the fire."

Jesse cursed. "You're kidding me?"

"I wish I was. Investigators will confirm." He hoped the information was wrong, but Wayne had been a chief for twenty years —the guy knew fires.

"I'll take some deputies down there and talk to the investigator," Jesse said. "Are you okay?"

His back teeth ground together as he looked out the window. "We put our lives on the line putting out these fires. Finding out this one was intentionally set feels like a kick in the gut."

Teddy grunted his agreement from the passenger seat.

"I know," Jesse said firmly. "You did your part by putting it out, and if it's confirmed this was arson, I'll do my part in finding the perp. I don't know what the hell's going on in this town. Someone's been breaking into houses and robbing people. Now someone's setting fires."

"Was there another break-in?"

"Last night. An elderly man's house. Fortunately, he had dogs who woke up barking and scared the perp off, but they still got away with some stuff."

Becket cursed.

"Anyway. That's *my* problem. I'll head down there now."

No. It was everyone's problem.

He hung up and radioed his team again. Once it was confirmed everyone was packed up and in the other engine, he and Teddy left.

Back at the station, Becket took a quick shower before heading to his office to write up the incident. A lot of people thought firefighters were always in the thick of the action, but that was a lie. Every incident had to be written up, and all the paperwork took hours. Some weeks, he spent way more time in front of his computer than putting out fires.

He was halfway through the report when he glanced at his phone for the hundredth damn time. He hadn't seen Sky since the dinner with her parents and Tony last weekend. They'd exchanged numbers after everyone left, but neither had used them…yet.

Fuck it.

Becket: Are you avoiding me, Peaches?

Her response was immediate.

Sky: No more than usual.

Becket: Still processing my earth-shattering kiss?

Sky: Still processing the loss of my tree.

Becket: You really need to move past that. It's not healthy to hang on to things for so long.

Sky: What's not healthy is telling my parents that I was too shy to ask you out a month ago because you're the fire chief. Talk about a big ego.

Becket: Nothing wrong with a healthy ego.

Sky: If you were with me right now, you'd be witnessing an eye roll.

Becket: I'd actually like to see that eye roll. Tonight?

Sky: Tonight I'm going out.

Becket: Where?

Sky: None of your business.

Becket: I'm your boyfriend, of course it's my business.

Sky: Fake boyfriend, so no, it isn't.

Becket: If you don't tell me where you're going, I might just get worried and call your parents looking for you.

Sky: You wouldn't. You don't even have their number.

Becket: I would, and I do. Your mom was all too happy to give it to me at dinner the other night. I think she's really warming up to me.

The three dots popped up then disappeared. His lips tugged up. He could just imagine the frustration on her face.

Sky: Fine. I'm going to CJ's with a friend, so no need to overreact and call my mother like a psycho.

Becket: Now it's not very nice to call your boyfriend names, is it?

Sky: I'm not replying anymore.

Becket: It's always so nice chatting with you, Peaches.

He was still smiling when a knock came at the door. Teddy leaned against the frame. "Hey."

"Hey, a few of us are ordering lunch from the diner. Want anything?

"A turkey sandwich would be great."

"Done."

Teddy was about to walk away when Becket called him back. "Ted?"

"Yeah, boss?"

"You busy tonight?"

His brows lifted. "On a Wednesday night? My plan was to have a beer on my deck."

"Want to have a beer with me at CJ's instead?"

"A beer with my boss at the bar so I can win some brownie points? Hell yeah, I do."

"See you there at eight."

Teddy nodded and wandered back down the hall. Becket turned back to his phone, about to text Sky that he'd see her there...but he stopped himself.

It would be a nice surprise for his girlfriend.

CHAPTER 10

Sky followed Kristina into the bar. It was busy. People-everywhere, couldn't-hear-yourself-think kind of busy. Her employee glanced over her shoulder. "Let's find a table."

Kristina had picked her up, and after the day she'd had, Sky was grateful, because it meant she could have a few drinks without worrying about driving home. Acupuncture had taken the edge off her anxiety, but the scent of smoke still lingered in the air around town, making that pit in her belly feel huge.

They did a circle of the bar, but every booth and table was taken.

"Maybe there's a spot at the bar," Sky suggested.

They were just turning when Sky spotted two women standing at a table.

Clara and her cousin Indie.

Clara grinned before waving Sky over.

Sky took Kristina's hand. "This way. Come meet some of my friends."

Well, technically it was just Clara who was her friend. She didn't know Indie that well, but the woman seemed lovely.

"Hey," Clara said, when Sky stopped at the table. She gestured to Indie. "Sky, you remember my cousin Indie."

Sky smiled at the other woman. "I do. Hi."

"It's good to see you again."

"You too." Sky turned to Kristina. "This is Kristina. She works at the doggy daycare and is new to town."

They exchanged greetings before Indie turned back to Sky. "Your ball was amazing. Did you raise a lot of money?"

"Thank you. We did, and I was so happy with how it went. The locals here in Amber Ridge are so generous when it comes to my fundraisers."

"You do them often?" Indie asked.

"I do. The next one will be a dog wash fundraiser. I'm hoping to do it outside and get coffee and food trucks to come out. Make a real day of it. We have so many dog owners here in Amber Ridge."

Kristina laughed. "You're not wrong. I can't believe how busy the doggy daycare gets."

Clara bumped Sky's hip. "And they all know you because you've built such a great business."

"I'm very lucky the people in our town trust me with their dogs." She studied the empty table. "No cocktails yet?"

"We just barely got the table." Indie laughed.

"Well, first round's on me."

Half an hour later, they had two jugs of strawberry mojitos in the center of the table, and Sky was already into her second glass.

"So, where have you come from, Kristina?" Clara asked.

"Connecticut. I liked it there, but I needed a fresh start and to do something new, so here I am." She sipped her drink before looking at Clara. "And you're an acupuncturist?"

"I am. And I will tell anyone who'll listen all about acupuncture's healing powers."

"She's a bit like that dad from *My Big Fat Greek Wedding* who believes Windex fixes everything," Indie said. "But her Windex is acupuncture."

Kristina laughed. "How'd you get into that?"

"Well, I was a lawyer, but then I got sick—cancer—and it kind of changed my whole life."

Sky's fingers tightened around her glass. Clara had shared that information with her a few months into their acupuncture appointments. She'd had stage four Hodgkin's Lymphoma and gone through chemotherapy. She couldn't even imagine how hard that would have been for Clara.

Kristina straightened. "Oh my God, I'm sorry."

Clara dipped her head. "Thank you. I lived in New York, and to say my job as a lawyer was stressful would be an understatement. Then I was diagnosed and it was like, 'What am I doing? I don't enjoy this. And I miss my mom and Amber Ridge and having time to take care of myself. Why am I wasting time that might be cut off tomorrow, living a life I don't love?' It was the reminder I needed that we don't live forever, so I have to make every day count."

"You're okay now though, aren't you?" Sky clarified.

"I'm okay now. I still get a lot of fatigue, and I get annual checks to make sure the cancer's still gone."

Indie slid an arm around Clara's shoulders. "You kicked cancer's ass!"

"Hell yes, I did."

"And thank God you moved back. I wouldn't know what to do without you."

"You don't have any siblings?" Sky asked.

"My brother's in the military and my sister lives in San Francisco." Something crossed over Indie's face. "I'm not close with my sister."

Clara gave her cousin a gentle smile before her gaze homed in on something behind Sky. She sucked in a breath and straightened.

Sky looked over her shoulder and spotted a man. He was tall. Probably as tall as Becket, and he had the same broad shoulders and thick arms. She'd seen him before...at the fundraiser ball.

She looked back at Clara. "That's Jesse's friend, right?"

Clara cleared her throat. "His best friend, Holden. He's a family friend, too."

Indie leaned forward. "Clara gets a little nervous around him."

"I do. I turn into a gigantic mess of nerves and can't say the right thing to save my life!" Clara groaned. "He's just so tall and beautiful, and he smells like peppermint and pine. And when he talks, his voice is this deep, gravelly—"

"Clara."

She stopped talking and looked at her cousin.

"Tell him how you feel."

Clara opened her mouth, clearly trying to say something, before snapping her lips shut. Then mumbling, "Maybe."

Sky glanced over her shoulder again—and this time it was *her* back that straightened. Because now, Holden wasn't alone. A guy with blond hair stood beside him...and Becket, who was looking right at her.

Her heart started to thump faster. Hard thumps that also quickened her breathing.

He wore a tight white shirt that made his biceps look even thicker, and the muscles in his chest stretched the material. But the thing that really stole her attention was his lips. Full red lips that just a few nights ago, had been kissing her.

She forced her gaze away.

"Oh no..." Clara inched closer. "I apologize in advance about my brother."

Sky could only nod.

She told herself not to look again, but her damn body had no self-restraint. She turned her head—and gasped to find Becket standing right beside her.

"Hi, Peaches." He slid an arm around her waist and kissed her cheek, as if he'd done it a thousand times before.

She couldn't breathe. He was so big and warm, and he smelled so good. But what the hell was he doing? They weren't supposed to fake date in front of *everyone*. Were they? They hadn't discussed it. God, why hadn't they discussed it?

She subtly elbowed him in the gut, but he didn't even flinch.

Clara's mouth opened and closed. "Um...why is your arm around Sky? And did you just *kiss* her?"

"We're dating," Becket said before she could say anything.

A thick silence surrounded the table. Even Holden, who'd moved around to stand on the other side of Clara, looked like someone had just dropped a bomb on him.

"You are not," Clara finally said. "You hate each other."

"I have *never* hated Sky," Becket said, sounding completely sincere.

"Um...will you excuse us for a second?" Sky grabbed Becket's arm and led him away. She waited until they reached the bar before spinning on him. "What the hell are you doing?"

"It's a small town. It's safer for everyone to think we're dating so the truth doesn't get back to your parents."

"Safer? You think it's *safer* to keep up this charade in front of everyone, including your family, who knows you would never date me?"

One side of his mouth lifted, and dammit, even that was sexy. "If my family thinks I wouldn't date someone as beautiful as you, they don't know me very well."

Her mouth went dry. He'd just called her beautiful. And why the hell did it make her belly give a funny kick?

"I just..." She shook her head. "I think it will be too hard to keep up the façade in front of everyone."

"Really?" He slid his arm around her waist again. "Was it hard to kiss me the other night?"

Every hair on her arms stood on end at his breath whispering across her skin. Too close. His mouth was too close. "Well…I mean…it wasn't *hard*, but it wasn't easy."

Ha. What hadn't been easy was ending the kiss. Walking away from him.

His mouth lowered to her ear, and his single word came out as a breathy whisper. "Liar."

She swallowed the lump in her throat. She *was* a liar.

"I'm doing this for you, Peaches. For the benefit of your parents and Tony. But say the word and I'll tell them the truth."

Her heart started to beat faster. She should tell him they were done. That this was over. But the words wouldn't come out.

"Sky."

Her head swung around to find Clara standing beside them.

Clara's gaze flickered between them before returning to her. "Is everything okay?"

Becket's arm tightened around her, his thumb slipping beneath the band of her jeans and swiping her skin.

The two words fell from her lips into the air. "We're dating."

* * *

BECKET LIFTED his beer to his mouth, his gaze returning to Sky for the fiftieth fucking time.

The women were working their way through their fifth jug of cocktail, and CJ did *not* hold back on the rum. He'd never thought of himself as a possessive guy, but right now, he wanted to march right over there, wrap his arm around her waist, and drag her out of the bar.

"Shit. You really are into her."

Becket shifted his gaze from Sky to Holden. Teddy had gone up to the bar with Sky's friend, and so far hadn't worked his way back to them.

"You sound surprised," Becket said.

Holden scoffed. "Uh, you made it sound like she was one argument away from murdering you in your sleep."

Becket grinned. "She probably still is."

"When did this happen?"

"At the ball."

There was a beat of silence. "When you were dancing? I was waiting for one of you to throw a drink at the other."

Becket laughed. He was also surprised that hadn't happened.

Sky glanced over and sent him a tight smile that said, "stop staring at me, you creep," before looking back at her friends.

He bit back another laugh before turning to Holden. "How's the woodworking going?"

Holden had bought a place in the mountains with a shed big enough to function as a workshop for his woodworking business. And he was damn good at it. He could make everything from dressers to an entire new kitchen.

"It's going well. Word's getting around town about what I can do, so there's been plenty of work."

"Good. And you're enjoying it here?"

"I am. It feels like home." His gaze returned to something across the room.

Becket followed his gaze to Clara. The two had always stared at each other more than either probably realized. They liked each other. That much was obvious. But as far as Becket knew, neither had ever made a move. Because Jesse was Holden's best friend?

Well, what was the point in dancing around the topic?

"Is there something going on with you and my sister?"

Holden's gaze flew back to Becket. "What?"

"You've been watching her a lot lately."

"I've just been worried about her. She pushes herself too hard and does too much."

"I've been worried about her too," Becket said, voice low, even though she wasn't close enough to hear. "She's got this 'experience life' mantra, and it's not always a good thing, but I can't tell *her* that because—"

"She wants people to think she can take care of herself," Holden cut in.

"Yeah."

Emotions flickered in Holden's eyes. Concern and something else…fear? "It's not a bad thing to have people looking out for you."

"You're right. But she doesn't want people to think she's not strong enough to do it herself."

"Not strong enough? She's the strongest person I know. But she *was* sick, so she needs to be careful that she doesn't push herself too hard."

Becket studied him. Was this just about Clara? Holden had been raised by his mother until she'd gotten sick when he was a teenager—lung cancer—and passed away not long after. Jesse had mentioned that her death had affected Holden on a deeper level than most. Partly because she'd been his only family, and he'd gone into foster care after she'd passed. And partly because she'd been sick for so long before she died that it had consumed his life.

Suddenly, Holden straightened. "Where'd they go?"

Becket's gaze shot back to the table—empty. Shit. He'd been planning on driving Sky home.

He glanced over at the bar to see Sky's friend and Teddy still talking. They stood close, Teddy's hand on her hip.

He crossed over to them. "Hey. Do you know where the women went?"

Her brows rose. "Yeah, they came over and said they were heading home. I said I'd stay."

Who the fuck was driving? They'd all been drinking.

He beelined for the door, Holden close behind. They found the women in the parking lot by Clara's car.

"Leaving?" Becket asked.

"We are," Clara said far too casually. "Why?"

"We'll take you guys home," Holden said.

"I hardly drank anything." Clara cocked her head. "You really think I'd drive drunk?"

Holden stepped closer. "I just think it's safer for me to drive you."

"I'm really okay. But thank you." She slid behind the wheel.

"She's fine to drive," Indie said before jumping into the passenger seat.

"Sky," Becket said, a warning in his voice. "I can take you home."

A half smile curved her lips. "Thank you, *boyfriend*. But no thanks."

"Honey, we live next door to each other."

"Oh, I know. There's been no avoiding you. Tell me the truth —did the last owner leave because of you?"

His lips twitched. "Let me take you home."

"Pizza."

Becket frowned. "Pizza?"

Clara rolled down the window. "We ordered a pizza from Burt."

"His pizza stinks," Holden said, frustration still brimming in his eyes.

"Not after a few drinks," Sky sang.

Oh, Jesus.

"I'll take you to pick up your pizza," Becket pushed.

"You're cute, but I choose Clara." Then she leaned against him, rose to her toes and whispered, "Safer option."

His back teeth ground together. He didn't seem to have a fucking choice. "Fine. Straight home after the pizza."

Clara rolled her eyes. "Oh, dang. Ruined my plans of bar hopping until we find a biker gang."

Sky pecked a kiss to his cheek. "See you later, *honey*."

He had to watch as she slid into the back seat of the car before Clara drove away.

Holden moved up beside him. "I'll follow them. You wait for Sky at home."

Thank fuck they were on the same page. Some might call it overprotective. Becket didn't give a damn.

"Thanks." He clenched Holden's shoulder in gratitude before moving to his car.

The trip home was quick, and once inside, he kicked off his shoes and waited.

It didn't take long. Fifteen minutes later, his phone buzzed with a text.

Holden: She's getting dropped off now.

Good. He'd give her a few minutes before checking on her.

But only a minute passed before a scratching noise sounded at his door.

What the hell was that?

Why wasn't the key going in? Sure, she'd had a few cocktails, and her vision was a bit all over the place, but the dang key should still fit.

She tried to push it in again. Same thing.

What the heck was going on?

She was about to try a third time when the door flew open.

Her jaw dropped. "Becket? What are you doing here?"

He lifted a brow, looking amused. "Peaches...this is my house."

His house? She stepped back and looked up. No second story. Then she glanced at the house beside it. Her house.

Shit.

She really should have stopped at the second jug of mojitos. Damn Indie for continuing to order more when Sky had zero self-restraint.

Becket opened the door wider. "Come in, Peaches."

"But it's your house."

"I'm aware."

She looked over at her place. It was so far...and she was so tired. And maybe a teeny tiny part of her wanted to see what Becket's place looked like.

She walked inside.

Interesting. Everything looked…normal. Well, normal for a man. A brown leather couch. A wooden coffee table. Black cabinetry in the kitchen, which she'd never been a fan of, but in his kitchen looked sleek.

The door closed behind her. "What are you thinking?"

"You have a nice place."

"Surprised?"

"A little." Why exactly, she wasn't sure. Maybe she'd expected him to have a pinboard with her face on it.

"What happened to the pizza?"

"We picked it up, took one bite each and threw it out. Turns out even alcohol can't make Burt's pizza edible." She looked longingly at the couch. And like her feet had a mind of their own, they just started making their way over there, and she collapsed onto the leather cushion.

Comfortable. Far too comfortable.

She closed her eyes. Immediately, her body relaxed and the room stopped swaying.

"Are you okay?"

His voice was close and deep.

Her eyes opened and, sure enough, he was sitting on the coffee table, right in front of her. She hadn't even heard him move.

"I'm sorry." The words were out before she could stop them.

"For what?"

"I've been angry, and I've been taking it out on you. Don't get me wrong, you're an arrogant dick sometimes, but I've probably been just as bad."

He didn't even crack a smile. Instead, his gaze was intense, almost like he was trying to figure her out. "Why have you been angry?"

He leaned forward and swept a lock of hair from her face. The warmth of his fingers against her skin had the words rolling out of her. "My life is the burnt toast theory."

"What's the burnt toast theory?"

"The theory that minor inconveniences or setbacks are blessings in disguise."

He frowned. "What was your inconvenience or setback?"

"My dog got sick and I didn't want to leave him, so I called one of the newer employees and asked if she could cover my shift at the dog café."

"How was that a blessing for you?"

"There was a fire." She closed her eyes, but nothing could really dull the pain from that day. "Eloise got trapped in the back room and died."

Becket cursed under his breath.

"I was so angry." That was an understatement. "Angry at how unfair it was, upset that she had died and so filled with guilt because she was there because of me. It should have been me."

"Hey."

She opened her eyes to see him leaning closer.

"It shouldn't have been *anyone*. Sometimes really shitty things happen for reasons no one can explain."

"This one could be explained. It was a sixteen-year-old kid who thought it would be funny to set a trash can on fire outside the café."

"Is he in jail?"

"She. And last I heard, she was awaiting trial."

His intense gaze burned into her. "That's why you left."

The alcohol started to burn in her belly. "Actually, no. I stayed for a while. I was stupid and thought I could move on."

"Why couldn't you?"

Her skin suddenly felt hot as the memory of the other flames danced in her mind. She closed her eyes again and shook her head. "It doesn't matter."

A lie. The weight of how much it mattered almost choked her. "Sky—"

"I'm sorry I tried to open your door with my key."

He cocked his head, clearly wanting to keep talking about her life in Cheyenne, but thankfully, he didn't push it. "If you hadn't come here, I would have come to your place."

After a moment, she frowned. "You called me Sky."

"I did."

One side of his mouth lifted. Was it possible a one-sided smile was sexier than a two-sided smile? Or was that the alcohol talking?

"I'm going to regret saying this in the morning…" she whispered. "But you're nice to look at."

The half smile turned into a full two-sided, dimples-and-everything smile.

Nope, she was wrong, this was better.

"You're not so bad yourself, Peaches."

Ugh, they were back to Peaches. Her eyes started to droop again. "I'm tired. I don't usually drink this much."

"Why did you tonight?"

"The smoke."

"What do you mean?"

"You don't want to know. Could you get me some water? Then I'll go."

Her eyes were now closed, and for a moment there was a heavy silence. Then the shuffle of his movement sounded.

She forced one eye open to see him entering the kitchen. His biceps flexed as he reached up for a glass. Why did he have to be so easy to look at? It made disliking him really hard.

Ha. It wasn't just the way he looked that made disliking him hard. When she put aside the fence, the tree and the camera stuff, he was actually kind of a nice guy.

Oh jeez, had Drunk Sky really just called Becket nice? At least it wasn't out loud.

Her eyes closed again, and suddenly her eyelids felt too heavy to lift. His couch was too comfortable, and somehow the leather smelled just like him.

Maybe she could stay just for a little bit.

* * *

BECKET'S MUSCLES WERE TENSE. All he could think was—it could have been *her* in the fire in Cheyenne. She could have lost her life and she wouldn't be here right now.

Fuck, he hated that thought.

There was more to her story that she wasn't sharing. How much more, he wasn't sure. Did it explain her cryptic statement about the smoke making her drink?

He filled a glass with water. Maybe there'd come a time when she'd trust him enough to open up about her past.

He moved back to the couch…and chuckled.

She was asleep. He shouldn't be surprised. She'd been struggling to keep her eyes open since the second she sat on his couch.

He set the water onto the coffee table and crouched in front of her. "Sky."

Nothing. Not even a flicker of her eyelids. She was completely out.

Unable to stop himself, he grazed another lock of hair off her face. Just like earlier, his fingertips ran over her skin, and all he could think about was how damn soft it was.

He blew out a breath and looked at his front door. He could take her home, but no part of him felt comfortable leaving her alone in her house after she'd drunk so much.

She could take his bed, and he'd take the couch.

He eyed the sofa. It was too damn small to be comfortable, but fuck, he'd slept in worse places during his time as a SEAL.

He went into his bedroom and pulled the sheets back on his bed before returning to the living room. Gently, he slipped his arms behind her back and knees. The second her body was settled against his, his gut gave a fucking kick.

Jesus, why did she feel so good against him?

He carried her down the hall and lowered her to the mattress. Carefully, he removed her shoes before pulling the covers over her. Immediately, she rolled into a ball on her side.

He was about to walk away when she mumbled something.

He frowned and stopped, listening.

Then she whispered again, *"Charlie."*

Who the fuck was Charlie? An ex?

The thought put a sour fucking taste in his mouth.

Back in the kitchen, he poured himself a shot of whiskey. The liquid burned his throat going down, and he grimaced.

He shouldn't care if she was saying an ex's name in her sleep. They weren't really dating, and they'd only kissed once. One fucking time. It shouldn't have had such an impact on him.

So why *did* he care?

He grabbed some blankets from the hall closet and moved back to the couch. Once the lights were off, he stripped to his briefs and lay down.

It would be a damn uncomfortable night. Not only because the couch was small, but because every part of him was hyper-aware of Sky a dozen feet away. Sleeping in his bed. Her soft curves tangled in his sheets.

Shut it down, Becket. He closed his eyes.

He didn't know how much time passed. An hour? Two? But he wasn't even close to falling asleep when a rustling somewhere in the house sounded...then footsteps.

The fuck?

He threw off the blankets and was about to get up when a figure appeared from the hall.

"Sky?"

She didn't respond. She didn't even look at him.

What the hell was going on? Even though it was dark, he could see the blue of her eyes seemed glazed.

"Peaches? Are you okay?"

Without a word, she moved toward him. It took her getting halfway across the room for him to realize she was sleepwalking.

Shit. He'd had a friend in the military who was a sleepwalker, and Sky's movements were eerily similar.

As he watched, she lowered beside him on the couch—then snuggled into his chest.

For a moment, he didn't move.

What the fuck was he supposed to do? Wake her?

His friend always told them not to wake him if he walked in his sleep. Something about triggering a stress response.

But he couldn't stay here. He had to get up…right?

She nuzzled her face into his shoulder before whispering three words.

"Don't leave me."

Even if he wanted to get up, her peachy scent pulled him in. And the way her soft curves melted into his hard edges—he didn't want to separate from her.

A few minutes passed before he pulled the blanket up over their bodies. He'd probably regret this in the morning, but he didn't care.

He closed his eyes, and finally, with her body pressed against his, Becket slept.

CHAPTER 12

There was someone behind Sky. Someone warm and hard. Their heavy arm was strung around her waist, weighing her down to the soft surface beneath her.

Her eyes flashed open to see a wooden coffee table in front of her. Not her wooden coffee table. Nothing in this room was hers. Everything was too dark, the tones too masculine. And was that a figurine of a dinosaur with a penis-shaped head?

She scrunched her eyes, recounting everything from last night. The bar. The cocktails. Clara dropping her off at home. Then…

She gasped—but then immediately wanted to slap her hand over her mouth.

Clara had dropped her at the wrong house. *Becket's* house.

Because she thought they were dating?

God, it didn't matter why. The point was, she had. Then Sky had told him about Eloise before falling asleep on his couch.

Stupid! Why had she drunk so much and let the alcohol turn her into a bumbling idiot?

But wait…she hadn't fallen asleep with Becket. She'd been

alone on the couch. So why was he wrapped around her like a pretzel? Had he decided to climb in after she was asleep?

Creep.

"Thinking pretty hard there, Peaches."

She elbowed him in the stomach, getting a very satisfying grunt in response, before scrambling off the couch. Of course, in her haste, she fell on the floor, almost hitting her head on the coffee table, but she didn't let that slow her down. She shot to her feet, the air whipping in and out of her lungs.

"What the hell, Hayes?" she yelled.

He sat up and rubbed his stomach. "You wake up all your boyfriends like that?"

"Only the fake kind who climb onto the couch with me while I'm unconscious and decide to have some nonconsensual cuddles."

He laughed. He freaking *laughed.*

What…the…heck?

He swung his bare feet onto the floor. "First of all, it was *you* who climbed onto the couch with *me*. And I'm pretty sure I felt you grab my arm and wrap it around your waist when you rolled onto your side."

"I might have been slightly drunk"—okay, more than slightly, but that wasn't important—"but I remember falling asleep on the couch *alone.*"

He stood, and dear Heavenly Father above, the man was only wearing briefs. And he was *shredded.* She'd known he was packing some muscle—one look at him in a T-shirt and anyone could see that—but this was muscle upon muscle.

How often did he work out?

"I put you in my bed and came out here to sleep on the couch," he said slowly, like she was a child who otherwise wouldn't understand. "But apparently, you can't stay away from me even when you're unconscious, because you sleepwalked right onto the couch with me."

No. No, no, no. That couldn't be true. It was too embarrassing. "That's not true."

"Afraid it is, Peaches."

She hadn't sleepwalked in a long time…almost a year. It was usually induced by stress.

And she *had* been stressed after smelling the smoke yesterday.

Dammit. "Okay, let's say I believe you. Why wouldn't you just get up and go back to your own bed?"

"Because you told me not to."

She swallowed. "You're lying."

He stepped closer, and it took every scrap of self-restraint she possessed to not move back and reinstate that semi-safe space between them. "You climbed onto the couch with me." Another step closer. "Wrapped your arm around me. And whispered, 'Don't leave me.'"

She felt sick. That post-humiliation, new-core-memory-created kind of sick.

He reached out and touched her hip. "I couldn't say no to that."

The deep, sexy tone of his voice combined with the way his touch made her lower belly quiver—it was too much. "I have to go."

"Stay for breakfast."

She took a quick step back, hitting the back of her legs against the coffee table. "No. I, uh, need to get to work."

It wasn't a lie. She was due in at nine, but she didn't even know what the time was.

She yanked her purse up from the coffee table, then ran—yes, ran—barefoot from his house. And she swore she heard the man laughing behind her.

Once inside her house, she slammed the door closed and rested her head against the wood.

Why? Why had she made an idiot of herself last night?

Because she liked running from a fake boyfriend's house? Because she enjoyed being humiliated?

Argh.

She pulled her phone from her purse and her jaw dropped. It was eight thirty. She started work in thirty freaking minutes.

Dropping her purse, she raced up the stairs and into her bedroom, where she stripped and took the fastest shower of her life.

It took her exactly twenty-one minutes to get ready, but that didn't include feeding herself. It was fine—she'd eat at work. She probably had an apple or something lying around at the office. And there was a coffee machine there. She didn't really feel like much more than coffee anyway.

She raced outside—only to run straight into a large chest.

She reared back, gasping. "Tony? What are you doing here?"

He cleared his throat. "Hi, Sky. I, um…well…I've been thinking about us."

Really? *Now?* He came over at almost nine on a weekday morning to talk about them?

"Us?"

He moved closer. "Yeah. I've been thinking about how we kind of grew up together. And how our families would always joke about how we would end up together."

Jesus. This was not happening.

She took a breath. "Tony, our families *were* good friends growing up. My parents still really like you, and yes, they would like to see us together because of your connection to the church. But we have nothing in common. And I'm with someone else. I'm sorry if that disappoints you."

A deep frown cut into his brow. "But—"

"I really need to get to work."

She tried to step around him, but he snagged her arm.

"Tony—"

"*Hey.*"

They both turned at the deep, angry voice.

* * *

BECKET TURNED OFF THE SHOWER. He was trying to think of something, *anything*, but Sky. The way her blue eyes had widened when he touched her. The curve of her waist beneath his palm.

Fuck, he was losing his goddamn mind. He needed to get her out of his head.

Maybe he'd go pound the shit out of the bag at the fire station. That always took the edge off.

He'd just pulled on a shirt and some jeans when his phone rang. It was his mother.

He answered on the second ring. "Hey, Mom."

"Becket James Hayes."

Shit. Why was his mother middle-naming him? The last time she'd done that, it was because he'd been away with his SEAL team for over three months and hadn't called her to check in. Was that it? Was he not checking in with her often enough?

No. He'd called her last week. "Whatever it is, Jesse did it."

"Becket," she scolded.

Well, it had always worked as a kid. "What's wrong, Mom?"

"Clara called."

He stopped beside his coffee machine in the kitchen. "And what did my darling sister have to say?"

"She told me that you're dating someone."

He cringed. He'd known it would get back to his mother, but he hadn't thought it would happen this quickly. He should have. This was a small town, and with all of his family members here, it made it feel even smaller.

He scrubbed a hand over his face. "Uh, yeah, I am."

"Who is she? And why haven't I met her?"

"It's new."

"It doesn't matter. My son, the child I gave life to, meets

someone he likes enough to date—which never happens, I might add—then I think I have a right to know about it."

She wasn't messing around when she dropped the "gave him life" card. He checked the pantry for coffee. "Mom. Just give me a month or so to settle into things."

Would they still be fake dating in a month? And why the hell did the possibility of the answer being a "no" feel like a gut punch?

"A month?" His mother's voice softened. "Becket, I love you, and I want to meet the woman who's made you proud enough to announce her as your girlfriend. So, Sunday night for dinner."

"I don't—"

"This isn't negotiable, Becket. I'm meeting her."

No coffee. He was getting a scolding from his mother, and he had no coffee.

"Okay." The second the word was out, he wanted to bite it back. Lying to everyone else was one thing, but his mother? She always saw right through him.

"Good. Let me know her favorite food and I'll make that. I love you."

"I love you too, Mom."

He hung up and blew out a long breath. Looked like Sky was having a meal with his family on Sunday. And now he needed a big cup of double-shot espresso.

He shoved his phone into his pocket and grabbed his keys as he headed out.

The car in front of her house was the first thing he saw. A blue Ford.

His gaze whipped over to Sky's front door to see the asshole standing in front of her.

Tony.

Becket was moving before he could stop himself, crossing his yard into hers, never taking his eyes off them. He was only a few feet away when Tony grabbed her arm.

The fuck?

"*Hey.*"

Both Sky and Tony looked up, the jerk's eyes narrowing on Becket. "Jesus Christ."

"Take your hand off her. *Now.*"

"We're having a conversation."

Did he really just fucking ignore Becket's command?

He grabbed the guy's wrist. "Final warning: release her before I make you."

"Will you just give us five—"

Becket squeezed, and the jerk cried out. The second his fingers released Sky, Becket twisted his arm behind his back and bent him over the porch railing.

Sky gasped. "Becket!"

Becket ignored Sky and leaned over Tony. "I'm going to let you go. But the next time I give you a warning and you don't listen, I won't be so forgiving."

He released Tony and stepped back, making sure he remained between the asshole and Sky.

Tony straightened, disbelief in his eyes as his gaze shifted from Becket to Sky. "You're really *dating* this guy?"

Sky's arms wrapped around her waist. "Yes."

"Go," Becket growled.

Tony's eyes narrowed on Becket before moving back to Sky. "This isn't over, Sky."

Yes, it fucking was.

Tony spun and marched back to his car.

Becket waited until he drove away before turning. "What the hell, Sky?"

She frowned. "What do you mean, what the hell?"

"Why didn't you shout out for help when he grabbed you? Or, I don't know, kick him in the balls?"

"I had it handled."

"Didn't look like it."

The wrong thing to say, if the tightening of her fists was anything to go by. "I didn't need your help. And now I need to go to work." She stormed off the porch.

He followed her. "You're not gonna say thank you?"

"Oh, sorry. Thank you for telling me I can't handle my business."

"I know you can handle your business. But as your boyfriend, I felt it appropriate to step in."

"*Fake* boyfriend. You keep missing the fake bit."

"Why do you seem fixated on that part?"

"Maybe because it's kind of important?"

"Nothing felt fake when you slid onto the couch with me last night."

She shot a disgusted look over her shoulder. "I was asleep."

"And you still couldn't keep away."

She stopped at her car and turned. "You need therapy, you know that? You think way too much of yourself."

"Can't possibly be as much as you think of me."

"Argh. You're impossible! I can't believe I was actually starting to like you."

"I think you started a long time ago, honey."

"I could strangle you. You know that?" She unlocked her car and dropped into the driver's seat. "I'm late for work. I'll see you later."

"Oh, by the way, my mom wants to have you over for dinner on Sunday."

She looked at him like he'd lost his mind, before slamming the car door.

He was going to take that as a maybe.

CHAPTER 13

"I'm so sorry about last night."

Sky glanced across the washroom at Kristina. "Sorry about what?"

"I totally ditched you."

Sky shook her head, her attention returning to drying Bella. "I just wanted you to have a good night out in Amber Ridge. And it looks like you did."

Stallion, the large Bulldog, shook his wet coat. Kristina laughed before looking back at Sky, a slow smile stretching her face. "I definitely did. Teddy asked for my number and has already texted three times today."

"Wow. You must have really made an impression." She threw the towel into the wash basket, and this time Bella shook her coat. Luckily, she was pretty dry.

"Seems that way." Kristina tilted her head. "So…Becket was kind of cute…"

Cute? She could use a lot of words to describe Becket, but cute wasn't one of them. Annoying. Arrogant. Tall and too sexy for his own good. Yeah, they all fit better.

Sky cleared her throat. "It's new. I don't even know how long we'll last."

"Ha. The way he was looking at you makes me think he won't let you go anytime soon."

How was he looking at her?

She shook her head. She shouldn't care. There was nothing going on between them. Well, nothing more than a fake relationship.

Besides, she was still mad at him because of the whole Tony incident that morning. "We'll see. I'm going to take Bella out front to wait for Rosemary. Enjoy washing Stallion."

Kristina laughed. "The names some people come up with for their pets never cease to amaze me."

"Ha. I've got some names that would knock your socks off."

She wasn't joking. Bark Twain was probably up there as the most memorable, but Chewbacca and Droolius Caesar weren't far behind.

She headed to the front. She was done for the day, and she could not wait to get home, put on her comfy, oversized pajamas and binge an entire season of *Brooklyn Nine-Nine*. Anything and everything to avoid Becket. And whatever happened, she *was not* going to think about how good his body had felt around hers on the couch this morning.

"Hey, Rosemary's not here yet?" Sky asked once she reached the front desk.

"Not yet." Dolly grinned at her. It was an I-know-something-you-probably-don't-want-me-to-know grin.

"What?"

"I heard a little rumor."

Oh, God. "Well, lucky it's just a rumor."

Dolly spun on her. "Sky Williams. Are you in bed with your sexy fire chief neighbor and didn't tell me?"

She rolled her eyes.

Thanks, Kristina.

Would it break Dolly's heart to hear that Becket was still the same six-plus feet of annoyance he was last week? "You don't need to get too excited. It's new and will probably be short-lived." About as short as Tony's stay in Amber Ridge.

"I knew it was just a matter of time. Love and hate often come hand in hand."

And where did overbearing and frustrating enter the mix?

The door opened and Rosemary came in. Her graying hair was pulled up into a ponytail, and she wore an oversized purple knitted sweater.

The older woman beamed down at Bella. "Hello, my darling."

Sky let go of the lead and the Chinese Crested ran into her owner's arms.

Rosemary picked her up before looking at Sky. "How was her day?"

"Great. She played. She ate. She pooped. We had a nice big wash."

"Wonderful. Thank you. I'm so grateful for your daycare. Bella just loves it here." Rosemary was retired, so she just brought Bella here half days while she shopped and ran errands.

"We love having her," Sky said. And it was true. She truly loved Bella.

"Well, I'll see you ladies later," Rosemary said as she left, squishing her face into Bella's neck.

Once the door closed behind them, Sky grabbed her bag from the storeroom. "I'm heading out now."

"Got some romantic plans with your sexy-as-sin firefighter?"

This is why she shouldn't have let Becket spread the word last night. Dolly wouldn't let her live it down. "Actually, I've got a pajama date with *Brooklyn Nine-Nine*."

Dolly's face turned into a frown.

Sky chuckled. "See you later."

As she walked toward her car, she pulled out her phone and saw a barrage of messages.

Mom: Darling, what happened between Becket and Tony? Tony

came home saying Becket put his hands on him.

Oh, man. Bet that weasel hadn't said what had come before that.

She opened the next one.

Tony: I think your boyfriend dislocated my shoulder. Is that really the type of person you want to date? I could press charges for his violence.

She snorted. Becket could have done far worse.

She opened the last text.

Becket: Call me when you've cooled off and we can talk about dinner at Mom's.

When she'd "cooled off"? God, the man was so infuriating, she wanted to kick him in the shins.

Her fingers flew over the screen.

Sky: How about you call me when you're ready to apologize for telling me I couldn't handle my own business this morning.

Becket: Come on, Peaches, don't pretend you're not grateful I'm in your life.

Jesus, he was crazy.

Sky: Let's all hope I never fall from the height of your ego to your IQ, because that would really hurt.

With a huff, she slid into her car. Her response was petty and immature, but dammit, he just brought that side out of her.

Her phone vibrated with more texts as she drove, but she didn't touch it. Her fingers just tightened around the wheel.

What had he written back? More stuff about how lucky she was to have him? About how lost she'd be without him?

God, she really needed more acupuncture. And maybe some meditation. She'd been so angry since returning to Amber Ridge. After Eloise's death, all the accidents, then losing Charlie, everything in her life had just felt infinitely unfair.

She pulled into her driveway but didn't immediately get out. Instead, she leaned her head back and closed her eyes, an image of Charlie flashing into her mind.

She'd never forgive herself for his death. Not if she ran a thousand fundraisers and helped a million animals.

It took a few deep breaths before she was ready to get out of the car, and she still ignored her phone until she got inside the house.

Becket: Don't worry, I'll catch you, honey. I'm in the business of saving people. Kind of like God.

And he finished the text with a wink emoji.

Infuriating.

She dropped her bag to the couch and angry texted as she marched upstairs.

Sky: I have never met anyone who has such a superiority complex.

Becket: Sexy, right?

She snorted. No. Not sexy. It wasn't even remotely sexy.

She reached the top of the stairs and was about to respond but stopped at a small rustling noise coming from...her bedroom?

Was it a breeze? Had she left a window open? No. She never left anything open. She was almost obsessive about closing everything up before leaving.

She took three more quiet steps toward the bedroom when something hit the floor with a clatter.

Her heart stopped.

Her phone vibrated again, and she absently looked down, the words blurring before her eyes.

Becket: Come on, you can admit I'm sexy. I won't tell anyone.

Her fingers moved quickly over the screen, the slight shake making it hard to get the words out.

Sky: I think someone's in my house.

The reply was instant.

Becket: Get out.

She turned and ran but had only made it down a couple of stairs when her foot caught the edge of a tread. She cried out and fell forward, trying to grab the railing but missing, and tumbled down the stairs.

* * *

Becket grinned as he hit send. He could just picture her eye roll at his self-declaration about being sexy.

He only played into this arrogant thing because it riled her up so much. All he wanted to do was unravel her. Peel back the layers and see who Sky truly was.

When she didn't immediately respond, his smile widened. Was he actually going to get the final word for once?

"What's put that smile on your face?" Irene asked as she entered the kitchen.

"Nothing." He sipped his coffee. For once he got to drink it hot. Too often he got interrupted and the damn stuff went cold.

Irene frowned at him before understanding crossed her features. "You're texting your neighbor slash girlfriend."

"How'd you know that?"

She snorted. "Teddy knew, which means everyone at the station knew five minutes later. I would like to know how it happened though. Last I heard, she hated you."

"She just realized that she'd rather kiss me than fight with me." His lips twitched at the memory of their kiss.

Damn, he needed to find out if a second kiss would be just as good.

"Hm." She looked like she didn't believe him.

Which was fair enough. Irene had heard all the stories.

He turned back to his phone and sent Sky another text.

Becket: Come on, you can admit I'm sexy. I won't tell anyone.

He was about to set his phone onto the table when Sky's response came through.

Sky: I think someone's in my house.

The mug almost slipped from his fingers as every fucking

muscle in his body locked.

Becket: Get out.

"What's wrong?" Irene asked, straightening.

"I need to go. Can you call Moose in to replace me?"

"Sure. But is everything okay?"

"I'm not sure."

Becket tried Sky's number as he ran to his car. When it rang out, acid churned in his gut. He pulled out of the parking lot and called his brother.

"Becket, I'm just in the middle of something, can I—"

"Someone's in Sky's house and now she's not answering."

"*What?*"

"I need you to get to her now."

Wind rushed over the line, like his brother was moving. "I'll be there in three minutes."

Becket hung up and pressed his foot to the floor, dialing Sky again.

Still nothing.

Fuck. Was this the asshole breaking into houses?

It took him too fucking long to get to her house, then he raced to the front door.

Locked. He could pick a lock, but it would take too long.

His gaze zeroed in on the group of potted plants near the front door. One by one, he quickly lifted them. A spare key was under the fifth pot. He grabbed it.

The door was barely open when he saw her—Sky lay on her back at the bottom of the stairs, completely still.

His heart shot into his throat, and he raced forward and dropped beside her. When he touched her pulse, a light thud beat beneath his fingertips. Good. He lowered his ear to her mouth. A whisper of air moved between her lips.

Thank God.

Gently, he cupped her cheek. "Sky? Can you hear me?"

A small feminine groan slipped from her throat. Her eyes

scrunched as she tried to roll to her side.

"Whoa, easy." He set a hand on her hip to still her.

She frowned as her eyes slowly opened. "Becket?"

"Yeah, honey, it's me. Can you tell me if anything hurts?"

Her frown deepened. "My head…"

He inspected the back of her head, and sure enough, blood soaked through her hair. Because someone had hit her? Or because she'd hit her skull on the stairs?

Fury heated his blood but he ignored it, focusing on her. Her pupils were wide and slightly unfocused. A concussion.

"Any nausea or pressure in your head?" he asked.

"No. Just an ache at the back."

Only pain from the site of the wound was good. "What about your back?"

"I think my back's okay. I'd like to sit up."

He gripped her upper arms and helped her, making sure she moved slowly.

"What happened?" He tried not to growl the words, but *fuck* he was angry. "Did they push you down the stairs?"

She cringed. "No. After you texted me to get out, I was in such a rush, I just ran and I fell down the stairs."

His gaze shot around the house. So there was a chance the asshole could still be here.

Shit.

Cars sounded from the road, and a few seconds later, his brother came in, deputies behind him.

Jesse held his pistol but lowered it when he saw them. "Are you okay?"

Sky nodded, only to cringe.

Becket grazed his thumb over her arm before looking back to Jesse. "Your deputies need to check the house. The guy might still be here."

His brother nodded toward his deputies, and they separated, some moving into the kitchen, others upstairs.

Sky started to push to her feet, and Becket gripped her arms again to take her weight before leading her over to the couch. "We need to get the bump checked out at the hospital."

"I'd prefer to wait and see how I feel."

"Sky—"

"I called an ambulance on my way here, in case one was needed," Jesse interrupted.

Good.

Jesse crouched in front of her. "Tell me what happened."

"There's not much to tell. I got home and was texting Becket. When I reached the top of the stairs, I heard a rustling in my bedroom and stopped. Then there was a crash, like something dropped to the floor. I texted Becket that I thought someone was here, and he told me to get out, but when I ran down the stairs, I was rushing and fell."

The idea of Sky unconscious on the floor, *vulnerable*, while an intruder was inside her house, made him feel fucking sick.

"And then you lost consciousness?" Jesse asked.

Sky nodded and looked at Becket. "Your cameras might have caught them."

His cameras only covered part of the front, and it was unlikely any thief would come in through the front, but he pulled out his phone and opened the app. "It didn't catch anyone."

"Jesse?"

They all looked up at the female deputy entering the room.

"Did you find something?" Jesse asked.

"The lock on the back door's broken, and the neighbor just got home and is saying someone broke into her place too. It looks like the person went to the neighbor first, then Sky's through the fence."

A visible shudder ran down Sky's spine, and Becket inched closer, slipping an arm around her shoulders.

He should have fixed that damn fence. He hadn't. So in his mind, this was as good as his fault.

CHAPTER 14

The warmth of the cup seeped into Sky's skin, chasing away the edge of the cold.

Someone had broken into her house. Stolen from her. They'd taken almost all her jewelry. Some cash she'd had lying around. Even some of her expensive shoes. But she didn't care about any of that. It was just stuff. She felt violated.

They'd also robbed the poor lady next door. At least she hadn't been home.

The worst part though, the part she really couldn't shake, was that the intruder would have had to pass her to get out of the house. They would have stepped over her unconscious body on the floor.

A shudder rolled down her spine at how vulnerable she'd been.

The back door opened with a click. She didn't need to look up to know it was Becket. She'd told him that he could leave, but he'd refused, and for once, she hadn't had the energy to fight him.

The second everyone had cleared out, he'd jumped into action, first fixing the lock on the back door, then the fence. He'd even muttered something about kicking his own ass for not fixing it sooner.

Honestly, she was glad he was here. The noise of him working was almost comforting because it reminded her she wasn't alone.

She glanced at her phone. She'd called her mother and then instantly wished she hadn't. Her mother had freaked out, told her father, then *he'd* freaked out. Fortunately, they were on a trip with their church, so they couldn't come over.

The couch beside her dipped, and she looked up to see Becket.

"Back door and fence are fixed," he said softly. It was probably the gentlest he'd ever spoken to her.

"Thank you." She really did mean that. If he hadn't been here to fix those things, she would have had to call someone, and there was no part of her that had the energy for that right now.

Concern darkened his eyes. "How are you feeling?"

"Relieved that the paramedic confirmed it was a mild concussion."

That was just the tip of the iceberg into what she was feeling, and by the furrowing of Becket's brow, he knew it.

She tilted her head. "How are *you* feeling?"

"Angry." His response was instant, and the muscles in his arms visibly tensed.

"I thought not much ruffled your feathers."

"I knew there was a thief in the area—"

"We all knew."

"I should have fixed your fence and checked your locks."

"They're my responsibilities."

A muscle ticked in his jaw. He didn't believe her. He looked so dark and angry and she hated it. But one thing was certain—this man would make a formidable enemy.

"Did I hear around town you were a SEAL before you were a firefighter?" she asked, suddenly wanting to know a bit more about him.

"Yeah. And I was good at it because I was driven to take down the scum we were assigned to."

Of course, he'd openly tell her that he was a good Navy SEAL. But that might not be hubris. Even becoming a SEAL was one of the hardest achievements there was. "I can picture you as a good SEAL."

"In that line of work, you have to be good or you don't make it out alive."

Her slight smile fled. The idea of this man defending the country by fighting the most dangerous people in the world was terrifying. "Why'd you leave?"

"It was time. I started losing my drive. My purpose. And out there, if you don't have those things, you're a sitting duck. You have to have pinpoint focus to stay alive."

"So you came home."

"So I came home."

Why did a little part of her feel unbelievably grateful for that? "Do you miss it?"

"Some days. But everything I liked about it, I still get as a firefighter."

"You like danger."

"I like the adrenaline rush. But more than that, I like feeling as if what I do matters."

It *did* matter. He was a hero. An ass a lot of the time…but also a hero.

"What about you?" he asked. "Do you miss Cheyenne?"

"No. I think I was trying to make myself fit into a town where I didn't belong. I was just so desperate for separation from my parents and their church and who I was here that I chose a random town and tried to force it. I love Mom and Dad…but I wanted to love them from afar."

"Why come back then?"

"Because it's familiar, and with the familiarity came a feeling of safety. And I needed that."

His brows flickered. "Who's Charlie?"

Air caught in her lungs. "How do you know about Charlie?"

"You said the name in your sleep."

Damn her and her inability to just sleep without walking or talking. "He was my Border Terrier."

"Was?"

"There was a fire at my house..." The flames flashed in her mind again, cutting off her words.

Her heart started to beat faster.

"How did the fire start?" Becket asked, pulling her attention back to him.

"It was an electrical fire. They said something about aged or faulty wiring. Honestly, all I could think about was Charlie. I didn't even care about my house."

"What happened to him?"

The familiar ache settled inside her chest. "I got him out of the house, but he'd inhaled too much smoke. He was old and already had lung problems. He passed away a few days later."

Her fault. His death had been her fault. Because that accident hadn't been the first. It was just the last of a string of incidents in Cheyenne. She'd known she wasn't safe to be around. Although, even if she had acknowledged it, she wasn't sure what she could have done.

When she looked up at Becket, it was to find him watching her closely.

She shook her head. "I know you're not a dog person, so you probably don't—"

"He was your family."

Tears gathered in her eyes. He was. And she'd let him down. "Running the doggy daycare and the fundraisers helps, but nothing completely takes the ache away."

"Nothing ever will. But you'll get better at living with it."

Her frown deepened. He said it like he understood. And so

few people ever understood. Not her parents. Not her friends in Cheyenne, who she didn't even talk to anymore.

She blinked back the tears. She did not want to cry. Not here, not now. "I'm going to get my wheat bag from my bedroom."

"Stay. Rest. I'll get it."

Why did kind, sympathetic Becket feel more dangerous than the jerk-next-door version?

She nodded and watched him move up the stairs, the thick muscles in his thighs stretching his jeans.

He'd only been gone a few seconds when a knock came at the door.

She wasn't expecting anyone. Could it be Jesse again?

She rose, and the second she opened the door, she regretted not looking in the peephole first.

Tony. Two visits in one day were far too many. "What are you doing here?"

"Your father called and told me what happened."

Her father had called Tony? Even after she'd told him she was fine and that Becket was with her and taking care of things?

Without a word from her, he walked inside and touched her arm. "Are you okay?"

"Tony—"

He tensed, his gaze going behind her.

Then warmth covered her back. And for the second time that day, Becket was there to save her from Tony.

* * *

Un-fucking-believable.

He was gone for two damn seconds and the asshole was inside Sky's house, *touching* her.

Becket narrowed his eyes at the hand on Sky's. This idiot was obviously smarter than he looked, because he dropped his hand and moved back.

"What are you doing here?" he asked, making damn sure to add just enough edge so the guy knew how close Becket was to losing his calm.

"Like I just told Sky," Tony said slowly, "I'm checking on her."

"No need. I'm here." *You know, her fucking boyfriend.* As far as Tony was aware, anyway.

Tony cleared his throat before looking back at Sky. "Do you need anything? Food? Coffee? Someone to talk to?"

Was he for real? Becket opened his mouth to tell him to fuck off, but Sky got in first.

"I'm okay. I've actually got a bit of a headache, and we were about to rest." Then she leaned into Becket, her arm wrapping around his waist as she rested her head on his chest. "Thank you for coming though."

Becket tightened his hold on her.

Frustration flickered in Tony's eyes. "Well, I'm glad you're okay."

He hadn't even finished turning when Becket slammed the door closed.

Sky gasped and frowned up at him. "Becket!"

"Come on, the asshole knew it was coming."

She rolled her eyes, and that simple action made some of the weight lift from his chest. Not all of it—someone had still broken into her house—but the eye roll was a small flash of her old self.

"How did he know about the break-in?" Becket asked.

"How do you think?"

"Your father."

"Yep. I should go to bed." Her gaze went to the stairs behind him. She nibbled her bottom lip. "Will you go up there with me?"

He held her close for an extra moment. "Come on."

They walked up the stairs together, but the second Sky stepped into the bedroom, she stopped.

Shit. He should have picked stuff up after fixing the fence and back door. They'd already been up here to check what was stolen, but she'd been in a haze then.

Someone had violated her personal space. This room would probably feel uncomfortable for a while.

He touched a hand to the small of her back. "I'll help you clean up."

She nodded, but her face was damn pale.

He grabbed a handful of T-shirts that had been pulled from her dresser, before looking at her. "So, we never finished the conversation about dinner at my mom's."

A small smile twitched at her lips as she bent to pick up some socks. "That's because you sprung it on me when I was in the middle of mentally murdering you."

"Really? What method did you go with?"

"Poison. I thought you'd beat me on strength, and I'd never be able to sneak up on you and stab you or anything, but watching you die slowly seemed kind of appealing."

He threw his head back and laughed. The woman definitely hadn't lost her sense of humor. "Smart."

"You said the dinner was Sunday?"

"Yeah, is that okay?"

"It is for me, but do you feel bad about lying to your mom?"

"No." Nervous? Yeah. Because she'd probably see right through it.

"Okay. Um, dinner sounds great. Unless you think I'll be grilled for information."

"Nah, that's not her style. She'll kill you with kindness and sneak the questions in so that you don't know you're being investigated."

"I'll have to be on my A game then so I don't let the truth slip." Sky grinned at him before cringing. "I'm sorry about the comment about your ego and IQ."

"Don't be. It made me laugh." A genuine, full belly laugh.

A few seconds of silence passed, but he didn't miss the side glances Sky shot his way.

He bit back the laugh. "What is it, Peaches?"

"Are we going to go back to hating each other tomorrow?"

"I have never hated you, nor will I ever hate you."

"Okay. But will we be enemy neighbors again?"

"No. Just neighbors who pretend to date while throwing out insults every other minute."

This time she laughed. "Jeez, we're complicated."

"Better than boring."

"Okay, one more question before I put my head down and really get to work."

"Shoot."

"Why do you have a penis sculpture in your living room?"

His mouth widened into a giant fucking smile. Whatever he'd thought she was going to ask, it wasn't that. "It's a replica of a sculpture in a park in Des Moines. I went there with my team between missions. I made a joke about it, and my buddy gave it to me as a joke present for my birthday."

"And now you put it up in your living room."

"When I look at it, it makes me smile. Not because of what it is, but because I remember how I felt when he gave it to me."

The smile slipped from her lips, and she frowned. "You're deeper than I thought." Then her eyes widened. Because she hadn't meant to say that out loud?

"Don't let anyone else know. It's my best-kept secret."

She shook her head, but even as they cleaned, she didn't stop looking his way. And he only knew that because of how often he looked at *her*.

"You know I'm sleeping on your couch, right?" he asked when they were almost finished.

"No, Becket, you don't need to do that."

"I do."

"No—"

"Sky. Just say thank you."

Her bottom lip disappeared between her teeth. She wanted him to sleep on the couch. She didn't need to say the words out loud for him to know that.

Finally, she dipped her head. "Thank you."

And that was his small win in an otherwise shitty day. That she trusted him enough to help her feel safe.

CHAPTER 15

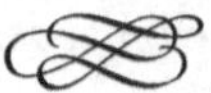

Sky ran her fingers over her pale blue cotton skirt as she stood in front of her bedroom mirror.

Dinner with Becket's family. Why did she feel guilty about lying to his mother? She hadn't felt guilty about tricking *her* parents. Heck, she hadn't felt guilty about lying to anyone else either. So why was his mother different?

She swallowed and turned, scanning her bedroom. A bedroom that was now clean and tidy but still felt different from how it had a week ago.

Becket had only slept on her couch the one night—her choice, not his—and man, that first night without him had been hard. Every whisper of sound, every creak and crack in the house, had set her pulse racing. How much sleep had she gotten? Two hours? Three?

Four nights later and she was a little better, but not a lot. She wouldn't be winning any competitions for how well rested she was, that was for sure.

She just needed Jesse and his deputies to find the thief, and she'd feel safe again.

She'd checked on her neighbor, and the older woman seemed fine. A lot finer than her.

One question kept ticking over in her head—had her house always been a target? Or had her neighbor's house been the original target, then the person had seen the broken fence and seized the opportunity?

Her phone rang, cutting into her thoughts.

She lifted it from the dresser and glanced at the screen before answering. "Hi, Mom. Are you and Dad back?"

"Yes, your father and I got home an hour ago. Tony's taken very good care of the house and even cooked us dinner."

Well, kudos to Tony. Thankfully, she hadn't seen him since his little visit after the break-in. "That's great, Mom."

"How are you?"

Her mother had called every day. Sky had actually expected multiple calls a day, so one had been a pleasant surprise. "I'm good. Really good." Okay, that was a stretch, but her mother was a worrier, and no good would come from adding to that worry.

"I'm glad. I hated not being here for you after the incident."

Her mother had tried to insist on coming back early, but thankfully, Sky had been able to talk her out of it. She hadn't had the energy to recover from the break-in *and* deal with her mother's hovering. Not to mention, her father might have dropped by and surprised her with Tony.

"I want to see you," her mother continued. "I'm coming over."

"Sorry, Mom. I'm actually going out tonight."

"Out? It hasn't even been a week since you got a concussion! Where are you going? Oh, don't tell me to the bar. No, you need to stay home. I'll bring some chicken soup and—"

"I'm having dinner with Becket's family."

There was a small pause. "Becket's family?"

"Yes." She grabbed her purse and popped her lipstick inside.

"I see. At his mother's house?"

"Yes, at his mother's house. It's my first time officially meeting her as the girlfriend, so it's kind of important."

Fake girlfriend. Small technicality. Although, the fake part had been feeling less accurate lately, with Becket's constant texts and check-ins. He'd honestly been like the perfect boyfriend.

"She'll love you, darling."

Sky frowned at her mother's tone. It sounded…off. "What is it?"

"Nothing."

"Mom…"

"I was just wondering when *I'll* meet his mother. I mean, my relationship with her is important, don't you think?"

Sky drew in a big belly breath. "Let me meet her first and make a good impression, then you and Dad can."

Her mother sighed. "Okay, that sounds practical. When will I see you then?"

"I'm working tomorrow, but you can come by and we can grab lunch?"

"Good. But I don't want that Chinese Crested licking me again."

She grinned. "That's Bella's way of showing love. But I can keep her away from you."

"Thank you. Okay, update me on how it goes tonight."

"I will. Thanks, Mom."

She'd just hung up when her phone vibrated with a text.

Becket: I'm downstairs, Peaches.

Her heart gave a little kick. She used to hate that nickname. But now? It felt kind of intimate. And whenever he used it, even if it was just in a text, her pulse took off in a sprint.

She dropped her phone into her purse and went downstairs. When she opened the door, a puff of air escaped her.

He looked good. *Really* good. He wore a white button-down shirt tonight. The sleeves were rolled up and the top couple of buttons were undone, showing just a hint of his muscled chest.

Hot. It was the only way to describe him.

"You look beautiful, Sky."

Her eyes flashed up, colliding with his dark brown gaze.

Sky…he rarely used her name, but she liked the way he said it. Deep and gravelly. "Thank you. You don't look too bad yourself."

One side of his mouth lifted. "That's almost a compliment."

Her fingers twitched, wanting to run down his chest. She fisted both hands. "Should we go?"

"Absolutely."

She cleared her throat. "I'll just grab the tiramisu."

She took the moment to turn away from him to breathe deeply.

Get a freaking hold of yourself, woman. He's just a man. Granted, a man with impeccable biceps and a voice that did funny things to her lady parts. Still…

The second she returned to Becket, he took the dessert from her fingers and put his other hand on the small of her back as he led her out of the house.

"You're still doing okay here by yourself?" he asked once they were in the car.

No. The word was a very unwelcome shout in her head. Because of course she wanted the former Navy SEAL to sleep on her couch and protect her from any future crimes. But she was a grown-ass woman, and she needed to suck it up and sleep in her house by herself. Plus, they weren't really dating, so it wasn't fair to keep relying on him.

"Yes." Okay, that hadn't come out with nearly enough conviction.

He nodded, but she didn't miss the way his fingers clenched around the wheel. He didn't believe her. She'd never been a good liar.

When they reached his mom's house, she nibbled her lip.

"Are you nervous?" he asked.

"Not nervous. For some reason, I feel guilty about lying to

your mom. Which is strange because with everyone else, the lie feels easy."

"Don't think about it as lying."

She frowned. "It is a lie though."

One side of his mouth lifted. "If it feels real to us, it'll feel real to her."

Her jaw dropped as he got out of the car. Was he insinuating it felt real to him?

She didn't have time to think about it before Becket was opening her door. He helped her out and grabbed the tiramisu. When his arm curved around her waist, warmth slid over her skin, and not just the parts that he touched.

What the hell was going on with her? She needed to get a damn grip!

Becket opened the front door without knocking, and they found everyone in the kitchen and living area.

Clara and Indie were filling wine glasses while Jesse was getting stuff out of the fridge, and Becket's mother and Aspen were setting the table. Everyone stopped and looked up.

"You're here!" his mother said first. She crossed the room and hugged her son before turning to Sky. "Hi, I'm Pam."

Then she pulled Sky right into a hug. The embrace was tight and warm.

"It's so good to properly meet you," Pam said before pulling away. "I was wondering if my son was ever going to bring a woman home."

Becket pulled Sky close again. "I hadn't found Sky yet."

Her heart gave a little thump.

His mother's smile widened. "Well, I'm glad you did, because I'm getting old. I need to see all my babies happy and in love."

Indie scoffed from the kitchen. "You don't need love to make you happy, Auntie Pam."

"No. But it makes me feel better knowing someone loves them as much as I do, in case anything happens to me."

Jesse growled from the fridge, "Nothing's happening to you, Mom. You're going to live to a hundred."

"A hundred and ten," Clara corrected. Her gaze went to the dish in Becket's hand. "Don't tell me you made that."

"I did."

Sky elbowed him in the side.

Becket grunted. "Hey. What was that for?"

"Taking the credit." She slipped the dish from his hold. "I made tiramisu for dessert."

Aspen gasped. "I love tiramisu. I haven't had it in years."

"Well, hopefully this one is as good as you remember."

Sky set the dessert onto the counter while Becket went to man-hug his brother.

"Can I help?" she asked Clara.

"Nope. We've got it all handled." Clara's voice lowered. "How are you feeling after the break-in and the fall?"

"Okay. Better every day."

"Good. Did our appointment help?"

Sky had booked an emergency acupuncture session yesterday. It had been very necessary, and it immediately took the edge off some of her stress. "It was the best night's sleep all week."

Not perfect, but better than previous nights.

Clara smiled. "Good."

"Has Becket been staying with you?" Indie asked.

She opened her mouth to say just the first night but stopped herself. If he were her real boyfriend, he would have camped out at her house all week. Either that or forced her to stay with him. "Um, yeah, he has."

"I've stayed with Mom a few nights," Clara said. "I didn't want her to be alone." She looked at Indie. "Have you been okay?"

"Well, Colt had a really good security system put in, so I always feel safe."

Sky glanced at the woman. "Who's Colt?"

"He's…" Indie shook her head. "*Was* my husband. We're separated. Not officially yet. We haven't signed any divorce papers, but in every other way."

Sky's brows rose. She hadn't realized the other woman was married. But by the look on her face and the sympathetic smile Clara sent her way, it was something she didn't want to discuss.

The front door opened, and Holden walked in. Sky felt the change in Clara immediately. Her back straightened and her eyes widened slightly.

"He looks good tonight, doesn't he?" Clara whispered before taking a big gulp of wine.

Indie lifted a shoulder. "He looks okay."

Holden wore a navy T-shirt that fit his sculpted physique nicely. And yeah, he looked good. But Sky couldn't help but keep looking at Becket. He was standing with Jesse and Aspen by the table, arms folded over his thick chest.

He glanced at her, and when he winked, her heart stopped.

He looked good. Dangerously good.

Indie leaned over and handed her a big glass of wine. "Welcome to our crazy family."

* * *

BECKET LEANED back in his seat as his family talked around him. He was smiling. A wide fucking smile, and not just because the food was good and the company was everyone he loved. He was smiling because when he touched Sky, she didn't pull away. When he leaned in close, she didn't look like she wanted to nail him in the gut. And when he spoke softly into her ear, he swore he saw a hint of something deeper there. Maybe some trust. Some attraction.

He slipped his arm behind her and swiped his thumb over her waist, and even though the noise of people talking around the table was loud, he still heard her sharp intake of breath.

"Where did you both end up on that fence?"

Becket's gaze shot up at his mother's question. "How do you know about that?"

"I hear things."

He shot a look at Clara, who was conveniently staring across the room as she sipped her drink. "You told her."

Clara lifted a shoulder. "Yes. I told her you were being a jerk to your neighbor and listed off all the things you did. But I'm glad that's changed."

"Me too." His mother nodded. "That would be so stressful, living next door to someone you didn't get along with."

"Really stressful," Sky agreed with a grin.

He tickled her waist, and she yelped, before he turned to his mother. "I'm actually a delightful neighbor. Ask anyone on the street."

Sky nodded. "It's true. Everyone else had great things to say about him. It was very confusing. He must have saved his less-favorable side for me."

"He was trying to hide how besotted he was with you." Clara sighed.

"Couldn't hide it for long, though," Indie added.

Okay, that was enough talk from the nosy women in his family.

"I'll start clearing the table." He rose to his feet, not missing the laughs that both Jesse and Holden were trying to hold back.

"I'll help." Sky moved to stand, but Becket set a hand onto her shoulder.

"You made dessert. I've done nothing, and my mother raised me right—if you don't cook, you clean."

Holden and his brother rose too.

He was rinsing dishes when Holden came to stand beside him. "Looks like things between you two are going well."

He glanced over at Sky. The women were laughing at some-thing Clara was saying. He'd become so used to her frowns and scowls during her time as his neighbor, every time he got a look at that full smile of hers, it squeezed the fucking air from his chest.

"Yeah," Becket finally answered. "Things are going well."

Jesse stood on his other side. As he started putting the leftover food in containers, his voice lowered. "In case you miss it on the local news, there was another break-in."

Becket stopped and looked at his brother. "Another break-in...but no arrest."

A muscle ticked in Jesse's jaw. "No. But they left something behind this time. A black cap."

He straightened. "Can it be used to identify the person?"

"There were some strands of hair inside. We've sent it away to see if we can get a DNA profile, but it will take over a week and if they're not in the system, it won't tell us much."

Jesus Christ. "Did anyone get hurt?"

"No. So far, Sky's the only one who was home during a theft, which makes me think even more that it was a crime of opportunity. They saw the broken back fence and got greedy."

And Sky was the one who'd paid the price. His back teeth ground together as he finished the dishes.

"Oh, Aspen, if you and Jesse are planning a trip away, you need to see these photos of Whistler." His mother pushed back from the table. "I took the kids when they were young so they could snowboard, and they loved it."

Becket dried his hands. "I'll get them, Mom. They're on a high shelf in the office."

"Thank you, darling." She turned toward the women. "Advantage of having tall boys."

He gently squeezed his mother's arm as he passed her and winked at Sky, whose cheeks turned a pretty rosy pink.

He smiled to himself. Yeah, things were definitely going well between them.

In the office, he studied the photo albums on the top shelf. His mother had documented every part of their childhood, and he loved her for that. For most of their childhoods, she'd raised them on her own and done a hell of a job.

He grabbed the album labeled "Whistler" and turned just as his mother entered the room.

"Hey. I've got it," he said.

"Thank you." She crossed the distance between them and gripped his arms. "I just need to tell you something."

"Something that needed to be said in private?" Shit, was he in trouble?

"No, it could have been said out there, but I wanted to say it in here." She tilted her head. "I like Sky. And I like that she makes you smile."

"Thanks, Mom, but we should—"

"And…I want you to know that it doesn't matter how things start. Hate can turn into love…and something that maybe didn't feel quite so real can turn into the most real thing in your life."

Becket almost pulled back. Did she know? How the hell did she know?

"You needed someone strong," his mother finished. "I'm glad you found her." She took the book from his hands and headed out of the room.

He stood there for another moment, shocked as hell, before shaking his head and returning to everyone. As he returned to the dining room, Sky's phone rang. She frowned at it, then excused herself and walked down the hall before answering.

Was it her mother? No. Sky had looked surprised by the name on the screen. Her mother called too often for her to be surprised.

Less than a minute later, Sky reentered the room.

He stepped in front of her. "Is everything okay?"

"That was Rosemary…Bella's missing."

CHAPTER 16

Sky swung the flashlight in a slow arc as she continued to call Bella's name. They'd been walking through the forest near Rosemary's home for the better part of an hour but still hadn't found the little dog. This had happened once before, and Rosemary had called her that day too, only that time, Sky had found Bella within fifteen minutes.

She knew Rosemary was getting old, but the woman really needed to make sure Bella didn't get out by herself.

"Why does she call you?" Becket asked.

She glanced at him, but the darkness kept most of his face shadowed. "I look after Bella a lot at the doggy daycare, and the dog likes me. Rosemary also doesn't have anyone else to turn to in town." She worried her bottom lip. "I found her a lot faster last time. What if—"

"We'll find her," he interrupted.

"I hope so. But she's getting old, and she doesn't see very well and it's dark. She could have made her way to the street and walked in front of a car."

"She won't walk in front of a car."

"You don't know that."

Becket stopped. "Hey, look at me."

She swallowed, taking a moment before looking up. Even in the darkness, she could see his eyes were shining with intensity, so focused on her it was almost as if the forest faded away around them. "We'll find her, and she'll be happy and healthy. Then we'll return her to Rosemary."

"You can't guarantee that."

"No, but my gut tells me it's true. And my gut's rarely wrong."

"Always so confident." She wished she could say the same about herself. A small smile lifted her lips. "If she skipped dinner, she won't be happy. I once gave her lunch twenty minutes late and she gave me the cold shoulder for a good hour after."

"So she's probably wanting to find us as much as we want to find her."

Sky nodded before searching with the flashlight again. She wished she was as positive as Becket. But she knew the pain of losing a pet, and right now, all she could think about was the worst-case scenario.

"I once had a goldfish."

She looked back at him. "You did?"

"Yep. I was in first grade and Billy Young had one. He talked about his fish all the damn time. I hated him."

She laughed. "Why did you hate him?"

"Because he was annoying. But he talked about that goddamn fish so much that I wanted one. Mom said I could have one, but I'd be one hundred percent responsible for him."

"Something tells me this story doesn't have a happy ending."

"He died."

"I knew it."

"Monsieur Claude ate him."

Sky frowned. "Who's Monsieur Claude?"

"He was Clara's dog."

"So that's why you hate dogs."

"I hate dogs because I'd wake up to Monsieur Claude's

disgusting dog breath in my face every morning. Because even though he was Clara's dog, I still had to pick up his shit every other week."

She tilted her head. "Small prices to pay for the kind of love you probably received. What happened to Monsieur Claude?"

"He lived to a ripe old age of sixteen before he passed away. Clara made us have a funeral. I didn't get a funeral for Jaws."

She choked back another laugh. "Your fish was named Jaws?"

"Yep. And he lived in a paradise tank."

Sky threw her head back and laughed. If Becket was trying to distract her, he was doing a good job. "Well, his life might have been short, but it sounds like he was loved."

She was still smiling when she spotted a shadow of movement behind a tree.

She stopped. "Did you see that?"

"What?"

She waited. Another slight movement.

She took off. Becket cursed from behind, but she ignored him as she raced forward, weaving around trees and jumping over branches.

Then she saw Bella. The poor thing was whimpering and trying to move, but her collar was stuck on a branch.

Sky dropped beside her. "Oh, Bells, what happened?"

Bella dug her head into Sky's chest.

Becket dropped beside them and carefully untangled Bella's collar from the branch

"There you go." Sky lifted Bella as she stood. "Want us to take you home for dinner?"

Bella's ears perked up, and Sky laughed as they headed back to Rosemary's house.

"I'll take her if she's too heavy." He reached forward to take the dog, but Bella growled at him.

Sky laughed. "I think she knows you don't like dogs." She handed him the flashlight instead.

"And people wonder why."

She grinned as she snuggled Bella closer to her chest.

As they neared the house, Sky scanned the dark patches of grass. "You said there was a fire here?"

"Yeah, Rosemary was burning off some old stuff. I asked her not to do it again."

Absolutely. This property was far too close to the forest.

The front door opened, and Rosemary gasped when she spotted them with Bella.

When Sky reached her, she handed Bella to the older woman.

Rosemary buried her face into Bella's furry head. "Oh, darling, are you okay?"

"She got her collar stuck on a branch," Sky explained.

"I think she's hungry," Becket added.

"Well, of course you're hungry. It's steak night."

Sky could have laughed. The dog ate better than most fully grown humans.

Rosemary glanced up. "Thank you! Both of you. Would you like to come in? I could make some coffee?"

Sky shook her head. "That's okay. We should head home. Have a good night." She gave Bella one last pat before turning away.

She was still smiling as they got back into the car. "Well, that's my good deed done for the day."

"It's nice that you helped her."

"I love Bella."

When they got back to her house, Becket walked her inside. Her awareness of him was like a pulse on her skin. The heat from his hand on her back. His pine scent surrounding her. Trying to ignore it, she dropped her purse on the hall table and focused on the happiness of finding Bella.

"Thank you for sharing your family with me tonight."

She turned—and her smile quickly slipped when she looked at Becket. He stood only a foot away, and the look on his face...it was dark and intense…and so fixed on her, she could barely breathe.

"You fit in well," he said quietly, taking a small step toward her. "Thank you for coming."

She swallowed—a big gulp of a swallow. He was so close. And he was making her want to do things that she should not be wanting. Like run her fingers down his chest. Put her mouth on his to see if he tasted as good as last time.

He inched another step forward. "Would you like me to go?"

"That would be smart…wouldn't it?"

"Maybe. But I don't always like to be smart. It's too safe. Sometimes it's nice to be a bit reckless."

Her heart pounded against her ribs as little wisps of air rushed in and out of her chest. "I've never been good at reckless."

She should back away, but her feet refused to move. It was like he'd locked her in place.

He brushed a lock of hair behind her ear, and the feel of his fingers against her cheek burned. "Do you want me to leave, Sky?"

Say yes, Sky. Close the door and watch him walk away.

But the words never reached air.

One more step forward. He was so close, she could feel the warmth of his body seeping into hers.

"Sky?"

"I don't know what I want."

A hint of a smile curved his lips. He lowered his head so that his mouth brushed her ear as he whispered, "Liar."

She *was* a liar. And with his mouth so close, she was forgetting why she was even bothering with the lie.

"I don't want you to go." The words were so quiet that she wasn't even sure they reached him. "I want…"

Oh, screw it.

She slipped her fingers into his hair, tugged his head down, and their mouths collided. It was a lips-sealed-together, body-against-body kiss that sent her blood rushing through her veins.

She groaned at the feel of his soft lips. Just as soft as before. And when his strong arms encircled her, pulled her closer, a craving grew in her body, throbbing inside her lower belly. A craving to sink deeper into him. A craving to taste and feel more of him.

His tongue ran over the seam of her lips, and she opened for him, letting him inside. Letting him tangle his tongue with hers while she melted.

What did he do to her? How did one kiss make her forget everything around them? Every argument that had come before this.

She ran her fingers over his chest. A chest so sculpted and muscled that it felt like stone.

Almost of their own accord, her fingers started to undo the buttons. One by one, she exposed his chest until his shirt was completely open and she was touching bare skin. Skin that made her want to groan and whimper and draw him closer all at the same time.

Suddenly his hands lowered, and he lifted her, turning them so that she was pressed to the wall…and then he was everywhere.

* * *

Fire burned through Becket's blood. Sky was in his arms, and she felt so good. Her soft curves melded against his hard edges, and the feel of her fingertips exploring his chest tormented him.

All he could think was…it wasn't enough. He needed *more* of this woman. He needed to taste every inch of her. To explore and lose himself in her.

He dropped his hands to the hem of her dress and tugged. She lifted her arms willingly, and he pulled the material over her head.

Black lace covering ample breasts turned his cock to stone.

Fuck, she was gorgeous.

He returned his mouth to hers, and she threaded her fingers through his hair. Tugging and pulling, seeming as desperate for him as he was for her.

His lips moved down her cheek, then her neck. When he reached her chest, he tugged one cup down to see a pretty pink nipple. He took it between his lips.

She cried out, her body arching into him, nipple thrusting farther into his mouth.

He swirled around the bud with his tongue before flicking it back and forth. When he sucked it like a candy, she groaned, and the sound wove itself inside him.

Everything about this woman called to him. Her body. The way she fit so perfectly against him.

Her hips rocked, her core pressing into his stomach, and he moved his hand from her waist to her other breast, finding the peak of her nipple through the material of her bra and rolling it between his thumb and forefinger.

"Becket," she moaned.

Fuck, his name had never sounded so good.

He ran his hand down her belly, his fingertips whispering against her skin. He was almost touching the V between her thighs when the ringing of a phone cut through the room. It was loud in the silence, and Sky's body immediately tensed, her softness turning hard.

"Becket." Two deep breaths from her. "Oh God, what are we doing?"

He could have laughed. "I think that's pretty obvious."

"We need to stop." She pushed at his chest, a request to put her down.

He closed his eyes, taking a second to breathe, before lifting his head. The phone was still ringing, and the apex of her thighs was still pressed against him. "Is that really what you want?"

Her eyes flared. It took three entire seconds before she finally whispered, "Yes."

He gently lifted the cup of her bra and lowered her to her feet. Immediately, she grabbed her dress from the floor. He reached for her purse on the table and handed it to her.

She fished out her phone. "It's my mom."

He nodded. "I should go then."

He wanted her to say no, and not just so he could taste her again. He wanted to stay. To be close, even if it was just on the couch.

But she nodded back.

Before walking out, he stepped closer and cupped her face. "Thank you for joining me tonight. It felt good to have you there." He swiped his thumb over her cheek. "Lock the door after me."

Another flaring of her eyes before she gave another small jerky nod.

He turned and stepped outside. The cold air slapped him in the face. He waited until he heard the click of her door locking before heading to his house. The second he stepped inside, the silence felt too fucking loud.

He ran his fingers through his hair. What the hell was going on with him? He liked living alone. He thrived on it. But now he was so aware of Sky next door that his house felt too empty.

He headed upstairs. What he needed was a cold damn shower.

CHAPTER 17

Sky grabbed her keys and her bag and rushed out of the house.

She was running late to work again. Really late.

Not only had she forgotten to set her alarm, she'd spilled coffee on her shirt, realized she'd run out of bread for toast, and tried to put her jeans on backward.

A mess. She was a *mess*.

Once she reached the car, she was tempted to put her foot to the floor. She didn't. She hated people who sped. All that did was increase the chance of accidents.

This wasn't the first time this week things like that had happened. She'd been out of sorts since that damn kiss three nights ago. Last night she'd forgotten about a quiche in the oven and set off the fire alarm. And the day before that, she'd left her phone at work and had to drive all the way back to get it.

How had one kiss upheaved her entire life? It hadn't even been that good.

Okay, it *had* been that good. And not just the kiss. The way he'd sandwiched her entire body between him and the wall, the way he'd touched her... Oh God, she was getting hot just thinking about it.

She hit the car's Bluetooth and called the daycare.

"Good morning, Sky's Doggy Daycare, Dolly speaking."

"Dolly, hi, it's Sky."

"Sky, I was just about to call you. Rosemary Symes came in with Bella, but she seemed annoyed that you weren't here. Said Bella needed a bath and you're the only one who does it properly."

Sky's lips twitched. "I think Kristina forgot to use Bella's own shampoo last time, and Pearl didn't blow dry her fur."

"Ugh, and now you're the chosen one. You *are* coming in, aren't you? I don't want to have to tell that woman you didn't bathe her dog. She kind of frightens me."

"Dog owners can be scary. I'm coming in, driving now. I'm just running late. I forgot to set an alarm."

"That's not like you."

"I know. It's not my week." She took a right turn.

"Mm, is a certain fire chief boyfriend keeping you up all night?"

She rolled her eyes. He *was* keeping her up, but not in the way Dolly meant. "I'm hanging up now."

"Oh, darling, you can hang up, but I'll just pester you at work."

Yeah, she knew that. "Bye."

She hung up as she neared the bridge. The bridge was short and high, stretching over the Willow Creek Reservoir, which was beautiful but cold and deep. When she was a kid, she'd always wanted to play in it. She'd asked her mother so many times, but the answer had alternated between "no, you'll freeze" and "no, you'll drown."

She accepted that now, but ten-year-old Sky had quite a hard time with it.

Suddenly, she noticed a white van speeding toward her.

Why were they driving so fast...?

She reached the bridge—and suddenly they swerved out of their lane and straight at her.

Sky screamed, instinctively turning her wheel, but there was nowhere to go except the bridge railing.

The airbag deployed. Her face slammed into it as the seat belt locked, cutting into her chest, then her head flew back and crashed against the seat.

Then, suddenly, there was stillness. Stillness and quiet. Everything hurt and something wet slipped down her temple, maybe from the airbag, or maybe from her window, which had completely smashed.

Eyes still closed, she tried to breathe. To slow the air moving in and out of her lungs.

Out. She needed to get out of the car.

With shaky fingers, Sky reached for her seat belt. She tried to release it, but it wouldn't budge. She was stuck. Her heart started to beat faster, panic and a sense of entrapment tightening her chest.

She looked up.

Her breath stopped. And that panic turned to cold, hard fear.

The car had gone through the railing and was hanging partially off the bridge so that all she could see was water and blue skies.

The edges of her vision started to haze, the tremble in her fingers expanding through her body, making everything shake.

She was having a panic attack. But she couldn't. Not right now!

She closed her eyes.

Breathe, Sky. Just breathe.

She drew in a deep breath and held it for a few seconds before letting it ease out.

Phone. She needed a phone so she could call for help. She checked the middle console but her cell wasn't there. It must have fallen during the crash. *Shit.*

A small whimper tried to escape, but she swallowed it down.

She couldn't get her seat belt off, so she couldn't search for her phone. But even if she could, she wouldn't. One small move and for all she knew, her entire car could go over the edge.

What was she supposed to do?

Suddenly, the sound of a car engine approached.

Hope hit her so hard that tears pressed against her eyes. A car door opened and closed. Then a voice.

"Oh my God! Is someone in there?"

She frowned. She knew that voice. Was it Joey? Garfield's owner?

"Joey?"

"Sky?"

Thank God. "Joey, I need you to call for help! Can you do that?"

"Y-yes. I'll do that right now! Are you okay?"

"Yes. But I need help, and I need it fast!"

* * *

"I DON'T KNOW, she's pretty fine if you ask me."

Becket slapped Teddy across the back of his head as he passed where he was sitting. "Don't talk about Sky like that."

"I told him," Moose said, lifting his coffee off the table.

Becket stopped at the coffee machine.

"Hey, a month ago, you wouldn't have cared," Teddy protested.

Actually, he probably would have. He just wouldn't have cared out loud. "A month ago, we weren't dating."

"Well, thanks to our little bar trip, I have a girl too."

"Yeah, yeah, Kristina. We know," Moose said, sounding bored.

"*You* know, but Beck doesn't."

Becket frowned. "Doesn't she work with Sky?"

"Yep, and she is *also* fine." Teddy grinned from ear to ear. "We've shared one date and a whole lot of dirty texts."

Jesus.

Becket turned back to the coffee machine and was just finishing a cup when his radio buzzed.

"Station 8, this is dispatch. There's an auto crash on Kento Bridge. The vehicle's hanging over the bridge and needs stabilization. A female in the driver's seat also needs extraction. We need all first responders immediately."

The alarm went off.

Becket cursed and deserted his coffee as he rushed to the apparatus bay. He pulled on his gear and jumped into an engine with Moose and Teddy. Some of the others jumped into another engine.

"If the car's hanging over the bridge, the first thing we need to do is stabilize the vehicle," Becket said as he sped out of the station.

Moose nodded. "Teddy and I will attach the chain."

"We'll then work on secondary stabilization," Teddy added.

"Good. I'll get the others to block traffic. Hopefully there isn't already a buildup blocking access." They needed a clear road to get the engine through.

When he grew closer, cars were lining the road leading to the bridge. He cursed and drove into the opposite lane, passing them.

A small blue Nissan on the bridge came into view. Then he saw a kid standing beside it, a terrier in his arms. The Nissan didn't look damaged, so it hadn't been part of the crash. The kid must have called it in.

As he drove onto the bridge, he got his first glimpse of the other car.

His world narrowed to pinpoint focus, and his chest felt like it was about to cave in. He knew that car. He saw it every damn day.

"Sky."

Moose's head whipped around. "*Sky?* That's Sky's car?"

Becket stopped the engine and threw himself out of the cab. He began to sprint toward the car, but Moose was suddenly there, the older man faster than Becket would have thought possible, grabbing his arm.

"Get off me, Moose! I don't want to hurt you. I need to see her!"

"*No.* You need to calm the hell down first."

He was about to shove Moose off when Teddy suddenly grabbed his other arm. "Becket—"

"That's Sky in there!" Becket growled.

Irene appeared in front of him from the other engine. She got really close, her voice lowering. "If that's Sky, then you need to get yourself under control. Her vehicle's sitting over the edge of the bridge. If anything bumps it or disrupts the balance, it could go over, and she'll go with it."

Fear gripped his limbs, despite his words. "I'm smarter than that and you know it."

"Emotions do funny things to all of us," Moose said.

Becket forced his muscles to relax. He could easily break out of the hold Moose and Teddy had on him—but they were right. He needed to be calm when he approached Sky. He needed to keep *her* calm so she didn't move.

"Fine," he finally conceded before taking a breath. "I'm okay."

Slowly, both men released him.

"I'm going to talk to her," Becket said firmly. "You guys stabilize the vehicle so it's secure enough to extract her. Irene, check there's no oil leak."

They all nodded and started to walk away, but Becket grabbed Moose's arm before he could leave. "And, Moose...do it fast."

Moose nodded before jogging back to the engine.

Becket crossed over to her car, his heart pounding so fucking hard he could just about hear it.

Then he crouched next to her window. "Peaches?"

CHAPTER 18

reathe in...breathe out.

The four words had become a mantra, repeating in her head over and over again, the only thing keeping her calm.

She didn't dare open her eyes. But anytime those four words faltered for any reason, the water would flash back into her head. The clear blue sky. The reminder of exactly where she sat and how close she was to going over the bridge.

She squeezed her eyes closed, the ache in her head fusing with other pain. The pain across her chest. Her legs. Everywhere.

"Joey..." she cried out softly.

"Help's coming, Sky. It won't be long."

Garfield barked, and the sound took a little bit of the pressure off her chest. Dogs had always been her comfort.

Breathe in...breathe out.

She'd just repeated those words again when sirens sounded, then engines. Her breaths sped up.

Help. It was here. Thank God!

Air was still whooshing in and out of her chest too fast as she heard doors opening and closing. Then she heard the distant hum of conversation. It was like white noise to the buzzing between her ears.

She kept her eyes closed.

Focus on your breath, Sky. That's your one job.

Another lungful of air—then she heard it.

"Peaches."

Her eyes flew open, blue sky and water once again filling her view. But this time she didn't focus on that. She turned her head.

"Becket." She could have cried. He was here. And just his presence alone took the edge off her panic.

"Yeah, honey, I'm here."

His warm, calm voice slid over her skin, chasing away some of the chill. "I can't get my seat belt off."

"Don't worry about that right now. My team is here and we're going to get you out. All I need from you is to remain really still. Can you do that, honey?"

"I think so." She swallowed. "It was a white van. They were driving really fast and they swerved to my side. Are they here?"

"No. But don't worry about that either. Focus on you."

She closed her eyes. "I'm sorry."

"What are you sorry for?"

"I haven't been nice to you."

His soft chuckle made some of the panic in her chest dissipate. "You haven't been that bad."

"Yes, I have. I've been angry at everyone. Because for a while, I've been feeling like the world is out to get me, which"—she laughed, but there was no humor in the sound—"this kind of proves it is. But I took it out on you."

"Sky. The day you moved in next door, my life got better."

She almost snorted. "I don't believe that."

"It's true. Fighting with you was the best part of my days... until I kissed you."

Despite everything, butterflies fluttered in her belly. "I kind of liked our kisses too."

"Kind of?"

Okay, more than kind of.

She opened her mouth to say that, but another bark sounded, which was closely followed by shouted voices.

Becket rose and turned before shouting, "Teddy, watch out!"

Suddenly, something hit the back of the car.

Her heart jackhammered.

Becket shouted, *"No!"*

Then the car tipped forward, sending her right into the reservoir.

* * *

A DOG BARKED, surprising Becket, and he whipped his head around. The owner of the Nissan had moved back to clear the scene, but as Becket stood up to see what was happening, the dog jumped out of his owner's arms and ran toward Teddy, who was hunched behind the car, attaching a chain.

"Teddy, watch out!"

But Becket's words came too late.

The dog hit Teddy at full speed, and Teddy fell into the car. The vehicle jerked. The chain was already attached but the undercarriage wasn't stable enough. It was the only anchor point.

Becket watched, helpless, as the undercarriage tore right off and the car fell off the bridge.

The splash of the vehicle hitting the water was loud, and it made a fear like Becket had never known slice through his limbs.

A collection of loud gasps sounded around him as Becket yanked off his helmet, jacket and boots.

"Becket, wait!"

He ignored Irene's shout, sprinting to the edge of the bridge and jumping off the edge.

Cool air whipped over his body as he sliced through the air, the years he'd spent as a Navy SEAL coming back to him. He sucked in a deep lungful of air before his feet hit the reservoir and he sank beneath the surface. Icy-cold water enveloped him, shocking his system. He ignored the urge to escape the cold, forced his mind to go black and his training to take over.

He spotted the car. It was sinking fast. His powerful strokes cut through the water, and he reached the vehicle in what felt like seconds.

Sky's eyes were closed, and her head was back.

He pulled his pocketknife and sliced through her seat belt. The second it was off, he locked his arm around her chest, maneuvered her out of the car, and kicked toward the surface.

As soon as his head broke through, he sucked in a lungful of air and turned Sky onto her back, then he swam her to the water's edge. It felt like it took too long, when in reality it was only a few seconds.

When he laid her on the bank, his skin chilled. She was too pale.

He placed the heel of his hand on the lower half of her breast-bone, right in the center of her chest, and his other hand on top, interlocking his fingers. He started compressions.

"Come on, Sky," he growled. "Open your eyes for me."

He needed to see the pretty blues staring back at him. He wanted her to wake up and yell at him. Scream. Fuck, *anything*.

When she didn't wake after thirty compressions, he tilted her head back. Once he'd opened her mouth, he sealed his lips over hers, pinched her nose, and blew a breath into her.

Her chest rose and she started to cough, water spluttering out of her mouth.

Yes!

Relief hit him so hard, he felt fucking weak with it. Quickly, he rolled her onto her side into a recovery position and rubbed her back.

"Easy, Peaches."

Coughs continued to rack her body. When they finally eased, she looked up at him. "Becket?"

"Yeah, I'm here, honey. Does anything hurt?" He rubbed her arms. Fuck, she was cold. He needed to get her to an ambulance, fast.

"Everything," she gasped, breaths shuddering.

His teeth ground together. "I'm going to pick you up, okay? Get you to help."

"O-okay."

Her teeth started to chatter, her skin not regaining any of its color.

Gently, he slid an arm behind her back and the other under her knees.

"You j-jumped in after me?" she whispered.

He began jogging back up to the road. "Of course I jumped in after you. You would have died otherwise." Saying the words out loud made acid fill his mouth.

"But *you* could have died."

"I was a Navy SEAL. I've done a million missions all more dangerous than this, honey."

At her silence, he looked down to see her frowning at him.

"You still should have—"

"Do *not* say I should have left you, Peaches. I'm already barely hanging on to my calm."

Calm? He didn't have any fucking calm.

There was a small pause. "Thank you."

"You don't need to thank me. I'll always jump in after you."

Her small intake of breath was sharp and loud. But then a shudder rocked her spine and she nuzzled deeper into his chest. He tightened his arms around her.

He jogged up the hill just as an ambulance and a sheriff's car pulled up. His brother climbed out of the vehicle. "Becket!"

Becket moved toward the ambulance. "Some asshole came at

her car from the other direction. She swerved and went into the bridge railing."

Jesse cursed and pulled his radio from his belt.

The paramedics pulled out the stretcher. "What happened?"

"Car collision with the bridge railing, followed by the vehicle going into the water. She lost consciousness and needed CPR."

"How long was she out?" the second paramedic asked.

"Not long. A couple minutes, tops." He laid her on a stretcher.

"Thanks. We've got it from here."

Sky quickly clutched his arm. "I want B-Becket to c-come with me."

"Ma'am—"

"I'm going with her," Becket pressed, the hardness in his voice proving he wasn't fucking backing down.

The paramedics sighed. "Get in."

CHAPTER 19

"*A*re you comfortable? Of course you're not comfortable. This pillow is the thickness of a sheet. Hang on, I'll go get you a new one."

"Mom." Sky grabbed her mother's hand before she could leave her bedside. "The pillow is fine. The people who work at this hospital are busy. They don't need to be rushing around, finding me a new pillow."

"Darling, you almost *died!*" Her mother closed her eyes and took a second to compose herself before opening them again. "It's their *job* to make you better, and a new pillow will—"

"Esther," her father interrupted. "Leave Sky alone."

Her mother turned and started arguing with him.

Sky sucked in a long breath. To say her rest had become a little less restful since her parents had arrived would be an understatement. She loved her mom, but the woman had walked into the room crying. Big, loud sobs that had probably been heard from the parking lot. And they'd lasted a while. Then had come the complaints—her room was too small, there were no open windows to allow fresh air.

She was grateful for her parents, but it was also exhausting.

At least they hadn't brought Tony.

Sky turned her gaze to the open doorway, and her heart gave a little thump. Becket stood there, somehow looking even bigger than usual. His arms were crossed, and he looked angry as he spoke to Jesse. The kind of anger that if directed at you, would make you run in the other direction.

He hadn't left her side. He'd even refused to go home to change into dry clothes, instead asking his sister to bring him some.

Her father had thanked Becket and had been slightly warmer to him. It wasn't quite at her mother's level, who'd thrown herself into Becket's arms, sobbing her gratitude.

Becket turned his head and his gaze collided with hers. He didn't smile. His lips didn't so much as twitch. He just watched her, the same intense expression on his face, like he was ready for whatever threat was about to come her way next.

A shiver ran over her skin.

"Darling, will you tell your father that you need more medication? You're in pain. I can see it."

She forced her attention back to her mother. "I don't need more medication. I'm okay."

"You're not okay, you almost *drowned*!"

When tears started to gather in her mother's eyes again, Sky reached out and touched her arm. "Mom...I know what happened to me has scared you. But I *didn't* drown, thanks to Becket. I'm here, I'm alive, and I'm okay."

Her mother closed her eyes and when she opened them, she nodded, clearly trying to pull herself together.

The doctor stepped into the room. "Miss Williams, how are you feeling?"

"A bit sore, but I don't feel too bad, considering." Probably due to all the drugs running through her system.

He nodded soberly. "You're lucky. This could have ended far worse."

She was so aware that this could have been worse. But lucky? No, she didn't feel close to lucky. She'd almost died today…and it wasn't the first time.

Everything that happened in Cheyenne started to creep back to her. The car incident. The fires.

Amber Ridge was supposed to be her fresh start. The place where her bad luck finally turned around. Was it starting all over again?

Her skin started to chill, and she once again searched out Becket in the hall. He was still standing with Jesse, but his attention was on her.

The doctor looked at her from over his glasses. "Now, I'm happy for you to go home as long as you have someone to stay with you tonight to monitor you."

"She's coming home with us," her mother said quickly.

Panic punched through Sky. "No, I'm not."

"Of course you are! I'm your mother. I need to take care of you."

She couldn't think of anything worse than going home with her parents. Her mother had only been by her side for an hour and she already felt more exhausted than when she'd arrived. And *Tony* was staying there.

"No."

Her mother blew out an exasperated breath. "Stop being silly, Sky. Roger, tell her she needs to come home with us so we can look after her."

"*I'm* looking after her."

Everyone's gaze flew to Becket.

Her father cleared his throat. "Now, young man, *we* are her parents—"

"And she's an adult," Becket cut in, so calm it was like he didn't feel a drop of the tension in the room. "So it's her choice."

Four sets of eyes locked on her. She didn't hesitate. "I'm going home with Becket."

Annoyance flared in her father's expression, and her mother just looked worried.

"Darling—" her mom started, but Sky cut her off.

"I need to sleep in my own bed, and Becket...he's my boyfriend, Mom. I choose him." She swallowed hard.

This time, it was hurt she saw on her mother's face.

The doctor nodded. "Okay, well, I'm going to leave you to it. Remember to come in if you start feeling unwell."

Sky dipped her head. "I will. Thank you."

When he stepped out of the room, she turned back to her parents. "Thank you for coming and bringing me clothes. I really appreciate everything."

"I don't want to leave you," her mother said, tears once again brimming.

"How about I call you later tonight, and tomorrow you come over and we'll spend the morning together?" Of course she'd have to use Becket's phone because her cell was at the bottom of the reservoir.

"Are you sure you'll be okay if we leave?"

"I'm certain."

Her mother sighed before leaning over and gently hugging her.

Her father stepped forward next and pressed a kiss to her temple. "Call if you need anything."

"I will."

When they left the room, she turned to Becket. "Thank you."

"You don't need to thank me."

He kept saying that, but it wasn't true. She was thoroughly indebted to this man and thanking him was all she had to give. "Did your brother have any information on the driver of the white van?"

Becket moved forward so that he stood beside the bed, touching her hand. His eyes were so dark they were almost black.

"No. But his deputies will speak to everyone they know in Amber Ridge who drives a white van."

She nodded, more focused on the warmth from Becket's touch than his words. She met his eyes. "Are *you* okay? You jumped off a bridge into freezing-cold water. Did you get checked?"

"I'm fine. I've done far worse in—"

"The military, I know. But you're still human. And you put yourself in danger for me." Nausea churned in her belly, memories of Charlie once again sending fear through her limbs.

Becket tightened his fingers on her hand. "I'm okay. I know my limits. Can I take you home?"

The thought of her own bed made some of the tension ease from her body. "I would love that."

"Do you need help changing?"

She glanced at the pile of clothes on the chair. When she'd brought clothes for her brother, Clara had also grabbed Sky some leggings and an oversized sweater. "No, I can do it."

His brows flickered. "I don't feel good leaving you to do it alone."

Her heart squeezed. How was this the same man she'd waged war with over a boundary fence? "I'll call out if I need help."

If the crease between his brows was anything to go by, he didn't like it. "I'll be right outside that door. If I hear anything I don't like, I'm coming in."

She nodded but the second he was gone, she wanted him back. Today, he'd saved her life. And in the process, he'd become more to her. The person she felt safest with. The person she wanted to keep closest. And she had a feeling that wouldn't be changing for a while.

* * *

BECKET'S FINGERS were tight around the wheel as he drove. Everything about this day made him cold with dread. And the anger…it was everywhere—in his skin, his bones, his clenched teeth. It made him want to drive the streets and find the fucking van owner and murder him.

They'd run Sky off a bridge, then left her, not caring if she lived or died.

The image of her car tipping into the water replayed over and over in his mind, tormenting him. The memory of her unconscious in her car at the bottom of the reservoir was like a nightmare he couldn't get out of his head.

She'd come so close to death today. Too fucking close. If he hadn't been there to jump in after her, there was a chance no one else would have. It was too much of a risk, even for a firefighter.

He shot a glance at the passenger seat. Sky's head was back, her eyes closed, but she wasn't asleep. There were deep circles under her eyes, and her skin still hadn't recovered much of its color.

He pulled into his driveway and turned off the engine.

"You don't have a car," he said, almost to himself.

"My parents have a spare I can use. They're dropping it off tomorrow."

Hell, he didn't even want her driving. He wanted her safe with him. "Your house or mine?"

"I'd love to shower in my bathroom and sleep in my own bed, if that's okay?"

If that was okay? Sky could ask him to sell his house and live with a hundred puppies and he'd probably agree right now.

He grazed a lock of hair behind her ear. "Done."

When he reached her side of the car, she went to climb out, but he slipped one arm under her knees and the other behind her back and lifted her.

Sky gasped. "Becket, I can walk."

"You were in a car crash today and went over a bridge. I want to carry you to your house."

He thought she'd argue. Instead, she sighed and leaned her head against his chest. And fuck, it felt good. *Holding her*, having her *trust him*, it all felt good, especially today.

On her porch, he lowered her to her feet, but only long enough to take the spare key from beneath the pot and unlock and open her front door. Her key was at the bottom of the lake, along with her car and everything else that had been in it.

His teeth clenched together again, and the second the door was open, he lifted her and carried her upstairs. It was almost eight. Usually too early for bed, but after Sky's day, she'd probably want to sleep as soon as possible.

When he reached her room, he set her on her feet before glancing at her bathroom, then back to her. "Are you going to be okay?"

There was a small lift of her lips. "I have to be. Because no way am I letting you shower with me."

A half smile curved his lips. "I'm offended."

"Don't be. It's basically a compliment."

"How's that?"

"I mean, if I'm naked, you have to be naked too, and then I'll want to do things we both know the doctor hasn't signed off on."

His dick twitched. "Fine. But only a short shower, because you need to rest."

"Got it, boss."

Jesus, this woman. She almost died and she was still giving him attitude.

He inched closer and cupped her cheek. "I'm being serious, Sky. Be careful. And yell if you need *anything*."

The smile slipped and her eyes flared. "I will."

"I'll make us food."

"I'm not hungry."

"You need to eat."

He got the feeling she wanted to roll her eyes, but she didn't.

Turning away from her was harder than it should have been. He forced himself to head downstairs and into her kitchen. Before he could check for food, his phone rang, his brother's name flashing on the screen.

He answered it straight away. "Jesse. Tell me you found the asshole."

"We paid a visit to everyone we know here in town who drives a white van. Everyone either had an alibi or denied any involvement."

"So someone's fucking lying."

Jesse sighed. "There's no evidence anyone hit her car. Therefore, no evidence linking them to the crime. I'm afraid I can't really do anything else."

"That's ridiculous." Anger blackened the room around Becket. "Someone caused a fucking car accident, then left the scene!"

"I know. I'm frustrated too, brother. If there was something else I could do, I would. I'm sorry."

Becket ran a hand over his face, frustration simmering in his gut.

"Are you home?" Jesse asked.

"I'm at Sky's house. I'm going to stay the night." Hopefully longer, if she'd let him.

"Good. How's she doing?"

"Pretty good, considering what happened. But I'm not sure if that's just for show because she wants me to think she's okay."

"It's possible." There was a small pause. "And how are you?"

He should be better than he was. This thing between him and Sky wasn't supposed to be real. He wasn't supposed to care this much. But what happened today had rocked him. "Not nearly as good. Which is stupid. I was a SEAL and I've been a firefighter for years. I should be better than this."

"It's different when it's someone you care about."

Jesse was right. He *did* care about her. Somehow, she'd gone from the neighbor he couldn't do anything but fight with to someone he struggled to be apart from.

A knock on the door had Becket lifting his head. Who the hell was that?

"I've got to go. Someone's here."

"I'll check in tomorrow."

"Thanks." He hung up and strode to the door, where he looked through the peephole.

"You have *got* to be shitting me," Becket muttered, even as he yanked the door open. "Was she not clear the first two fucking times? She doesn't want you here."

Tony glared. "Where's Sky?"

"That's none of your business. Answer my question."

"I brought her food. I wanted to go to the hospital, but her mother asked me to wait."

"Good."

"You know, whether you like it or not, we're old family friends. So I made her favorite meal." He cocked his head. "Do *you* know her favorite meal?"

"I know she'd prefer it if you weren't here."

Tony laughed, but there was no humor in the sound. "Fine. Just give this to her for me."

Becket took the dish and slammed the door closed. In the kitchen, he peeled off the foil to reveal enchiladas.

He shouldn't feel jealous that the asshole knew her favorite food and he didn't.

He'd lost his fucking appetite.

He put the dish in the fridge before heading back upstairs. When he reached her room, he stopped at her doorway to see her climbing into bed. She wore an oversized shirt that reached mid-thigh. The salt lamp beside her bed was on, casting a dim glow over the room.

She frowned when she looked at him. "Hey. Are you okay?"

"I should be asking you that."

"I've been asked that a million times today. I'm all okayed out. And I kind of feel like a new person after the shower."

He sat on the edge of her bed. "Tony dropped by."

Her nose wrinkled. "Why?"

"He wanted to drop off some food. Your favorite, apparently."

"What's my favorite?"

"Enchiladas."

She laughed. "I *like* enchiladas. I wouldn't say they're my favorite. I'm more of a plain-Jane, toast-and-avocado-with-a-little-bit-of-salt kind of girl."

He'd made her toast and avocado the morning after the break-in. "I'll go get you some."

She shook her head. "I'm still not hungry. But I was wondering…"

"Anything."

"Would you share the bed with me tonight? I know it might be weird, but it's big and—"

"Yes. Besides, the couch is kind of uncomfortable."

The air rushed from her chest on a big sigh. "Thank you."

"I'll just take a shower and lock up."

She nodded, and he squeezed her hand before rising and moving out of the room.

He used the hall bathroom to shower, and it was the quickest of his life because he didn't want her to be alone. Once everything was locked up and turned off, he returned to her, sliding into the other side of the bed.

Every muscle in his body itched to reach over and tug her against him. But he didn't have to. *She* inched backward, until her back was pressed against his side. He rolled to spoon her and slipped an arm around her waist.

She sighed. "Thank you again for saving me today."

"Always, Peaches."

CHAPTER 20

Sky watched as the steam from her coffee curled into the air. It was still dark, and the kitchen counter was cool beneath her while she watched the sun rise through the window. It was early. Too early to be up. But she couldn't get the events of yesterday out of her head.

If Becket had been a few seconds later getting her out of that water...

She sucked in a sharp breath and closed her eyes.

She'd dreamed about the accident last night. But when she'd hit the water, instead of feeling cold, she'd felt this burning heat. Then she'd smelled smoke, and she was back in her house in Cheyenne the night it had caught on fire.

She shook her head, trying to chase the memory away. But she couldn't. Everything that had happened in Cheyenne was alive inside her.

At first she'd thought she was crazy to believe the universe was out to get her. But after that last house fire, and then losing Charlie less than a week later...she hadn't been able to run from the truth any longer.

Amber Ridge was supposed to be her sanctuary. But first the

break-in, then being run off the bridge. And just when Becket and his team were working to save her, Garfield jumped onto the firefighter, causing her car to fall off the bridge.

That wasn't ordinary bad luck. It was the universe working against her.

Because she'd survived that initial fire in the café? Because Eloise had wrongly died in her place and destiny was determined to get her?

"What are you doing up so early?"

She jumped at Becket's voice, the hot coffee almost spilling onto her hands.

He was shirtless, and God, his chest...it was muscled and tanned and so hard to look away from.

"Hey," she started softly, "I couldn't sleep and didn't want to wake you."

He stopped in front of her, so close she could almost feel the heat radiating off him. "I'm surprised I didn't wake when you got up. I usually wake at everything."

"I'm pretty stealthy."

He gave her a small smile.

She frowned at the cut on his chest. Gently, she reached out and grazed her fingertip across the minor wound. "Is this from yesterday?"

"Must be."

Her frown deepened, again reminded that it wasn't just *her* life that had been on the line yesterday. That yet again, her bad luck was affecting those closest to her.

"Hey."

Her eyes flashed up to his.

"What are you thinking?" he asked quietly.

"That I hate that you put yourself at risk to save me yesterday."

He stepped closer, his hands going to the counter on either side of her hips. "What happened wasn't your fault."

"I know. But I kind of feel like the world's out to get me again."

An intense frown cut into his brow.

She looked down at her coffee before glancing back up. "You know how I told you my life is the burnt toast theory, and Eloise died in my place?"

"Yeah. And I told you her death wasn't your fault."

"Well, after she died…things started happening."

"What do you mean?" His voice was deeper now, a dangerous edge to it.

"A month after her death, my brakes failed. I was turning a corner and if I'd been driving any faster, it could have been really bad." She swallowed. "A few weeks later, my engine literally blew up. There was so much smoke, and I barely got Charlie and myself out in time. Then there was my house fire, which I told you about."

A shudder rolled down her spine. She hated remembering that day.

"You came here to escape the accidents."

"I did. But now I'm not sure running did anything. They could be starting again."

"Hey." He tilted her chin up. "If you're trying to tell me you're cursed or something, you're wrong."

"Maybe not cursed. More like I escaped my fate that day at the café, and now destiny's out to get me."

"No. That's not how it works. What happened yesterday was a shitty driver causing an accident. You are *safe*. And I will stay with you for as long as you need so that you *feel* safe."

She was shaking her head before he finished speaking. "No. I already feel bad that you've had to look after me so much. Besides, I promised my mom I'd spend the day with her."

"I can spend the day with her too."

She laughed. "You don't want to spend the day with my mother."

"Why not?"

"Because you'll go crazy. *I* go crazy and I love the woman."

"I'd do it for you."

Those familiar butterflies took off in her belly again.

"Becket," she whispered. "What are we doing?"

"Well, I'm not sure about you, but I'm standing in front of a beautiful woman, wondering what she'd do if I kissed her again."

For a second, she couldn't speak. She had to roll his words around in her head a few times, convince herself he really had said them.

She opened her mouth to remind him that they weren't really dating…but she wasn't sure if that was true anymore.

And hell, even if it was true…she'd almost died yesterday. If she wanted to kiss the man, she should just kiss him.

Slowly, she set the mug onto the counter and slipped her fingers into his hair. "She'd probably kiss you back."

Heat flared in his eyes. Then he lowered his head and kissed her. A gentle graze of his mouth on hers. A touch that she felt in more places than just her lips.

His mouth swiped against hers again, softening her. Teasing.

This kiss was different than the last. It wasn't desperate and fast…it was gentle and safe. A slow coaxing until her lips parted and his tongue slipped inside so he could taste her.

A deep throb began in her lower belly. A sensation that had become so infinitely tied to Becket.

He slid her to the edge of the counter, and she wrapped her legs around his waist.

How he sent her from zero to a hundred in a matter of seconds, she had no idea. But it didn't matter. All that mattered was kissing him. Holding him. Accepting everything he offered her.

With one hand still in his hair, she swept the other down his chest, brushing her fingertips against every hard ridge. Letting them unravel her and drive her wild.

When he lifted his head, his mouth parting from hers, it was too soon.

She groaned, and he chuckled. "You need to rest, Peaches."

"No. I need more kisses." She tugged his head back to her and kissed him again, slipping her tongue straight inside his mouth and caressing his.

God, he tasted good. She could drown in his kisses and never want for air.

Again, he pulled away. "Sky…"

And again she groaned.

Then a phone he'd set on the kitchen island rang. A ring that was completely unwelcome in this moment.

Man, the universe really *was* out to get her.

He sighed as he turned and grabbed it. "It's work."

She felt her chest rise on a deep inhale, trying to pull herself together even though her skin felt like it was on fire. "Answer it."

He pressed one firm kiss to her forehead before turning away.

She dropped her head and breathed.

Pull yourself together, Sky. He's just a man and it was just a kiss.

But it wasn't just a kiss. Every time he touched her, he burrowed that much deeper into her life.

When he hung up and turned back to her, she knew it was bad news. "There's a fire in the mountains. They need me."

"Go. I'll be okay."

He stepped back between her legs, his eyes boring into hers. "Rest while I'm gone. Please?"

"Don't worry, my mother won't let me lift a finger."

"Good." One more kiss before he turned, and the second he walked away, she had to fist her hands to stop from dragging him back.

* * *

RED-HOT FLAMES DANCED in front of Becket's eyes, heat radiating all around him.

Another damn forest fire. The second in the past month, but this one was bigger.

He moved around his crew, making sure everyone was where they needed to be while watching for spot fires. Every time they thought the blaze was under control, another spot fire would pop up, or the wind would change and spread the flames.

He lifted his radio. "Copter 312, we need that water drop. What's your ETA?"

He'd ordered the water drop when they'd arrived and the damn thing still wasn't here.

His radio sounded. "Station 8, this is Copter 312. We're four minutes away."

It wasn't good enough. Four minutes could mean the difference between a fire being contained or becoming uncontrollable.

"A few more minutes until the drop," Becket yelled to his crew.

"They better be quick," Moose yelled. "Wind changes direction again and the whole mountain could go up."

Becket fucking knew that.

Those minutes took a long fucking time to pass. Then his radio finally sounded again. "Flying over now."

"Water drop," Becket yelled.

He and his crew dropped flat to the ground, heads down and hands going over their helmets as the water fell over them.

They all remained on the ground for a few seconds before pushing to their feet.

The last of the flames seemed to be out. Thank God.

"All right, let's spread out and make sure it's all gone," he called.

Becket grabbed an extinguisher and moved through the debris. When footsteps sounded behind him, he turned to see Teddy jogging over. "Beck. Wait up."

Becket kept walking. "Everything okay?"

"Yeah, I just…we haven't really talked about yesterday," Teddy said as he caught up.

His jaw clenched. "Now isn't the time."

"I'm sorry."

Becket's fingers tightened around his extinguisher. "Teddy—"

"I should have been more efficient yesterday. And I should have been more aware of my surroundings and braced when that dog jumped on me."

Becket stopped and turned, fighting for calm that he didn't have. "Did you check the undercarriage before attaching the chain?"

"I…" He swallowed. "No. I'm sorry. I should have."

"Yeah, you should have. That's the difference between people living and dying in our line of work."

Teddy's mouth opened and closed. "I'm sorry."

"Get back to work, Teddy." Fury tightened his chest.

What happened wasn't all Teddy's fault. But if he'd examined the undercarriage to see if it was compromised like he should have, Sky's vehicle would've been secure.

He moved faster. When he was done checking his area of the forest, he returned to the engine to find his brother talking to a fire investigator. When Jesse saw him, he shook the investigator's hand before crossing the space between them.

"Hey. I heard your crew took care of the fire."

Becket nodded. "It's out, but I want to know how it started. This is the second vegetation fire in our forest in the past month. The last one was arson. Was this the same?"

"They're still investigating the cause," Jesse said.

"Call me as soon as you know."

"Will do."

When his crew was done, they climbed into the engine cab, Becket taking the seat behind the wheel.

Irene leaned her head back. "It's been a big month."

"Huge," Moose agreed.

"Hopefully it means we're due a few quiet ones," Becket said, even though something told him that was wishful fucking thinking.

When they got back to the station, he hung up his helmet and jacket, grabbed a clean uniform and called dibs on a shower. Before getting in, he sent a text to Sky. She'd messaged him earlier that day with a new number from a cell her mother had picked up for her. Thank God, because he needed an easy way to get in contact with her.

Becket: Hey. Just checking in. Are you doing okay?

He hit send and jumped into the shower. He hated being away from her. But the fire was big and his crew needed him. Irene was the second in charge, but he still liked to take the lead on such significant fires.

Once he was out, he pulled on his clean clothes. His phone buzzed on the way to his office.

Sky: I'm being force fed. And every time I try to get up, I'm physically pushed back down. How my mother's so strong, I have no idea.

Becket: Force feeding and rest doesn't sound terrible.

Sky: I'm losing my mind. And she won't leave until you get back. When are you getting back?

Becket: A few hours.

Sky: Sigh.

Becket: Want me to pick up something for dinner?

Sky: If by dinner you mean pie from The Tea House, then yes...yes I do.

He chuckled.

Becket: Done.

In his office, he dropped into his seat. The reports he had to do after incidents were the worst part of the job. They were long and tedious. The only thing that got him through the damn things was the knowledge that it was important. And coffee.

Fuck, why didn't he have a coffee?

He'd just turned on his computer and was about to get back up to go to the kitchen when his phone rang, his brother's name on the screen. "Jesse. You know what caused the fire?"

"Yeah, but you're not going to like it."

"Tell me."

"Someone used paint thinner as an accelerant."

Becket cursed. Paint thinner was often used by arsonists because it was available in containers that were small and easy to transport. It also didn't raise any red flags when bought. "You think it's the same person?"

"Two forest fires set within a few miles of each other? Yeah, I think it was the same person."

It was too big of a coincidence not to be. "Why would they use two different accelerants though?"

"Maybe gasoline didn't have the effect they liked."

"Maybe. Or maybe they were scared to be pulled over with gasoline in their car near the mountains after the first fire."

"Whatever it was, I'll be getting my deputies to do drives through the most wooded areas as often as possible."

That wouldn't be enough. The forest was huge. "Jesse...if we hadn't gotten to today's fire when we had, it could have been really bad. The fire could have become completely uncontrollable."

He could almost hear his brother's heavy inhale. "We'd better not let this person start another one then."

Absolutely not. They were lucky no one had gotten hurt yet. They may not be so lucky a third time.

CHAPTER 21

Sky stood under the warm stream of water, one thing on her mind. The same thing that had been on her mind for the last week. Well, not so much a thing but a person.

Becket.

He was downstairs cooking dinner while she washed off the smell of dogs. In fact, unless one of them was at work, he literally hadn't left her side since the incident on the bridge. He'd been sleeping here, making her food, caring for her.

She sucked in a sharp breath. He'd been…God, he'd been so much more for her than she'd ever expected.

The cocky, know-it-all-Becket was gone, and in his place was this kind, gentle, *protective* version of him. He'd even taken her to another family dinner, and every touch and intimate glance her way had felt real.

Was it real? At some point, had they shifted from fake dating to real dating and just not discussed it?

She closed her eyes, letting the water beat down on her face and chest.

They weren't friends. Friends didn't share a bed, right? Friends didn't wake up in each other's embrace with his hard stomach pressed to her back or her cheek on his chest. And they weren't enemies anymore.

She just needed to ask him and get it over with.

Mind made up, she turned off the water and stepped out. As she dried, her gaze caught on her reflection in the mirror. On the bruises that were fading from her arms. The healing scratches splattered across her body. After the car accident, she'd been covered in them. Now, you almost wouldn't be able to tell anything had happened.

She still couldn't believe Becket had jumped in after her. Because that was crazy, right? He'd jumped off a freaking bridge and risked his life for her.

Fear kicked at her ribs. The same fear that had been living inside her for the last week. *He'd risked his life for her.* He could have drowned trying to get her out.

She shook her head. Nothing was going to happen to him because of her. And her bad luck *was not* returning.

Ha. Maybe if she repeated that enough she might believe it.

She left the bathroom and stopped at the sight of broad shoulders and a very muscled back in the bedroom.

Desire slammed into her belly. Even from behind, he was the most beautiful man she'd ever seen.

Becket turned, and his washboard abs made her skin feel sensitive and tingly. She forced her gaze up to his eyes. Eyes that were darker than usual as they took her in just as she'd done to him.

"Hey," she said softly.

"Hey. Sorry, I got pasta sauce on my shirt."

He'd started leaving some of his things here. Clothes. Toiletries. Little bits and pieces of his life so that even when he wasn't here, it felt like he was. "That's not like you. Usually, you're the cleanest cook I know." Actually, he was the cleanest *guy* she knew. He said it was a military thing. She was pretty sure it was just a Becket thing.

"Guess I was distracted."

His gaze lowered to the towel wrapped around her body. Her breasts suddenly felt heavy. She liked it when he looked at her. It made her feel beautiful and desirable. And it made her want things that part of her whispered she shouldn't want.

"Is this real?" The quiet question was out before she could stop it.

Slowly, he crossed the space between them. "Does it feel real?"

"Yes."

He stopped in front of her. "It feels real to me too."

"You haven't tried to kiss me in the last week." She almost cringed. That kind of sounded desperate.

So gently she barely felt it, he ran his fingers down her arm. "I wanted to give you space to heal."

"I feel good. Thank you for taking care of me."

"Always."

His fingers ran back down her arm, all the way to her wrist. She shuddered. Then he lowered his head and kissed her bare shoulder, making her abdomen flare to life.

"Becket..." she breathed.

"Mm." He kissed her again, but this time her neck. On the third kiss, she tilted her head to give him better access. "So soft."

Her eyes shuttered and she pressed her palms to his hard stomach, anchoring herself.

His lips moved over her cheek, slowly growing closer to her mouth. She could almost feel his lips on hers...but suddenly he stopped and lifted his head. Just a fraction, but it was enough to make her want to groan in disappointment.

His dark eyes bored into hers. "Do you want this, Sky?"

"I want you," she whispered, the words truer than any other she'd spoken. Then, to prove her point, she rose to her toes and kissed him.

The second their mouths sealed together, her entire body

came to life. It was like a beam of electricity shooting into her. That was what he did to her.

A deep growl rippled from his throat. He tugged her closer so her body was flush against his. She gasped, and he slipped his tongue inside her mouth.

The second she tasted him, she wanted more. It was only their fourth kiss, yet he tasted so infinitely familiar.

She slid one hand behind his head, threading her fingers through his hair. Hair that was far softer than she would have thought. She smoothed her other hand down his chest, feeling the steady thumps of his heart beneath her palm. So strong, just like the rest of him.

In one swift move, he lifted her, and she instinctively wrapped her legs around his waist. He turned and lay her on the bed, his warmth above her...surrounding her. Light kisses grazed down her neck. When he reached the towel, he loosened the top and tugged it open.

She watched the heat in his eyes turn molten as he took her in.

"Fucking gorgeous," he whispered. She didn't have time to think before he lowered his head and took one pebbled nipple between his lips and sucked.

She cried out and arched, pressing her nipple deeper into his mouth.

He licked and sucked, his teeth grazing across her bud, driving her wild.

Then he switched to her other breast and did it all over again. Flicking her nipple back and forth, then running his tongue in a circle.

The throbbing in her core intensified, beating through her belly. She craved this man. She craved to be touched and kissed and *loved* by him.

Like he heard her thoughts, he released her nipple and trailed kisses down her belly then her hip bone. When he hovered over the apex between her thighs, the air in her lungs stalled.

He parted her thighs, wrapping his thick arms around them, and lowered his head. Then his tongue ran over her clit, and her entire body jolted. He did it again, but this time he placed a hand over her belly, keeping her exactly where he wanted her.

Every time he licked and tasted her, the room hazed and swirled. She fisted the bed sheets as he played with her, the need and desire building, making her *ache* for him.

When Becket wrapped his lips around her clit and sucked, she almost toppled over the edge. Desperately, she grabbed at his arms, tugging him up. He rose, only to crash his lips back to hers. The kiss was hungry and raw. It was a collision of mouth against mouth, tongue against tongue.

She reached between them, popping the button of his jeans, then lowering the zipper. She reached inside his briefs and wrapped her fingers around his cock. The shift in him was immediate. His muscles tensed, a new stillness taking over his limbs.

She started to explore, moving her palm over his length. When she reached his tip, she rolled her thumb over him.

He hung his head, and the growl that escaped his chest was primal. "Sky…you're killing me."

The warmth of his breath whispering over her skin sent goose bumps trailing over her throat. She quickened her strokes and adjusted her pressure, learning what he liked by the shifts in his breathing. The tightness of his muscles.

Only a few more seconds passed before he released another long, deep growl. His mouth dropped to hers again, tongue plunging inside.

When he pushed off the bed, she wanted to cry out and haul him back. He quickly shoved down his jeans and briefs, and her mouth went dry. God, he was gorgeous. And so incredibly big… every inch of him.

He reached into his jeans pocket and pulled a condom from his wallet. His eyes never left hers as he opened it and rolled it over his length, and every second that passed had her heart beating a little faster.

When he returned to her, she could feel him between her thighs, nudging at her entrance.

"This is real," he whispered.

She cupped his cheek. "More real than anything."

Another darkening of his eyes. Then, slowly, he pushed inside. Filling her. Stretching her. Making her his.

* * *

BECKET CLOSED HIS EYES, trying like hell to calm the fucking storm inside him.

She was tight. And she felt too damn good clamped around his cock.

His heart beat so hard he could hear it. And it was taking every ounce of self-restraint he had to remain still. The heat of her walls around him, combined with the feel of her beneath him, was fucking torment.

He took advantage of her exposed neck and sucked, rewarded with a feminine moan. Every sound from her made lava burn through his veins.

With his mouth still on her, he reached for her breast and rolled his thumb over her nipple. More earth-shattering cries. She wrapped a leg around his waist and tugged him deeper.

Fuck. That last bit of control snapped. He lifted his hips and thrust into her, hard.

Her nails bit into his shoulder, and he plunged into her again and again, sinking so deep that the heat of her body surrounded him on every return.

Perfect. She was fucking *perfect*.

She rocked her hips, matching his thrusts. Deepening them.

When she nipped at his lips, he growled. She did it again, this time following it up with a soft graze of her lips against his, almost teasing.

He dropped his head and crashed his mouth to hers, getting lost in her. Fuck, he loved kissing her. Everything about this woman called to him, and he was fucking helpless.

When he pinched her nipple, she cried out, her nails digging deeper into his flesh.

He quickened his pace, moving harder. Faster.

Need danced between them, the sounds of their breathing and movements loud in the otherwise quiet room.

The muscles in his arms vibrated, and he told himself to slow down. To take his time and stretch this out. But he physically couldn't. Not with Sky making those sweet sounds. Not with her legs tangled around him and her hips lifting to meet his.

He slipped his hand between their bodies and rubbed his thumb over her clit in a circular motion.

She grabbed his upper arms and arched, keening as she fell. Shattering beneath him.

When she screamed his name, it almost broke him.

He pumped harder, stroking her, prolonging her orgasm. Watching as she completely abandoned all inhibition.

He kept thrusting until his own body finally tensed and he exploded, growling as he dug his head into the crook of her neck.

When he finally stilled, they both breathed deeply, every one of his inhales a breath of her. Her sweet scent that at some point he'd become utterly addicted to.

A few more breaths and he lifted his head to see her eyes hooded, a slow smile curving her lips. "Why did we waste so much time fighting when we could have been doing *that*?"

He laughed. He could barely fucking speak, and she came out with that?

He rolled to the side, dragging her into him. "I don't know, Peaches. It was our mistake."

"A huge mistake." They lay there for a few seconds before she gasped. "Your pasta!"

"I took it off the heat. It's probably just gone cold."

"Sex and cold pasta, that's my kind of evening."

"Yeah? You know what *my* kind of night is?"

She looked up at him, her cheeks still a pretty pink, eyes still half closed. "What?"

"Anything that includes you."

CHAPTER 22

Sky sank deeper into the warm sheets.

Mm. Bed felt good this morning. Warm and cozy. Far too comfortable to get up.

She rolled to the side and an ache between her thighs had the previous night slamming back to her mind.

Her eyes sprang open.

Becket. She'd had sex with Becket. But he wasn't in the bed with her now. Her room was empty. Not a huge surprise. He'd woken before her every morning for the last week, usually to make them coffee.

She bit her bottom lip, nerves fluttering in her belly.

Was he down there? What was he thinking? Did he regret anything?

She sat up, pulling the sheet over her chest.

If someone had told her a few months ago that she'd have sex with her stubborn, tree-destroying neighbor, she'd have thought they were insane. But now? He felt like a different person. They felt like *two* different people. He wasn't her stubborn, tree-destroying neighbor anymore. He was the man who'd jumped into a reservoir to save her life. He was the guy who'd refused to leave her side for a week to help her recover.

Now, he was just Becket.

She threw back the covers. She needed coffee. A big, gigantic mug of coffee to wake her up.

Maybe he'd run home and she'd have a chance to down a coffee and feel semi-human before they saw each other and had the post-sex chat.

Wishful thinking?

She grabbed a shirt from the floor and threw it over her body. Becket's shirt. His pine scent hit her nose, making her lower belly give a funny little kick and memories of the previous night once again play in her head.

She scrunched her eyes, her body growing hot just thinking about it.

She was halfway down the stairs when she heard the sizzle of something frying. The shuffle of footsteps.

He was still here…and not just to make coffee.

She stepped off the stairs and turned to see a very bare-chested, very sculpted Becket making breakfast. And man, oh, man, that profile looked good, with his low-hanging track pants and day-old stubble.

He turned his head, and the sexiest grin she'd ever seen immediately spread across his face. "Morning, Peaches. Nice shirt."

"You're making breakfast."

The smile widened. "Bacon, eggs and waffles."

She moved slowly into the kitchen, looking at the array of food. "I didn't have any of those ingredients."

"Actually, you supplied the eggs. And fortunately, I live close." He winked before turning back to the frying pan. "I'll make you coffee."

She rounded the counter. "You're actually making waffles?"

"You sound surprised."

"You don't look like a waffle-making kind of guy."

One side of his mouth lifted, showing off a sexy dimple. "What do I look like?"

A million things, and all of them good, but her brain wasn't working well enough to articulate any of them. "There are too many options to name one. Thank you."

"And thank *you* for wearing my shirt." He turned from the coffee maker, his arm curling around her. Then he lowered his head to her neck while his other hand went to her thigh, pushing up the material of the shirt. "It looks better on you than me."

She ran her fingers down his chest. "I like you in this shirt… but I like you better without it."

He growled, his teeth nipping the bottom of her ear. "Tell me you've got today off."

"I'm working." But suddenly she wished she wasn't.

"Be late."

She groaned as he kissed a sensitive spot beneath her ear. "I can't. I've already missed too many days."

"You're the boss. You can do whatever you want."

"Nope. Some of our dog owners are fussy about certain things."

He kissed down her neck, then nudged the shirt aside before kissing her shoulder.

"Becket…when you do that, I can't think."

"Good." Before she knew what was happening, he'd boosted her onto the counter and his mouth crashed to hers.

She gasped, and his tongue plunged inside her mouth, tangling with hers. The shirt was now bunched at her waist, and he stood right between her thighs, his hard cock pressing against her core.

And suddenly she wanted him all over again. When he kissed her, she didn't care about work or breakfast or anything outside of the two of them. All she cared about was holding him tighter, pulling him closer. Prolonging the kiss.

She rocked her hips, rewarded with a deep growl. His fingers tightened on her hips before one hand slipped beneath her shirt and trailed up. When he cupped her naked breast, she had to swallow a cry.

He'd just found her nipple with his thumb when he stiffened and pulled away. The sound of his curse pulled her out of her haze, and she followed his gaze to the stovetop.

Flames. They were bright as they rose over the frying pan.

The flames were too hot. Too bright.

Charlie...where was he?

She glanced around her bedroom, searching. He wasn't there. She looked at the bedroom door again, where the flames were alive and angry. He was out there.

"Sky."

She blinked.

The fire in the pan was gone, and Becket was in front of her again, concern in his eyes.

"Are you okay?"

Instead of answering his question, she swallowed. "You put the fire out?"

"Yeah, I turned the heat off and threw a lid on." His brows flickered. "Where'd you go?"

"I—" She stopped, the words not making it out. Her heart was beating too fast and her stomach was still doing little rolls. She hadn't had a flashback for months. "I should get ready for work."

She slid off the counter and took a step toward the stairs, but Becket gently caught her wrist, stopping her. It took her three long seconds to turn back toward him.

His brows were still slashed together. "You didn't answer my question. Are you okay?"

No. But if she told him that, she'd have to reveal other things. Things about fear creeping inside her. But not for her safety—his.

"I just need to get ready for work."

* * *

Becket's fingers were tense around the wheel as he made his way to The Tea House. He was meeting his brother and sister for coffee, but he couldn't get Sky off his mind.

That wasn't the first time she'd reacted like that to flames. The fear had been so palpable that he'd almost felt it. And damn if her skin hadn't gone pale. Because of her house fire in Cheyenne? Because it had caused her to lose Charlie?

He wished she'd talk to him about it. Was it a flashback she'd experienced? Did she get them often? He had so many damn questions.

Last night had been… Fuck, it had been everything. And he'd thought it would bring them closer.

So why couldn't she talk to him about what she was feeling this morning?

He pulled into the parking lot of The Tea House and took out his phone to text her.

Becket: Hey, Peaches. You get to work okay?

Her three dots appeared immediately.

Sky: I did. No thanks to you.

He chuckled, because she wasn't wrong. Once breakfast was ready, he'd gone upstairs and found her in the shower.

Becket: I'm pretty sure you're the one who told me to get in the shower with you.

Sky: You opened the door and stood there shirtless… You set me up.

His dick twitched at the memory of her naked and wet beneath the spray of water.

Becket: I'd do it again.

She responded with an eye roll emoji. He chuckled.

Becket: Have a good day, Peaches. If something makes you unhappy, just think of me naked in the shower and it will turn your day around.

This time her reply was three eye rolls, and he laughed before shoving his cell into his pocket and climbing out of the car.

He was halfway across the parking lot when he spotted his sister getting out of her red Volkswagen Beetle. He fucking hated that thing. It was too small and not safe enough. She needed a Mazda CX-90 or a Toyota Highlander. Something big enough so that if she crashed, her car wouldn't compress to fucking nothing. But was she receptive to any advice from him?

Hell no.

She hated him or Jesse giving her any advice. And yeah, after she'd gotten sick, they'd been pretty overbearing anytime they were home from the military. But fuck, when you got told your sister had stage four cancer, everything changed. It was natural to then want to keep her as safe as possible.

He stopped beside her car. "Still driving this cardboard death trap, I see."

Yep, there was the glare. "If by cardboard death trap you mean Sally the Beast, then yes, she is still my ride or die."

"You named your car Sally the Beast?"

"Or just Sally for short."

He shook his head as they headed toward the café. Since her diagnosis, his sister had changed. She didn't take life so seriously. In fact, she took a hell of a lot more chances. Just last year she'd gone skydiving, and the year before that she'd gone snorkeling in the Great Barrier Reef in Australia.

"No Sky this morning?" Clara asked.

"No, she has work. So just me and our charming brother."

"Well, charming compared to you." She laughed, nudging him with her hip before stepping into the café.

Becket tried to grab her, but she knew him too well and slipped beneath his arm like a damn ninja. She dropped into the booth opposite Jesse and Aspen, and her "I win" grin was too damn wide.

Jesse frowned, though humor danced in his eyes. "Everything okay?"

"It's great," Clara said, lifting the menu.

Becket slid into the booth, shuffling Clara over and getting an elbow to the ribs. "Our sister thinks she's a comedian."

"Please, I'm far funnier," she corrected.

Aspen grinned. "I find you funny."

"See?" Clara bumped his shoulder.

Women. They were always ganging up on him.

Mrs. Gerald stopped at their table. "Hi. Would everyone like their usual?"

They obviously all came here too often, but it was the only place in town that sold decent coffee.

"Actually," Clara said. "I'll have an affogato."

Jesse frowned. "That's a dessert. It's not even nine yet."

Clara lifted a shoulder. "Life's short. I may as well eat dessert in the morning."

"Actually," Aspen parroted. "I'll have one too."

Jesse sighed.

Mrs. Gerald nodded. "Coming right up."

Clara watched someone across the café, and Becket followed her gaze to see a woman with short brown hair, red-rimmed glasses, and a laptop bag slung over her shoulder standing near the counter.

"Who's that?" Becket asked.

"Scarlett."

Aspen turned to look also. "The roommate who doesn't talk to you?"

Jesse frowned. "She doesn't talk to you?"

"Nope. But that's her loss."

"Why do you keep her if you don't get along?" Jesse asked.

"We don't not get along. We just don't talk," Clara clarified. "And I need a roommate because I make a conscious effort to only work the number of hours I want, so financially, I need her. Plus, she's quiet and always out, so it suits me."

The woman turned, coffee in hand, and as she headed toward the door, she glanced Clara's way. His sister smiled and waved, but the woman only gave a brief nod before stepping outside.

That was a bit cold.

"What did you do to her?" Becket asked.

"I told you, we're just not friends. It's fine. Life's too short to care about who likes who, and it's certainly nothing either of my big bad brothers needs to intervene in."

Jesse lifted a shoulder. "I don't know. I could pull her up on some technicality and scare her."

Clara snorted. "You? Mr. Play by the Book?"

"It's true," Becket confirmed. "I'm the intimidating one out of the two of us."

Jesse shook his head, a hint of a smile on his face.

Becket chuckled, but the smile dropped when he spotted Teddy and Kristina by the counter. Teddy looked his way but didn't smile, just gave a small chin lift, and Becket returned it.

They'd barely talked since the argument after the bridge incident. And yeah, Becket needed to find a way to move on and let it go. Maybe even apologize to Teddy. Because what had happened hadn't only been his fault. And they worked together, for Christ's sake.

But, damn, it was hard. Sky had almost died that day, and it wasn't something he'd be forgetting for a while, if ever.

CHAPTER 23

*S*omething pulled Sky from her sleep. What? A sound? A smell?

It was nearly impossible to open her eyes, exhaustion trying to pull her back under, but she frowned on her next inhale.

What was that? Smoke?

A crackling noise had her eyes shooting open. Then she saw the light. Bright light from the doorway.

She shot up to a sitting position, and the world narrowed to the flames. Bright, angry flames that, even from her bed, she could see engulfed her hallway.

Fear and panic and shock snapped over her skin, making her breaths come faster and her heart thump harder.

Charlie!

She glanced around the room.

"Charlie?" she called.

He wasn't there.

The fear turned into something else. Something stronger and so visceral that she could feel it with every part of her body.

She jumped out of bed and grabbed her phone. The call had barely rung before the operator picked up.

"Nine-one-one, what's your emergency?"

"There's a fire in my house! A big one. I need the fire department here as quickly as possible." She rattled off her address before hanging up, not even waiting for the lady over the line to respond.

She moved toward the doorway, coughs starting to rack her chest.

Her stomach dropped. It wasn't just her hall that was enveloped in flames. It was everything. There was no way through!

The ice in her veins competed with the heat around her.

If Charlie wasn't with her, he'd likely be in the laundry room with his food and water bowl. Her gaze flew to her bedroom window. There was an external window in the laundry. She could access the room from outside. It was locked but she could break the glass.

She slammed her bedroom door closed, grabbed a towel from her bathroom and sprinted toward her bedroom window. Cool, fresh air blew into the room the second she got it open, sending goose bumps running over her arms.

She jumped out, the grass cold beneath her feet. Then she ran, sprinting around her house, ignoring the air that burned as it whipped in and out of her already sore lungs. When she reached the laundry window at the back of her house, the panic almost swallowed her.

The kitchen was completely alight, and the flames were close to the laundry room. Too close.

Desperately, she searched the ground around her for something— anything that could break the glass. A large rock lay at the edge of her yard.

She sprinted toward it. It was heavy. So heavy she needed two hands to lift the thing.

Good. The heavier the better.

When she reached the laundry again, she lifted the rock above her head and smashed it against the window. The glass shattered, a few small fragments flying back and cutting into her skin.

She ignored the little stabs of pain and used the rock to clear the shards of glass around the edges. Then she spread the towel on the bottom of the window and climbed inside. A few sharp edges still cut into her skin, but she was so focused on Charlie she barely felt the scrapes.

She hit the floor inside the laundry, pieces of glass cutting into her feet—only to stop. Where was he? There was no laundry room door, but surely he wouldn't have run out into the fire?

The smoke was thick, burning her lungs more with each cough. She dropped to her knees, ignoring the sear of glass cutting into them.

There was a gap between her washer and dryer...and that was where she found Charlie. He'd burrowed right to the back.

Thank God!

"Charlie, come on, boy, I need you to come out."

He whimpered, his little limbs trembling as he pushed himself farther back.

"Charlie, honey. I can get you out. Trust me." She kept her voice soft and gentle, coaxing him.

He took a small step forward.

"Yes, that's it, honey, keep coming."

A little closer. His legs shook, but he continued to move forward until finally he was in her arms.

Tears stung her eyes as she cuddled him against her chest. He was okay. Now they had to get out.

She stood and was about to turn toward the window—only to stop at the sight of the figure in her kitchen. A large, dark figure.

Becket.

She frowned. That didn't make sense. She was in Cheyenne.

But he was there...standing in the middle of the flames, not moving.

"Becket! Get out!"

But even as she cried the words, she knew there was nowhere for him to go. Flames surrounded him. He was stuck. Stuck in her house in the middle of a blazing fire.

"Becket—"

"You did this." He didn't yell, but somehow his words carried over *the flames, punching right into her. "You knew you weren't safe to be around, yet you allowed me to stay. You killed me. Just like you killed Charlie."*

She stumbled back, only to gasp when she realized her arms were empty.

"Charlie?"

"He's gone," Becket said.

Her head shot up.

Becket lifted a shoulder. "You let us get close. You killed us."

She turned, searching. "Charlie? Where are you?"

"Sky? Can you hear me?"

"Where is he?"

"Sky..."

The next time she looked up, Becket was gone.

She screamed.

* * *

A LOUD WHIMPER pierced the air, and Becket's eyes shot open. Beside him, Sky's head thrashed from side to side, her chest rising and falling with quick, shallow breaths, but her eyes were closed.

She was having a bad dream. He'd seen lots of nightmares before. Some guys in the military had suffered from pretty bad ones and this looked identical.

"Sky?"

Nothing. Her head continued to toss and her breathing grew more erratic by the second.

He pushed up into a sitting position. "Sky...can you hear me?"

Fear cut across her features and she frowned in her sleep.

"Sky." He called her name with a bit more force.

If possible, her chest heaved faster—and she screamed.

Fuck.

He gripped her arms and gently shook her. "Wake up, Peaches. *Now.*"

Her eyes popped open, and the mix of panic and terror and just sheer fucking darkness on her face gutted him.

"Becket?" Her voice was a pained whisper.

"Yeah, honey, it's me."

Slowly, she pushed up, her arms trembling, while she scanned him from head to waist. "You're okay."

His brows twitched. "I'm okay."

She looked around the room. "I'm in Amber Ridge."

"Where were you a second ago?"

Her gaze flew back to him, and he could have sworn he saw ghosts in her eyes. "Cheyenne. It was the night my home caught on fire. I had to climb out of my window, then break the laundry window to get Charlie out."

The thought of her breaking back into a house that was on fire made his skin crawl. "Do you dream about that night often?"

"I used to. Especially after Charlie passed away. But usually the nightmare follows the night exactly."

"It didn't this time?"

"No, this time..." She frowned, something he couldn't place passing through her expression. Something that made his stomach drop. She lowered her head into her hands. "I'm sorry."

"Why are you sorry?"

"I woke you with a silly dream and—"

"Hey. It's not silly. It's something that happened to you. Something that still affects you. What can I do to help?"

"Can you get me some water?"

"Sure."

Becket leaned over and pressed a firm kiss to her temple before climbing out of bed. Even when he got downstairs, his chest was still too tight. He could barely breathe. He *hated* that she'd been caught in a fire. That she'd had to escape then reenter to save her dog, only for Charlie to die less than a week later. And he hated that the event stayed with her. That she had nightmares about it.

Had this nightmare been caused by the small grease fire in the kitchen a couple of mornings ago?

He filled a glass with water.

There was something about the way she'd looked at him though. She'd been relieved when she'd first seen him, but then that fear returned to her eyes. Why? And how had her dream been different than usual?

He took the water back up the stairs, only to stop at the doorway. Sky was still sitting on the bed, sheets pulled up around her chest, but she was looking out the window, an intense frown carved into her brow.

She was so deep in thought, she didn't hear him come in.

"Hey."

She jolted and turned to face him. "Hey."

He perched beside her on the bed. "Are you doing okay?"

She nodded. He didn't believe her for a second.

He brushed a lock of hair from her cheek. "Sky. You can talk to me."

Her brows flickered. "Thank you."

Becket sighed. He wished she'd talk to him. But he couldn't force her. He just had to hope that when she was ready, she'd open up about her nightmares and flashbacks.

"Let's get some rest," he said gently.

She nodded and sipped her water. When she curled back up under the blankets, she was right on the edge of the mattress. He could have laughed. There was an entire bed between his side and hers. No way were they staying like that.

He turned off the light, and the second he was beneath the sheets, he curved an arm around her waist and pulled her back against him. At first she was tense. Then he kissed the back of her neck, and whispered, "Sleep. You're safe."

A second passed, and she relaxed into him. But he still didn't feel okay. Something was going on in her mind that she didn't feel she could share. He needed to know what…and he needed to know soon.

"Oh, hello, my darling," Ivory Hanks said as she scooped her Shih Tzu off the floor and into her arms. "Did you have a nice day today?"

The Shih Tzu licked her face.

Ivory was in her forties, never married and no kids, and her dog was her entire world. She looked up at Sky and Dolly. "Did Miss Penelope enjoy her cooked liver today?"

Sky nodded. "She did. I think liver's her favorite."

"I do too," Ivory agreed. "It used to be chicken thighs, but we're not such a fan of those anymore."

Ivory sent Penelope to doggy daycare with home-cooked meals labeled with very specific heating instructions, and as such, Penelope had to be the best-fed dog in the place. Probably the best fed in Montana.

"Did she play with her friends?" Ivory asked.

"Oh, yes," Dolly answered. "Penelope is the most popular dog at daycare. She plays with everyone."

Ivory beamed at them while Sky bit back a grin.

Dolly was good at her job because she knew what dog owners

wanted to hear, which was basically that their dog was the cutest, best-behaved and most-loved animal ever.

"Is that right?" Ivory asked Penelope. "I did watch you on the doggy cam."

Sky's lips twitched again. She knew the woman watched the live-stream feed of the outdoor area obsessively. In fact, Sky had heard through small-town gossip that Ivory kept the dog cam on all day beside her computer while she was at her desk job.

"Well, we'll see you tomorrow." Ivory walked out just as Rosemary walked in.

Sky smiled at the older woman. "Hey, Rosemary. I'll go get Bella."

"Thank you, dear."

She turned, and the second she was away from the desk, the smile dropped from her mouth. Her cheeks hurt from pretending she was okay. In fact, her entire head hurt.

She hadn't been able to get the nightmare out of her head all day. The vision of Becket in those flames…the words he'd said to her.

Dread twisted in her belly as she opened the back door. She didn't even need to call Bella. The Chinese Crested ran straight up to her and jumped into her arms.

She chuckled. "Hey, girl. Mama's here to get you."

Pearl looked up from the other side of the yard. "Hey. Are you finishing soon?"

"Yeah, Becket's coming to get me. We're going to walk to The Tea House."

"Oh, I've been dreaming of their coffee. I might grab one on my way home. Enjoy."

She *would* enjoy it. She'd be ordering the largest freaking cup the woman had…maybe two. "Thanks."

She took Bella back to the front, only to stop abruptly at the sight of Tony standing beside Rosemary.

He straightened when he spotted her. "Hey."

"Tony…I'm working."

Dolly cleared her throat and stood behind the front desk, taking Bella from her hands and giving her to Rosemary. "Here you go. Now, I'm going to check on our dog shampoo order on the office computer."

Rosemary shot a curious glance between her and Tony before waving goodbye, while Dolly disappeared into the back room.

Tony stepped toward the desk. "You haven't been answering my calls."

"I know. Because we're not friends. We're not anything." Plus, she didn't want to encourage all of his dropping-by-her-house stuff. She hadn't thought he'd then resort to dropping by her work.

His lips thinned with a scowl, and he looked down, pushing his hands into his pockets. When he glanced up again, there was resolve in his eyes. "Look, I just came to tell you that I've changed my plans and I'm leaving soon, so this is your last chance."

"My last chance for what?"

"You *know* what. Us."

Was he actually serious? "Tony, I don't know how else to say this. There has never been, and will never be, an *us*."

His jaw clenched. "It was *always* supposed to be us. You didn't even give me a chance! You're really throwing it away for that steroid-using bodybuilder?"

"Get out."

He stepped closer.

"Get. Out!"

"You're making a mistake," he seethed before turning and storming out of the center.

Sky swallowed, taking several deep breaths to push down her anger. She'd just turned away from the door when the ding of it opening sounded again.

"Tony, I—" She spun around and stopped at the sight of Becket.

His eyes narrowed. "Tony was here?"

"No...I mean, yes, he was, but he's gone now."

The muscles in Becket's arms bulged, and he looked like he wanted to turn around and go find the man.

Sky quickly moved forward, touching his arm. "Hey. I'm okay."

He studied her face. And suddenly, with him so close, the scent of him surrounding her, the nightmare from last night hit her at full force. The flames. The heat. Becket in the middle of it all.

"Sky?"

She blinked to see Becket looking down at her, now frowning. "Sorry. I'll just get my bag and we can go." She hurried toward the office before Becket could ask if she was okay...because she wasn't.

But she should be. It was just a nightmare. And she needed to shake it off.

Dolly sat in the corner of the room, filing her nails. She looked up. "Oh, done with Mr. Not So Right?"

"Done. And Becket's here, so I'm heading out now."

"Full house today. No worries, darlin'. I'll see you tomorrow."

"See you tomorrow."

As soon as she returned to the foyer and saw Becket again, that familiar nausea hit her belly.

Stop it, Sky. It was just a dream. The past isn't repeating itself.

She forced a smile to her lips. "Ready to go."

"Great."

They stepped outside, and he slipped his fingers through hers.

"How was your day off?" she asked.

"Good. After coffee, I went to the station with Jesse."

She glanced up at him. "Everything okay?"

"Yeah. There have been a few fires lately."

She almost tripped on the sidewalk. "Fires?"

"Jesse's on it. He'll figure out who's been setting them. Me and the other firefighters just need to be on guard until he does."

Figure out who's *setting* them? So it was arson. Someone in the small town of Amber Ridge was setting fires.

That was a big coincidence, wasn't it? That's she'd left Cheyenne after a fire at her work, *then* her home, and now fires were being set in her hometown?

Her pulse picked up speed, and she was so caught up in her head that she didn't see the step down to the road in front of her. She stumbled and would have fallen flat on her face if Becket hadn't caught her. Although, her bag wasn't so lucky. She dropped it, and its contents scattered everywhere.

"Whoa, Peaches, are you okay?"

She swallowed. "Yeah. Sorry, I wasn't looking where I was walking."

His brows drew in, but he nodded. Together, they gathered up everything from the street. She was standing when she saw her lip balm near the center of the road. She started toward it just as a car raced around the corner.

She opened her mouth to scream as a body hit hers, throwing her out of the way. She hit the asphalt hard but ignored the ache to her backside, looking up just in time to see Becket get sideswiped by the car, his body flying and hitting the asphalt.

Everything in her stopped. Every movement. Every breath. Even her heart felt like it had halted in her chest.

Then reality hit, panic rushing through her system, and she pushed to her feet and ran.

Other cars stopped around them. People climbing out, a couple of them pulling out phones and making calls.

But she could only focus on Becket.

Sky dropped beside him. "Becket! Are you okay?"

He growled as he pushed up. "I'm fine. Are you?" He scanned her body, looking for injuries.

"I wasn't hit by a *car*." Her voice broke on the last word.

When red started to seep through his shirt, she reached out and tugged up the material to see a large scrape across his stomach, bleeding.

He wasn't okay. He'd thrown her out of the way of a speeding car, and in the process had been hit.

She'd been right to be scared. It was happening again. The accidents...those around her getting hurt.

* * *

THE HUSTLE of footsteps and the smell of antiseptic surrounded Becket as the nurse busied herself wrapping his wound. He should be focused on her. On what she was saying about caring for the patch of road rash.

He'd barely heard a word she'd said. It was a scratch, and he'd had far worse injuries in his life.

Sky took all his attention. She stood a few steps away, arms wrapped around her body, nails digging into her waist. Her skin was too pale. Her eyes too worried. And she was staring at his wound. *Frowning* at it.

What was going on in her mind? She'd barely said two words to him since the incident.

Incident...no. It wasn't a fucking incident. Someone had sped around the corner and almost hit Sky. Rage tightened his throat. Sky had come so damn close to being hit. Too close. And with the speed that car had been driving, she might not have made it out alive.

The nurse stepped back. "Okay, all done. Any questions?"

He shook his head. He had no idea what instructions she'd given him, but he had enough medical training to look after himself.

"Great." She tugged off her gloves. "You're free to go when you're ready."

He dipped his head. "Thank you."

The second the nurse was gone, he rose, but Sky's eyes widened at his movement and she rushed forward, pushing him back down. "Becket! Slowly. You just got hit by a car."

"Sideswiped."

"Same thing."

"Not the same thing."

She huffed an exasperated breath. "You can still go slowly."

"I need to find out what's going on in your head."

Her eyes flared, something akin to fear flicking over her face. "What do you mean?"

"You're pale." He gripped her hips. "I've barely heard you say anything, except for when you forced me to come here. And your nails have been digging so deep into your waist, I've been scared you're going to break skin."

She wet her lips, her gaze lowering to his shoulder. "I just hate what happened today."

"No. It's more than that." He touched a finger to her chin and tilted her face up. "Tell me...please."

Her gaze shifted between his eyes. "I—"

The door opened and his brother walked in.

Goddammit.

Sky pushed against his chest and took a hurried step back, forcing his hands to drop.

Jesse stopped. "Sorry. Am I interrupting?"

Becket's "yes" came out at the same time as Sky's "no."

"I can come back—"

"No," Sky said again, cutting him off. "This is important. Come in. Did you find the car?"

Jesse moved into the room, his gaze shifting from Sky to Becket. "Unfortunately, a gray Toyota wasn't enough to go by."

Fuck, Becket wanted to kick his own ass for not getting the plates. But he'd been too focused on Sky.

"No one reported a speeding Toyota past that point."

Becket's eyes narrowed. So the asshole had only sped on that street, at *them*. Coincidence?

"There have been too many incidents in the last couple months." He stood. "Her break-in. The bridge. And today's almost hit-and-run."

Sky paled further and he watched as her breathing quickened.

Becket's jaw clenched. He just wanted some fucking answers. It felt like Sky was being targeted, and he didn't like it. He scrubbed a hand over his face. "Thanks, Jess."

Jesse nodded. "Your stomach okay?"

Sky's gaze flew back to him, and she visibly swallowed.

"It's just a graze," he said firmly.

Jesse nodded. "Good. Okay, call if you need anything."

The door closed behind Jesse, and Becket turned back to her. "Sky—"

"We should go."

He gritted his teeth in frustration. He wanted to push. To demand to know if she was just rocked by the accident or if there was more...and he *would* push, just not here and now.

"Okay, Peaches. Let's go."

As they left the hospital, he tugged Sky into his side and scanned the parking lot.

Three incidents in the span of a month, all involving Sky, and all of which could have ended really badly for her.

It all left an acid taste in his mouth. He'd wanted to talk about it more with his brother, but Sky had already been too pale, so that wasn't the time.

He'd call Jesse later. He'd also make sure Sky stayed by his side. He didn't want the woman out of his sight until they got to the bottom of this.

Sky insisted on driving, and she kept her focus on the road.

When they reached their houses, she pulled into her driveway but walked toward his house, and he followed. He didn't care which damn house they spoke in. They just needed to talk.

Inside, she went straight to the kitchen. "I'll make you some coffee."

He closed the door and dropped his keys before walking slowly to the kitchen. "I need you to tell me what's going on in your head, Sky."

She stilled, back ramrod straight.

"Something's not right." A few more slow steps forward. "I need to know what you're thinking."

"We have to stop seeing each other."

Her words slammed into his midsection, making him flinch.

"I'm not talking about just dating." She shook her head, her words running into each other. "I'm not even sure if we *are* dating. But we need to stop all contact."

"Turn around, Sky."

She didn't. She clenched the kitchen counter so tightly that her knuckles turned white.

"Sky…" He stopped behind her, hands going to her waist. "I need to see your face."

One more second and finally, she turned. There was the glint of tears in her eyes, and so much sadness that he could have fucking drowned in it. "Tell me what's going on."

"I told you, we can't see each other anymore."

"Why?"

"Because you were hit by a freaking car today, Becket!" She pulled out of his hold.

If she thought he was letting her walk away from him without so much as an explanation, she was dead wrong.

He caught her arm before she could leave the kitchen. "What does the car sideswiping me have to do with us seeing each other? If anything, it's reason for me to stick closer."

A tear fell down her cheek. "It's not just the car. You also jumped into a river to save me."

"I'm well-trained to do things like that."

"I'm not safe to be around."

What the hell was she talking about? "Sky—"

"Ever since Eloise died, bad things have been happening to me. I told you that. It feels like I was supposed to die, and because I didn't, the world is coming for me!"

"You know that's ridiculous, Sky."

She shook her head, another tear rolling down her cheek as she pulled her arm free. "No, it's not. In Cheyenne, there were so many incidents after Eloise's death. I ignored them, and Charlie died. What if I ignore them again and *you* die too?"

"I'm not going to die," Becket growled.

"I'm leaving, and you have to let me go."

"*No.*"

"You don't have a choice." She turned and moved quickly toward the door.

He sure as hell *did* have a choice. He moved after her and gripped her hips before she reached his door. "Sky…don't do this. I can protect both of us."

"I dreamed about the fire in Cheyenne. But it changed. You were stuck in the flames and there was no way out."

That's what her nightmare had been about last night? "It was a just dream."

"If anything happened to you because of me—"

"*Nothing* will happen to me. Don't do this."

She hung her head again, her hands touching his.

Take it back, Sky. Tell me we can handle this together.

"I'm sorry. I have to go. Please just…give me some space." Then she grabbed his hands and gently pulled them off her before stepping out of his house.

CHAPTER 25

Becket hit the bag hard and watched it tremble under the force. Air hissed between his teeth and his blood pumped fast.

He hit the bag again, ignoring the exhaustion that pulled at his limbs.

How long had he been at this? Thirty minutes? Forty? It didn't matter. He wanted to exhaust his body. Dull the fury inside him. The frustration that was the last few days without Sky.

She'd ended things between them. Broken up with him, *for* him, to keep him safe, and nothing he'd said had changed her mind.

He hit the bag harder.

He'd tried calling her. He needed to hear her voice and talk some damn sense into her. But she wouldn't answer. And she hadn't responded to a single text. When he'd gone over to her place before work today, her car was gone.

She was scared. He got that. He understood her fear. Charlie had died because of an accident she'd been involved in, and now she was convinced he was at risk too. But pushing him away wasn't the answer.

A throat cleared behind him, and he turned his head to see Teddy standing in the doorway.

Becket looked back at the bag and hit it again. "What is it, Teddy?"

"Just checking in. You didn't seem yourself at training this morning."

His back teeth ground together. The team had done some sprint training this morning, and yeah, he'd been short with the entire crew. "I'm fine."

"You're not fine. You almost bit Irene's head off when she told you to ease up."

Three more punches.

"Is it Sky?" Teddy asked. "Did something happen?"

Another punch, and this time the bag swung back violently. "We broke up."

Teddy cursed. "I'm sorry, man."

Several more hits, each harder than the last.

Teddy cleared his throat again. "Okay, well…call if you need anything."

He left the room, and Becket dropped his hands and used his teeth to undo one glove. He pulled it off and tapped his phone.

Nothing. No missed calls from Sky. No texts.

He was losing his goddamn mind.

He pulled the glove back on and continued to punch the bag. Another ten minutes passed before someone entered the room again.

"Teddy, I told you, I'm—" He stopped at the sight of Jesse. "What the hell took you so long?" Yeah, he was being an ass. He didn't care.

Jesse lifted a brow. "We were busy at the station. Moose said you've been in here hitting the bag for over an hour, after you already trained with the crew this morning."

"Sounds about right." And he'd have thought that would be enough to exhaust his mind and body. It wasn't.

"You were hit by a car a couple days ago. You should be resting."

"I'm fine. I keep telling everyone I'm *fine*. It would be great if someone listened." His mother and his sister had brought food over yesterday. On a normal day, he'd be lapping up the attention. But nothing about these last few days felt normal.

"What's going on, Beck?"

Two more jabs. "Sky broke up with me."

There was a small pause before Jesse spoke. "Stop hitting the bag."

"No."

"You want me to fucking tackle you to the floor? Because I will."

He hit the bag again. A fight with his former special ops brother didn't sound so bad. Maybe *that* would take the edge off.

"Last chance, Beck—stop or I'll stop you."

Becket growled and turned. "I'm *angry*."

"I can see that."

"Sky was almost hit by a fucking car this week!"

"I know."

"And before that, her car went over a *bridge* with her inside, and she almost drowned."

"I know that too."

"And before *that*," Becket hissed, "someone broke into her house, and she fell down the fucking stairs. This isn't just a string of unfortunate events."

"I agree."

Becket frowned. "You agree?"

"One person can't have that much bad luck."

"You didn't say anything at the hospital."

"Neither did you. I assumed it was because Sky wasn't doing too good, and we didn't have any solid evidence yet."

Jesus, he should have known his brother was on the same page.

"Shower, change and we'll go get a coffee at The Tea House," Jesse said.

"I can't. I—"

"I spoke to Irene. Told her about your injury, and she agreed you were an idiot for pushing your body so hard today. Apparently, you didn't tell anyone what happened. She'll cover for you."

No, he hadn't told anyone. Instead, all he'd been doing was barking instructions at people.

And now that he'd stopped exerting himself, the wound on his stomach burned.

"Fine."

He pulled off his gloves, picked up his phone and headed for the showers, grabbing a clean set of clothes on the way. When he was done, he found his brother waiting for him by the exit.

The Tea House was just around the corner. They'd barely started walking when Jesse asked the question Becket was waiting for.

"Tell me everything you know."

Becket ran his fingers through his hair. "This started before the break-in."

"What are you talking about?"

"Things happened in Cheyenne. Sky's dog got sick, so she called in someone else to take her shift at work."

"How does that—"

"There was a fire. The coworker who was called in got stuck in the back room and died."

Jesse cursed.

"After that, these *incidents* started occurring," Becket continued. "The brakes on her car failed. Then her car engine exploded. And a few weeks after that, there was a fire at her house. Her dog inhaled too much smoke and passed away not long after."

"Jesus Christ."

"She believes it's the universe trying to deliver the fate she avoided at the café, but—"

"Someone close to the woman who died is targeting her."

Becket nodded. "That's what I'm thinking. Her name was Eloise and the café was called Canine and Coffee. I don't know her last name, but if you look up the fire at the café from a year ago, I'm sure you'll find her."

"I will find her."

"Thanks. I'd appreciate it."

When they reached The Tea House, Becket's attention immediately went to two women sitting at a table in the center of the room. Esther Williams…and Sky. Sky looked up, and her eyes locked with his.

* * *

"Darling, I just don't know if you're going to have enough volunteers."

Sky frowned at the list of names on the laptop screen that was angled so both she and her mother could see it. "What are you talking about? We have rotating shifts of people. A few from your church. A few from the doggy daycare. And Clara, Indie, Jesse and Aspen." Or at least, she hoped she still had them, even though she wasn't with Becket anymore.

Had he told his family? What had they said?

She shook her head. It didn't matter. They'd barely been dating anyway.

The Tea House was quiet today, which worked for her. She hadn't felt like staying at home but she needed to finish organizing this fundraiser. She'd actually moved this fundraiser forward because she needed something to keep her busy.

Home just felt too close to Becket at the moment. Even when he was out, she found her attention going to the windows far too often, waiting for him to get home.

She still wasn't sure if she'd made the right decision breaking up with him, but every time she started to question herself, the image of Becket being hit by that car played in her mind. Of him at the hospital, that huge scrape across his stomach.

No, this was safer...even if it did break her heart.

Her mother frowned. "Wait...Becket's not on the list."

She'd been waiting for her mother to notice that. "No, he's... busy." Yeah, busy being separated from her. Would she actually need to tell him that his help was no longer required? Or would he just know that, since they weren't dating, he shouldn't come?

She'd have to tell him. Dammit.

Her mother straightened. "What on earth could be more important than supporting his partner during a fundraiser she's organized?"

"It doesn't matter. Can we get back to this? Do you think these time slots work for your church friends?"

"I'll ask them, but I'm sure they're fine. The council has approved you using the park and public water?"

She nodded. "It's all taken care of."

She'd originally planned to run the fundraiser at her doggy daycare, where she already had all the dog-washing equipment, but the fundraiser had grown to include food carts and coffee stalls, so they'd needed an outdoor space.

"Good." Her mother frowned and angled her head, her gaze moving over Sky.

Oh, God. Her Mom only did that when she was trying to figure something out. And the only thing she could be trying to work out right now was—

"Something's off with you today."

"No, it isn't." She lifted her mug and took a big, burn-her-tongue sip.

"It is." Her mother leaned closer. "What is it?"

"Nothing."

"It involves Becket, doesn't it?"

"Mom—"

"Don't *Mom* me. I gave you life. The least you can do is tell me when something's wrong."

Jesus. She hadn't told her mother about Becket because she didn't want to hear the "I told you so" that would inevitably follow.

Suddenly, her mother gasped. "You broke up, didn't you?"

Shit.

"He's not on the list to help," her mother continued, putting the pieces together. "You haven't mentioned him since you got here, and you've been in a terrible mood."

"Yes, we broke up."

Her mother's jaw dropped.

"And I didn't tell you because I didn't want to hear you say that it was always going to end this way, and I should have listened to you and Dad."

"I wouldn't say that."

Sky tilted her head. "Really? You're not biting your tongue right now to stop yourself from telling me that if I'd chosen someone from your church, like Tony, I would be happy?"

"Sky, I know your father and I pushed Tony on you a bit—"

"A bit?"

"But…then we saw you with Becket. And I know your father's had a hard time with it, and I did at the start, but now…"

Sky frowned. "Now what?"

"Well, after I saw how happy you were together, he grew on me. Your happiness is all I've ever wanted, darling. Of course, as your parents, we sometimes think we know best."

"*Sometimes?*"

"But you showed us that we don't."

Sky swallowed, the pit in her belly deepening.

Her mother leaned forward, asking quietly, "What happened?"

Man, she really didn't want to get into it. Her mother knew everything that had happened in Cheyenne, and she would just try to convince Sky that she was wrong about the whole "the world's out to get me" thing.

She hadn't told her mother about the incident outside her doggy daycare either. All her parents would do was worry.

She opened her mouth, not sure what words were about to slip out, when the door to The Tea House opened and Becket and Jesse walked inside. Becket's gaze found her like a laser, his eyes dark and intense.

Her breath stopped, her stomach doing a funny roll.

For a moment, he didn't move. He just stood there, watching her.

Then Jesse grabbed his arm and guided him toward a booth. The second his gaze wasn't on her anymore, air whooshed into her chest.

Somehow she wanted to cry and scream and rage all at the same time. And mostly at herself for breaking up with him.

She didn't. She turned back to the laptop, almost unseeing. "We've got enough volunteers."

There was a heavy pause that stretched until she finally looked up to see her mother watching her so closely that Sky felt like she was being dissected.

"What?" she asked.

"You should talk to him."

Her heart thumped. There was a reason she hadn't answered a single one of his calls these last few days—because she knew she'd crumble.

"About what?"

"About whatever misunderstanding broke you up."

"You know, I think everything's ready for the dog wash. I'm going to head home now."

Her mother straightened. "Wait."

"What?"

"Can you go to the counter and order your father a double-shot latte and a piece of rhubarb pie? He gets so disappointed when I return home with nothing for him."

"There's table service."

"I know. But Mrs. Gerald is right there at the coffee machine, and my knee's not great so…"

Sky was tempted to tell her mother that her knee was perfectly capable of the three steps to the counter, but that would just end in more arguing.

With a sigh, she rose and crossed to the counter, careful not to look Becket's way. To not even glance in the vicinity of his booth.

Mrs. Gerald looked up from the coffee machine. "Hi, Sky. Something else?"

"Would I be able to grab a double-shot latte and a piece of your rhubarb pie to go?"

"Of course. Won't be long."

"Thanks."

Someone stepped up beside her, and she knew—not just from his pine scent, but his familiar warmth—exactly who it was.

"Hey, Peaches."

She tried to get her suddenly uneven breathing steady before finally looking up. Mistake. Big mistake. His eyes were too dark and too beautiful. "Hey."

"How's your day been?"

Really? He was asking about her day? "Fine."

"Mine hasn't been great either."

Because of her? Were those his unspoken words?

Her heart started to beat faster, the hair on her arms standing on end. "I can wait at the—"

"You don't have to do this." He stepped closer, his fingers curling around her waist.

"I do," she whispered.

"No, you don't. I can take care of myself."

"You can't outrun a car, Becket. You're not superhuman."

His jaw clenched. "I miss you."

"It's only been a couple of days."

"It feels longer."

It really did. Who knew a couple of days could be so torturous?

That thumb on her waist caressed her, making a cascade of butterflies take off in her belly.

The words "I miss you too" were on the tip of her tongue. And other words…like "I made a mistake" and "I need you back." But she swallowed them, keeping them buried deep inside her. Because she couldn't be selfish and take him back, only to lose him like she'd lost Charlie.

"Here you go, Sky."

Thank God. She swung around and paid for the drink and pie. "Thank you." She forced her attention back to Becket. "I have to go."

"Don't run from this, Sky."

Without another word, she went back to the table. She wasn't running. She was sprinting, barely feeling the ground beneath her feet.

CHAPTER 26

It was actually too busy. They'd put up too many fliers. Let too many people know about the dog wash fundraiser. She'd thought four people per shift would be enough, but the event was only an hour in and there was already a long wait. There were dogs and their owners *everywhere*. People had come from all over Amber Ridge and from as far away as Bozeman to support the cause.

She rushed to get more shampoo from behind the makeshift reception desk.

Of course, it didn't help that she'd barely slept the last few nights. What had she gotten? Three hours of sleep per night? Maybe four? Her mind had been a busy mess. Every time she closed her eyes, she had another dream about that fire in Cheyenne. Sometimes Becket was there. Sometimes just Charlie. And when she wasn't dreaming about fires, she was dreaming about Becket. About the day she'd broken up with him. The pain in his eyes.

She gritted her teeth, grabbed a bottle of shampoo and ran it back to Kristina.

"Thanks." Kristina took the bottle and squeezed it all over

Penelope, the Shih Tzu. "You know she's watching my every move, right?"

Sky shot a look over her shoulder to see Ivory Hanks sitting by the coffee cart, Styrofoam cup in hand, and yeah, watching very intently. Most dog owners had gotten a drink or some food and gone for a walk...not Ivory.

Sky smiled at her before looking back at Kristina. "Penelope's like her child."

"Yeah, well, she's making me nervous. I'm waiting for her to march over here and tell me what I'm doing wrong."

It probably wouldn't take long either. Not that she was going to tell Kristina that. "You're doing a great job. Can I get you anything? A coffee? Some water?"

"A bottle of water would be amazing."

"Done."

She returned to the folding table Dolly sat behind.

"Sky, just look at all these people!" Dolly said. "Another successful fundraiser."

"Yeah, too much of a success. There are like six dogs waiting."

Dolly scoffed. "Let them wait. They'll get their turns soon enough."

"They're not getting angry?"

"Of course they are. People are impatient and rude. I've just been killing them with kindness."

Sky chuckled. God, she was glad to have the woman on her team. She crouched and opened the cooler before taking out a handful of waters, one for each dog washer.

Dolly straightened in her seat. "Well, hello there, Mr. Tall, Dark and Handsome."

Sky stood and turned to see who she was talking to—only to gasp at the sight of Becket on the other side of the table.

"Becket." She hadn't seen him in days, but God, had he been on her mind.

A sexy smile curved his lips. "Hey." He wore a tight white T-shirt and looked as good as always. Dangerously good.

"What…what are you doing here?"

"I'm here to wash some dogs. I know, I'm early."

She shook her head. "No, I texted you saying you didn't need to come."

"And I texted back that I wanted to help."

"Then *I* texted back that we didn't need you."

His smile widened. "You see, I knew we'd just end up in a texting war, so that's when I stopped replying and decided to come anyway."

"You hate dogs."

"But *you* don't."

She swallowed. "You aren't needed."

He lifted a brow and turned his head, very obviously looking at the half dozen people waiting with their dogs.

"Fine," Sky huffed. "We need help, but we don't have any more hoses or buckets."

"Oh, Sky, don't be silly, we can work it out," Dolly scolded. "Grab a dog, find some water, and start washing."

Damn it, Dolly. Sure, what she said was correct. But her butting in was another thing that wasn't needed.

"Thanks, Dolly." Becket looked back at her. "Is that okay, Sky?"

No. But she couldn't say that. They *did* need his help, and her insisting otherwise would just be immature and…not smart.

When she didn't respond, he stepped closer, that pine scent once again toying with her. "It's just a dog wash."

"I know." She squirmed under his scrutiny. "Fine. There are buckets of water at each washer's station, and Dolly will give you some shampoo."

"Here you go, darlin'."

He took the bottle from Dolly and dipped his head. "Thanks."

Sky nibbled her bottom lip and watched him walk away. All

million feet of him.

She shook her head. *Snap out of it, Sky. You've got a fundraiser to run.*

Over the next hour, they moved through dogs a little more quickly, and a new round of volunteers arrived, including Clara and Indie. She should've been focusing on what a huge success the fundraiser was and all the money they were raising. But too much of her attention was going to how good Becket's shirt looked when it was soaked and stuck to his muscled chest.

Why did she find him even more attractive with a dog in his arms?

She gritted her teeth and walked over to Clara and Indie's station. "Hey. Are you two doing okay?"

"Oh my gosh, I am in doggy heaven!" Clara gushed, as she cuddled Mr. Bruno's Puli dogs. The dogs required special care to rinse and shampoo out their cords, so Clara and Indie had been given very specific instructions.

"I must admit," Indie said. "I'm starting to think you have the best job in the world. You just get to hang out with these guys all day."

Sky grinned. "I'm definitely lucky."

Clara wet her lips and looked behind her before returning her gaze to Sky. "Are you and Becket okay? I couldn't help but notice that you haven't really spoken to each other."

He hadn't told them? "We're working through some things, but we're okay."

If "okay" included barely talking to each other.

Clara's brows flickered. "If you ever want to talk about it, I'm a great listener. And I'll always take your side."

Sky chuckled. "Thanks." She shot a look over her shoulder. Yep, he was still looking far too good in his wet shirt. But now he wasn't alone. Holden was with him. He briefly clenched Becket's shoulder before heading in their direction.

Sky looked back at Clara, whose eyes had grown wide.

"I didn't know he'd be here," Clara said quietly.

"Um, yeah, Jesse volunteered him. Is that okay?"

Clara's mouth opened and closed. "Of course. Why wouldn't it be?"

Holden stopped beside them. "Hey."

Indie grinned, while Clara seemed to struggle for words.

"Hey," she finally said, the word far too quiet.

"Clara." There was a softness to Holden's voice when he said her name.

Had they dated? And if not, why not? They definitely seemed interested in each other.

Sky cleared her throat. "Hey, Holden. Thank you so much for coming."

"Happy to help." He smiled at Sky before shifting his gaze back to Clara. "Maybe you could show me the ropes."

Clara nodded. She was definitely nervous, and Indie now seemed to be biting back a laugh.

"Sure, I can help you," she finally said.

One side of Holden's mouth lifted. "I'd like that."

Sky grinned too. Then, without her permission, her attention once again returned to Becket. Immediately, his eyes locked with hers.

Her smile dropped, and something hot slipped over her skin.

She was so screwed.

* * *

BECKET LEANED back as Bella shook her furry head, getting him even wetter than he already was.

How he'd ended up with the little Chinese Crested, he had no idea. Bella had made it damn clear she didn't like him by the number of times she'd growled at him from the moment he got his hands on her.

As if she'd heard his thoughts, she looked up and growled

again as he began shampooing her fur.

"Yeah, well, guess what? I'm not your biggest fan either," Becket muttered. And not just because Bella was a dog. Also because her owner had given him a million instructions on the way Bella liked to be washed.

She was a *dog*, for Christ's sake. He'd damn well wash her the same way he'd washed the last ten.

Someone chuckled behind him, and he turned to see his brother standing there with a wide grin on his face.

"What?" Yeah, Becket growled it, but he didn't care.

"She doesn't seem to be your biggest fan. I don't know why. You're a pleasure to be around."

Becket barely held off the eye roll. "Sky gave her to me on purpose. She knows Bella doesn't like me."

Humor danced in Jesse's eyes. "So she did it to torture you."

"Hell yes, she did."

"Maybe she's testing you. Seeing how far you'll go for her."

He glanced behind Jesse toward Sky, who was now standing with Aspen as she washed a terrier. Sky was watching him too, but the second their gazes met, she looked away. Because she didn't want him to know she was watching?

He could have laughed.

"All the way, my brother," Becket finally said. "I would go all the way for her."

One side of Jesse's mouth lifted. "Well, she'll find that out then, won't she?"

Becket lowered his voice. "Have you looked into that girl who died?"

The humor dropped from Jesse's face, and he moved closer. "I found the news reports. Her name was Eloise Porter. She had two living parents but no siblings. There was, however, a boyfriend."

Becket's muscles locked. "Did you look into him?"

"Yes."

Something dark flashed over Jesse's face, and Becket knew he wasn't going to like what was coming.

"He's a firefighter," Jesse finally said. "And he was part of the crew that went to the café fire."

Becket's entire frame stiffened. So he'd attended the fire that had killed his girlfriend. "That would have a massive fucking effect on him."

"It would," Jesse agreed. "Maybe even make him angry enough to seek revenge."

Becket's jaw clicked and he looked back at Sky again. "Do you know where he is now?"

"I plan to get in contact with the fire department and ask to speak to him."

"Thank you."

"I'll let you know when I have more." Jesse squeezed his shoulder and headed over to Aspen.

Becket's muscles remained tense while he finished shampooing Bella. And maybe Bella realized, because she didn't growl or splash water on him again.

Sky came up, bucket of water in hand. "Here you go."

"Thanks." When he took it from her, their hands grazed, and it shot awareness all the way through his body.

"You're welcome." Sky gave Bella a pat before stepping back. "You know, most people only did a two-hour shift."

How long had Becket been here? Four hours? More? It was the only place he wanted to be, but that had nothing to do with the dogs. "Guess I'm more committed to the cause."

Sky rolled her eyes, but there was a hint of a grin on her face.

"It's going well," Becket said as he looked around the park.

Her eyes lit up. "It's been so much busier than I thought. I don't know why, but I always worry I won't raise much money with these fundraisers, and then they do a lot better than I think."

"Because you put a lot of yourself into them. And you do it for Charlie, right?"

Her chest rose, surprise flickering in her eyes. "Yeah. I do it for Charlie."

"I saw your mom earlier. She came by and said hi. Even told me I was doing a great job."

She shook her head. "Yeah, she's been helping. Seems she doesn't hate you."

"Very few do."

Sky scoffed.

He rinsed the shampoo from Bella's fur. "What does she think about our…breakup?" Fuck, that was hard to say.

She frowned. "You'll be happy to know she was quite surprised. She even tried to convince me that I should get back together with you."

"I knew I liked your mom."

Sky laughed, and the sound was light and airy. "It surprised me."

They held each other's gazes for another second, and her smile slipped.

"Sky—"

"We're starting to pack up now, so Bella should be your last dog. Thank you again for volunteering your time today."

He dipped his chin. "Of course."

She walked away, and he was left feeling like the air no longer moved so freely in his lungs when she wasn't close by.

Damn, he was losing his mind.

He looked down at Bella. "What do you think, Bells? Am I losing my mind without her?"

Bella barked.

He was going to take that as a yes.

When Bella was done, Becket returned her to Rosemary.

She patted his shoulder. "Thank you, young man. You did a good job. Not the best job, but good enough."

Well, that kind of sounded like a compliment. "You're welcome."

After that, he said a quick goodbye to his brother and Aspen before he started grabbing the buckets scattered around the bath stations.

"What are you doing?"

He lifted another bucket and turned. "Building the Great Wall of China."

Sky's frown deepened. "You don't need to help pack up."

"I already am."

"Becket—"

"I was actually wondering if you could give me a lift home."

There was a short pause. "You need a ride home?"

"Clara brought me, so it would save her a trip." It was a damn lie, his truck was around the corner, but he'd deal with that later. Right now, he needed an excuse to get her alone.

A conflicted expression crossed her face, and she turned her head as if searching for someone else who could give him a ride.

He almost laughed. "Come on, Peaches. It's just a lift. We're right next door to each other."

She sighed. "Okay. I'll give you a ride home."

Not the most gracious agreement, but he'd take it. "Thanks."

Her eyes held his for one more beat before she moved back to the folding table.

They spent the next twenty minutes packing everything up, and in that time, Sky didn't talk to him again. In fact, she seemed do everything she could to avoid him.

When they finally got into her car, her hands were shaking. Was she nervous?

He set a hand on her arm. "Hey."

Her gaze shot to him.

"Like I said before…it's just a ride."

She nodded quickly and took a deep breath. "I know."

She pulled onto the street, and he waited a couple of minutes before breaking the silence. "Can I ask you something?"

Her fingers visibly tightened around the wheel. "As long as it's not about us getting back together, sure."

Oh, they would be getting back together, and deep down, she probably knew that too. "Eloise, the woman who died in Cheyenne—did you know her family?"

Sky's chest rose on a sharp inhale. "No. She was new at the dog café. None of us really knew her well."

"Did she have a boyfriend?"

"Uh, yeah, I think so, but I only know that because she mentioned him once or twice. I never met him." She glanced at him again. "Why are you asking?"

He should probably wait until they got home to mention this, but hell, this might be the only time she gave him. "There have been too many accidents for them to actually be *accidents*…and I think you know that."

This time, it wasn't just the fingers around the wheel that tightened. It was every muscle in both arms and the muscles in her neck. "What are you talking about?"

"You know what I'm talking about. The fire. The car crash. The car engine. One person can't be that unlucky."

"Becket, there have been moments where I've wondered exactly that. But I just can't allow myself to believe someone could have followed me."

"Why not? You didn't move across the country. You moved from one state straight up to the next one. And you would be easy to find. A simple Google search. You're named as the owner right on the business website. You even have your picture there. Plus, social media pages for the doggy daycare…"

"No. I mean, I can't allow myself to believe it because that's crazy."

"There are a lot of crazy people out there, Sky."

She pulled into her drive, grabbed her keys and opened her door. "No."

He followed her out. "Why?"

"Because that means someone's so obsessed with hurting me,

killing me, that they've uprooted their entire life just to get me."
She marched toward her front door. "It means Charlie's death
wasn't an accident, that someone *killed* him."

"I know it hurts—"

At the front door, she spun to face him. "It doesn't hurt! It's
more than that. It's so painful that I *can't* believe it."

He inched closer. "Sky, you need to face reality before—"

"Before what? Before they finally kill me?"

"Yes."

Fear flashed in her eyes. He didn't want to scare her, but he
needed her to grasp the danger she was in.

"I can't do this right now." She turned back to her door. "I'm
going inside."

"You shouldn't be alone," he said through gritted teeth.

She tried to put her key in the door, but she missed. Then she
missed again. Her shoulders trembled, her breaths growing
shallow.

He put a hand on her waist and reached the other around her
body, wrapping his fingers around her hand. "Jesse and I are
looking into it, okay?"

Her chest continued to heave, and her chin lowered to her
chest. "You don't need—"

"I do."

One deep, shaky inhale before she whispered, "Thank you."

He slotted the key into the lock and turned it before kissing
the top of her head and stepping back. "Keep your house
locked up."

She opened the door and turned. There was the hint of tears
in her eyes, and it looked like she wanted to say something, but
she just nodded and went inside.

The door closed…and fuck, if that separation didn't feel
wrong. And every step toward his house felt even more wrong.
All he wanted to do was be close to her. Protect her. But he
couldn't do that until she stopped pushing him away.

CHAPTER 27

Sky tipped her head back and let the soothing shower water run down her chest. She'd been in the shower far too long, but she was distracted. Distracted by everything Becket had said…and the fear that had accompanied it.

But it hadn't just been fear she'd felt. There'd also been a feeling of safety when his arms had been wrapped around her. Safety that had left her pretty damn quickly the second she was alone and cold reality had set in…

Someone could be targeting her. Someone could have followed her here all the way from Cheyenne.

Despite the warmth of the water, a deep shiver ran down her spine.

There'd always been this voice in the back of her head that whispered that was likely the case. But she'd shut it down or ignored it. Because that was too malicious. Too vindictive to believe.

It was natural to feel anger over the way Eloise had died. But to blame Sky to the point of wanting to *murder* her? She couldn't fathom it.

Her heart thumped. She blamed herself too. It was an awful

feeling, knowing she'd lived and someone else had died in her place. But for someone to then target her? Who? The boyfriend? Eloise had talked about him a lot. A firefighter she'd been dating since high school. Apparently, he'd been on the scene that day.

The thought made her feel sick. She couldn't imagine being called out for a fire, only to discover your partner was trapped inside the structure.

She was drying off when a text dinged from her phone.

Becket? Staying away from him was so hard. And today he'd been perfect. Helping for almost the entire fundraiser. Cleaning up. God, he didn't even like dogs!

There was also something about such a big alpha man washing small dogs that was ridiculously sexy.

Argh. She wrapped a towel around her chest and stepped into the bedroom. She hadn't looked at her phone all afternoon, and there were four messages waiting for her.

Kristina: Great day today. I hope you raised lots of money.

Clara: What a fun fundraiser! Thank you for letting me join. Squishing those puppies' little wet faces was the best.

Mom: Congratulations, darling. Today was wonderful. And so nice to see Becket there. Did he stay until the end?

Becket: Can you message me before you go to bed, so I know you're safe?

Her belly gave a little kick at the last message.

Taking a breath, she responded to each text, thanking Kristina and Clara for volunteering their time, and confirming for her mother that Becket had stayed for the remainder of the event but not to read too much into it.

When she got to Becket, she paused. She wrote a text but then scrunched her nose and deleted it. Then she wrote another text, this time hitting send.

Sky: All safe. Will be going to bed soon.

Becket: Good. And you did an amazing job today, Peaches. Charlie's smiling down at you right now.

She sucked in a sharp breath at the mention of Charlie.

Sky: If my house fire in Cheyenne was arson, do you think they knew Charlie was in there?

Tear pressed at her eyes. That would make them a monster.

Becket: I hope not.

Sky: Me too.

Becket: Get some rest, honey.

She nodded, even though he wasn't here. And suddenly, despite all the pushing away and avoiding of Becket that she'd done over the last week, she wished he was there.

With a shake of her head, she plugged her phone into the charger and changed into pajamas. Well, not actually pajamas. A T-shirt Becket had left here during one of his stays. Yes, it was kind of pathetic. She should have returned it to him. That's what most normal people would do. Not her. She was the insane, wear-an-ex's-shirt-to-bed kind of woman.

And yet, no one could have paid her to take it off.

She left her bedroom and was halfway down the stairs when she stopped at the sound of movement. From her kitchen?

The fine hairs on her arms stood on end and every muscle in her body locked. *Not again!*

Had she really heard it? Or was everything that had happened just messing with her head?

For a moment, she didn't move. Just stood there on the stairs, waiting. A part of her wanted to go down and check. But the other part? The part that had already experienced someone breaking into her home screamed *run*.

She took one more step down—and the second she did, the click of her back door opening sounded.

A deadly mix of fear and panic swirled in her belly, and she ran.

Sprinted down the stairs without even glancing behind her and pushed out of her front door.

The door that had been locked—and was now unlocked.

She sprinted toward Becket's house, not stopping until she reached his front door, then frantically banged her fist against the wood.

"Becket!" She hit the wood again and again, her throat actually hurting from screaming his name just once.

The door flew open. "Sky? What's wrong?"

"Someone's in my house!"

His eyes narrowed, darkness slipping over his features. He grabbed her wrist and pulled her inside his house before locking the door.

"Wait here."

She opened her mouth to ask where he was going, but he'd already disappeared down the hall. When he returned, he held a gun.

He stopped in front of her and cupped her cheek. "Lock the door after me, Peaches."

Then he was gone.

* * *

BECKET RAN QUICKLY and quietly across the lawn to Sky's front door. As he moved, he scanned the street, spotting an unfamiliar blue Ford sedan. Not parked directly in front of Sky's house, but across the road and a house back.

So they wouldn't be seen?

The door was open when he got there. Because Sky had left it open or because the asshole had run?

He inched inside, Glock at the ready.

Silence. It surrounded him. Dim light filtered into the living room from the kitchen, but he heard no movement.

He didn't make a sound as he crossed the living area into the kitchen. The back door was closed and nothing seemed to be out of place. He stilled and listened. Again, there was nothing. Not even the sound of a breeze from an open window.

He turned and made his way up the stairs, where he checked every room and every closet.

There was no one up there. And every window was locked.

When he returned downstairs, he pulled out his phone and accessed his external cameras, playing over the last few minutes.

His muscles contracted at the sight of a man climbing out of the blue Ford. He wore a black jacket with a hood pulled over his head. That, in combination with the darkness, made it impossible to see his face.

The man knocked on Sky's door, but he only waited for a second before lifting a pot on the porch.

Fuck. He knew exactly where her spare key was. And he used it to unlock the door and step right in. Why the hell hadn't Becket made sure Sky removed the spare key?

Suddenly, there was the click of the back door, loud in the otherwise quiet house.

Becket pushed his phone into his pocket and moved into the kitchen, aiming his gun at the back door as it opened.

The second the man stepped through, Becket grabbed his arm and spun him around.

The guy cried out.

"Who are you and what the fuck are you doing here?" Becket yelled, forcing the man over the counter.

"Get off me!"

Becket scowled. He knew that voice.

He spun the guy and yanked his hood down. "Tony?"

A gasp sounded by the front door, and Becket turned, keeping one hand on Tony's arm. He cursed. "Sky! What the hell are you doing? I told you to stay at my house."

She held a big knife in her hand and her eyes were wide. "I was worried! You were taking a long time." She stepped closer, eyes on Tony. "Why are you in my house?"

"I'll tell you once *he* gets off me."

"No," Becket growled. "Tell us why you broke into Sky's house first."

"I didn't break in! I knocked. No one answered. So I used the spare key her dad told me about. Her car was in the drive and the lights were on, so I was worried when she didn't answer the door. When she wasn't downstairs, I went to check outside."

"You don't just enter a fucking house," Becket said through gritted teeth, barely holding on to his damn temper.

Sky crossed the room, knife still in hand. "Tony, just tell me why you're here."

He scowled at Becket before looking at Sky. "I'm leaving tomorrow morning. Going home. And I just wanted to say goodbye."

Her brows flickered.

"You broke into her house to say goodbye?" Becket growled.

"I didn't *break in*," Tony pushed. "I used the spare key!"

"Becket...let him go," Sky said quietly.

That was the last fucking thing he wanted to do. In fact, he was tempted to call his brother to have the asshole arrested.

"Please."

How the hell was he supposed to say no to that? Becket released the asshole, and Tony straightened and looked back at Sky. "Can I talk to you?"

"You *are* talking to me."

"Alone."

Fuck no. He opened his mouth to tell the guy that, but Sky spoke first. "Anything you have to say to me, you can say in front of Becket."

Tony's lips thinned. "Fine. I came to tell you that even though I'd hoped things would end differently between us, and your dad made me think there was still a chance...I get it. For some reason, you're into him. So I'm leaving, and I won't be back."

Finally! The jerk finally got it.

"I'm sorry my dad led you to believe things might be different between us."

Tony just grunted. "I'll see myself out."

Sky followed him to the door, and Becket didn't take his fucking eyes off them. When she touched his arm, Becket's muscles tensed, but the guy just stepped out and Sky locked the door behind him.

She turned and sighed. "Thank God."

He eyed the knife in her hand. "You came over to stab the intruder?"

"Why do you say it like it's a bad thing?" She crossed into the kitchen. "Would you have preferred me to come over unarmed?"

"I'd prefer you hadn't come at all. Do you know how close you have to be to stab someone?"

"I could hazard a guess."

"Too close." He lowered the gun and slipped the knife from her fingers. "Next time, you stay locked in my house. You don't go looking for a fight."

"I wasn't looking for a fight. I was trying to protect you."

Jesus Christ. He was a former fucking Navy SEAL and *she'd* come over here with a kitchen knife to protect him.

He pinched the bridge of his nose. "We're getting rid of that spare key."

"I know. I should have done it already. Sorry about running over to your house like a crazy person."

"I'm not." When her eyes lowered, he touched her chin, tilting her head up so he could see those beautiful eyes. "I always want you to come to me if you feel unsafe or need help."

Her gaze shifted between his eyes. His hand itched to curve over her cheek. Every part of him wanted to kiss her. The need was like a living, breathing thing inside him, consuming his every breath.

"Becket..." The soft whisper of her voice called to him.

He inched closer, his thighs touching hers. "I miss you."

"It hasn't been that long."

"It has." Far too fucking long. Unable to stop himself, he lowered his head, grazing her cheek with his lips. "Tell me I can kiss you."

Her breathing grew louder. "I can't."

"You can. Trust me to be able to protect us both."

He kissed a spot behind her ear, feeling the shudder roll down her body.

"What if something happens to you, like it happened to Charlie?" Sky whispered.

"It's possible."

She started to draw back, but he slipped an arm around her waist and tugged her back to him.

"But it's not likely, because I *can* take care of both of us." Another kiss, this time on her cheek. "I'm going crazy without you."

When she touched his chest, he thought she was going to push him away. But a few seconds later, she ran her palms over him like she was exploring.

Another kiss, this time closer to her mouth. Then her hands wrapped around his neck and she pulled his mouth to hers.

Immediately, he slipped his tongue inside, tasting her. Refamiliarizing himself with all that was Sky. The kiss was everything he'd been missing in the last week and more.

He gripped her waist and lifted her, spinning her around and setting her onto the counter. Her thighs hugged him, bringing him closer.

He wanted to touch all of her but also wanted to keep his arms so tightly around her that there was no space for her to get away.

The hands on her waist slipped beneath her shirt, sliding up.

She groaned and leaned into him, the sound so fucking sweet he wanted to bottle it up.

When he reached one of her bare breasts, he cupped her,

feeling the hard peak of her nipple pushing into his palm. This was heaven. Sky and the feel of her in his arms and her taste. It was everything he both wanted and needed. Everything he'd craved.

He started to graze his hand down her belly when she suddenly pressed at his chest.

He wanted to groan. No part of him wanted to let her go. But he did. He lifted his head and took her in with his eyes.

"We shouldn't be doing this," she whispered.

"Why not?" And if she said something about keeping him safe, he was going to fight her on it until his last breath. It was *his* job to keep *her* safe, not the other way around.

"Becket, my head's a mess. So much of me is screaming yes, but there's still this hesitation and I don't know how to move past it."

He fucking hated that. "Okay, Peaches. Not tonight. Would you like me to go?"

Say no. Not just because he liked being close to her, but because with everything going on, he *needed* to be close.

She nibbled her bottom lip like she wasn't sure.

He lifted a lock of hair from her face. "Let me sleep on your couch."

Another short beat of silence passed before, finally, she nodded. "Okay. I'd like that."

Thank God.

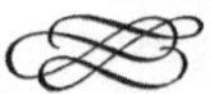

CHAPTER 28

Becket couldn't sleep. It was late. Or probably early, depending on which way you looked at it. The damn couch was small and hard and all he could think about was Sky. He wanted to be closer to her. He wanted her in his arms, wanted to be holding her.

He rolled to his other side, punching the pillow like that would somehow help him sleep.

The most frustrating part was that she wanted him too. But she was scared. And he didn't blame her for being scared. She'd lost her dog, and that dog had been her best friend. With everything going on, she was scared to risk losing anyone else.

He flipped to his back and threw an elbow over his eyes.

He wasn't going to sleep. He knew that.

Ten more minutes passed and a noise sounded from the top of the stairs. He grabbed his Glock from beneath the couch and shot up into a sitting position.

The room was dark, with only the dull light of the moon through the gap in the curtains allowing him to see.

A figure appeared at the top of the stairs.

"Sky?"

She didn't say anything. Just gripped the railing as she slowly came down the stairs toward him.

He sat there watching her for another three seconds before it hit him—she was sleepwalking again.

She reached the bottom and crossed the space between them.

He set the Glock back under the couch, then stretched out. The couch was small, but she managed to lay half on top of him, one arm slipping around his waist.

For a single second, he just lay there, caught up in her scent and the feel of her warmth and soft curves around him. Then he pulled himself together and wrapped his arm around her. A small hum slipped from her chest.

She needed him just like he needed her. Even in her sleep, she sought him out.

There was no running from this for either of them.

* * *

WARMTH WRAPPED around Sky's body. It tried to keep her asleep. To lull her back into the dream about Becket. About lying on the couch with him, his arms around her like a thick blanket.

She wriggled back into the heat...only to freeze. Something hard pressed into her butt. Something that felt an awful lot like—

Her eyes popped open, but it wasn't her bedside table and lamp in front of her. It was the coffee table. She was in the living room on her couch, and Becket was wrapped around her like a damn pretzel.

Shit. It hadn't been a dream. She'd walked her butt all the way downstairs, right into his arms...*again.*

Had he woken up? Of course he had. So why hadn't he sent her back to bed?

Well, that was a stupid question. *He* hadn't been the one who wanted to break up.

His arm was heavy around her waist, and when his thumb grazed her belly, hot liquid pooled between her thighs.

No. No, no, no. She should not be getting turned on by his erection pressing into her or his thumb on her belly. She needed to be immune to all of it.

Time to get up, Sky.

But she didn't move. He was so warm, and he felt so dang good.

Goddammit, Sky. Get the heck up!

She clenched her teeth and was still mid pep talk when his mouth suddenly touched her neck. A gentle kiss pressed to her skin, the graze of his day-old stubble making her skin tingle.

A stifled groan tried to slip from her lips.

"Mm, you taste good in the morning," he moaned.

The deep gravel of his voice made the throbbing in her lower belly intensify. "I should get up."

"Should you?" Another kiss, this time behind her ear exactly where he knew she liked.

"Y-yes." Damn her lack of conviction.

Because her traitorous body had a mind of its own, she wiggled her butt into him, and he growled.

"You're killing me, honey."

He kissed her again, and she reached back and slipped her fingers through his hair. It exposed more of her neck, and he took advantage, peppering kisses across her skin.

The hand on her belly wasn't moving, so she set her palm on top of his. She told herself she was trying to remove his hand from her body, but then, almost of its own accord, her hand started guiding his down.

The closer he grew to the apex of her thighs, the more the throbbing in her lower belly intensified.

Slowly, so slowly it stole her breath, he slipped his fingers inside her panties. Her thighs parted and he swiped her clit.

It was like a bolt of lightning through her body, and her head tossed back into his chest.

"So sensitive," he whispered, the heat in his breath sending a trail of fire over her skin.

He swiped her again, then ran a circle around her clit.

Fire burned inside her, so hot. She arched into him, rubbing circles against his cock with her ass.

His other arm snaked beneath her side and slipped under the material of her sleep shirt. The air in her lungs stalled. Slowly, his hand moved up, whispering against her skin. Then he cupped her, finding the hard point of her nipple and rolling it between his thumb and forefinger.

She cried out, the sound so primal that she didn't recognize it as her own.

More…she needed more of this man. Even if it made her selfish. Even if it wasn't smart. She didn't care.

The fingers on her clit continued to move, her ass continuing to grind against him. After another thirty torturous seconds, his fingers slipped to her entrance, and her breath caught.

He pushed two fingers inside her, and she opened her mouth to scream but no sound came out. Because she had nothing left. Everything she had was his.

Her walls clenched around his fingers, squeezing as he thrust and played.

He was everywhere. Behind her, inside her. Even his mouth had reattached to her neck. There wasn't anywhere to go, and she was finally realizing, there was nowhere she *wanted* to go.

* * *

Sky's sweet cries slipped into the air. The softness of her body called to him, and the way she hummed and shook at every touch screamed *his*.

Every inch of her was perfect.

She pushed her ass into him, and he growled. He was so hard he hurt. Never had he needed a woman like he needed Sky. He fucking craved her.

As if she heard him, she reached behind her back and slipped her hand into his briefs. When she wrapped her fingers around him, his cock turned to stone.

Jesus Christ, she was going to kill him.

His fingers stilled inside her, his palm unmoving on her breast. It was just his forehead that shifted to the nook of her neck as his eyes squeezed shut.

Her hand slid up and down his cock like fucking torture. When she rotated her palm over his tip, it took everything inside him to remain exactly as he was. To not grab and roll her. Take her then and there.

Fuck, she made him crazy.

He slipped his fingers out of her and was moments away from snagging her wrist and stopping her when she suddenly released him and shimmied out of her panties.

Her bare ass pressed into him, making the muscles in his body go so tight it felt like they'd snap. She slipped her hand behind her again, pulled his cock from his briefs and pressed his tip to her entrance, where his fingers had been.

Blood roared between his ears, deafening the world around him.

She started to push back, but he gripped her hips. "Peaches… I'm not wearing anything."

"I went on the pill a month ago."

The fire in his veins roared, and when she eased back into him, pushing his tip inside her, the world blackened around him. Sky groaned, her fingers once again reaching up and tangling though his hair. Scratching and pulling.

He latched onto her neck and sucked before pulling her hips back until he was deep inside her.

She moaned.

Fuck, she was tight. And so fucking wet for him.

He pulled back and thrust into her, once again palming her breast. Every sound she made, every cry and hum and scream, called to him.

She tugged his head back to her, kissing him. A long, deep kiss as he continued to move in and out of her.

His pumps became faster. And he once again found that bundle of nerves between her thighs and stroked her.

Her groans grew wild, her hips moving, pushing back into him, meeting him thrust for thrust.

He trailed his mouth to her ear, nipping it before whispering, "Come for me, Peaches."

Her entire body tensed, then she broke. Her scream was loud and fierce as it roared through the room. He kept thrusting, moving in and out of her, feeling her walls throb around him. Her body trembled in his arms.

Perfect. Every fucking inch of her.

Three more pumps and he couldn't hold off any longer. He shattered, shouting her name as he lost any sense of the world around him.

When his thrusts finally slowed, there was only stillness in the room. Neither of them spoke, and they remained exactly as they were, connected in the most intimate way, unmoving for a long minute until Sky pulled away and shifted onto her back.

A slow smile curved her lips. "Hey."

"Hey, yourself."

"We had sex."

He chuckled. "We did." And now he was praying she wasn't about to kick him out and tell him it was a mistake or that they couldn't do it again.

She bit her bottom lip. "I want you. I want to kiss you and touch you. I want you in my life. And that probably makes me really selfish when I likely have someone gunning for me."

"It doesn't make you selfish." He cupped her cheek. "I know

that losing Charlie hurt you, but it wasn't your fault. And nothing is going to happen to me."

"It could."

"It won't. Don't push me away anymore. Please."

She met his eyes. "Even if I wanted to, I don't think I could."

Thank fuck. He dropped his head and kissed her again, finally feeling a small semblance of peace in knowing that she was finally his.

CHAPTER 29

The breeze was cool as it blew between Sky's fingers. It was a better week. There'd been no more incidents, no more home intruders, and things between her and Becket had been good. Really good. Even though the urge to protect him by pushing him away was still there, the need to keep him close was stronger.

So he'd remained close. Every night for the last week, either he'd been at her house or she'd been at his. He'd been driving her to work, picking her up.

He squeezed her thigh. "Hey. You look deep in your own head."

She turned from the window to look at him. The long fingers of his other hand curled around the wheel, and the muscles in his arm rippled. But it was the day-old stubble that had her wanting to reach out and touch.

She set her palm over his. "I was just thinking that it's been a good week."

"*Good* doesn't come close to describing it." He turned his hand and lifted hers to his mouth.

She shuddered at the kiss. But then her mind went to the

evening ahead. "I can't believe my parents are coming to your family dinner. It's so weird."

"Why's it weird?"

"Because it feels like two worlds colliding." She angled her body toward him. "You know that episode of *Seinfeld* where Elaine starts hanging out with Susan, George's girlfriend, and George loses his mind, saying that his two worlds are colliding and he doesn't like it?"

"I've never watched *Seinfeld* before."

Her mouth dropped open. "You hate dogs and you've never watched *Seinfeld*? Do you hate rainbows and ice cream too?"

"Some days." He grinned at her. "But I like you every day."

"Good answer."

He squeezed her hand. "Today will be great."

"Really? I'm already in defense mode over the looks my father will throw your way."

"I can handle your father."

"I know. It's *me* who feels the urge to strangle him, and I can't do that in front of your mother and the town sheriff."

He pulled up in front of his mother's house. Half a dozen cars were parked on the street, one of them being her parents'.

So. Weird.

They climbed out and Sky grabbed her pasta salad from the back.

Then Becket slipped an arm around her waist. "So, in *Seinfeld*...why doesn't George like Susan hanging out with Elaine?"

"Because when he's with his friends, he's Independent George, and with Susan he's Relationship George. If those two worlds collide, Relationship George will kill Independent George."

Becket frowned. "This doesn't sound like a show I would watch."

"You *will* be watching it. We're starting season one tonight."

"How many seasons are there?"

"Nine."

He chuckled as they stopped at the door and he tugged her into him. "You know I'd do anything for you, right? Even sit through hours of mindless TV."

"*Seinfeld* is not mindless."

He lowered his head, his mouth hovering over hers. "It doesn't really matter, because with you beside me, I don't know how much concentrating I'll be doing."

"Hmm, I guess you'll just have to try hard."

"*Really* hard."

He lowered his head and kissed her. His tongue swept across her lips, making her groan. He'd just slipped his tongue inside her mouth when the door opened.

She jolted, shoving at Becket's chest. "Dad!"

Her father's gaze moved between them. "Skylar. Becket. It's good to see you both."

Ha. She didn't believe that for a second. And the almost warning in his tone when he'd said Becket's name didn't help convince her.

Becket dipped his head. "It's good to see you too, Mr. Williams."

Her father cleared his throat. "Your mother left her glasses in the car. Everyone's in the backyard."

"We'll see you out there." Becket nudged her out of the way and her father passed them.

Yep, that was about as awkward as she'd expected.

They joined everyone out back. Becket's mother, sister and brother. Aspen, Holden, and Sky's mom. She went around to greet everyone. When she reached her mother, the woman gave the tightest hug.

"Oh, darling, it was so nice of Pam to invite your father and me." She pulled back. "She's just lovely. The entire family is."

Sky snuck a peek behind her to see her father hadn't returned yet. "Is Dad being nice?"

"Of course." Her mother's brows shot up. "He wouldn't come to someone else's house and be rude."

Hm. Maybe. "And Tony's not here?"

"Tony went home."

Relief whooshed from her chest. He'd told her he was going, and she was glad that he was true to his word.

"He didn't say goodbye?"

"He did. I just wasn't sure exactly when he was leaving."

"A few days ago." Her mother glanced around the yard before she looked back at Sky and lowered her voice. "I think your father's really coming around to Becket."

She almost snorted. "Mom—"

"I'm serious, Skylar. He was talking about inviting him over for dinner."

Well, of course he was. Becket's mother had invited Sky over a few times now—it would be impolite not to return the favor. "Well, if he does, that will be lovely."

"I agree."

"I'm just going to get a drink." She squeezed her mother's hand before heading to the drinks table.

"She hates me," Clara said quietly.

Indie shook her head. "No one hates you."

"Well, she does."

Sky filled a glass with soda water.

Clara turned toward her. "Sky, I need your opinion."

"Of course."

"I've been trying to bond with my newish roommate. She's an investigative journalist, so I made the effort to read one of her articles on technology's role in journalism. Then, this morning, I made her some really nice waffles and coffee and when she came into the kitchen, I offered her both and started talking about AI and automation, and their impact on journalism."

"You sound like the perfect roommate."

"That's what I thought," Clara said. "But she swallowed a mouthful of coffee, grabbed a waffle and flew out of the house with barely a word."

"She sounds busy," Indie said.

"Yeah, but she's quiet and barely around, so I can't complain." Clara sipped her drink. "Now, excuse me, I'm going to talk to people who do have time to like me." She turned—only to walk straight into Holden, the red liquid in her cup splashing all over his white shirt.

Clara gasped. "Oh my God...I'm *so* sorry. Look at your shirt. It's ruined! And it's all my fault."

Holden glanced down at his soaked shirt, the material stuck to his chest, and grinned. "It's okay, Clara."

She turned and grabbed some napkins, then started dabbing his chest. "I didn't see you there. I mean, of course I didn't, otherwise I wouldn't have spilled wine all over you. I don't want you to think I did it on purpose, because I didn't. That would be crazy. But then, if anyone should have a shirt sticking to their chest, it would be you, because you have a nice chest." She closed her eyes and shook her head. "Not that I'm looking at your chest, I—"

"Clara." He touched her arm and waited until she looked at him. His tone was warm and gentle. "It's okay."

Indie scooted next to Sky and sighed. "Ah...that pre-relationship crush goodness. Bet it's the one thing about being in a relationship with Becket that you're going to miss."

Sky scoffed. "We did *not* start out like that. The opposite, actually."

"It's usually one way or the other."

She studied Indie. "You're not dating anyone?"

Something flashed over her face. Regret? "No, my separation from Colt is still new...too new." She almost looked pained when she said the word separation.

Sky gently touched her arm. "I'm sorry."

"Me too." Indie smiled, but it didn't come close to reaching her eyes.

Whatever had happened between Indie and her husband, the woman was still hurting.

* * *

"Tell me you found something on the boyfriend."

"I found something on the boyfriend."

Becket's fingers tightened around his beer. He shot a glance at Sky across the lawn, then looked back at his brother. "Tell me."

"I called the fire station in Cheyenne...told them I needed to speak to Mateo Flores about official sheriff business. They said he quit two months after a fire that had killed his girlfriend, then he left town."

"That would line up with when Sky moved home."

"Yeah, doesn't look good for him." Jesse pulled out his cell and searched for something before handing it over to Becket. "A photo of him."

Becket studied the guy's brown eyes, hair and fair skin. "I haven't seen him around town."

"Neither have I, and neither have any of my deputies. But we'll keep an eye out for him and also keep digging. I'll see if I can find a trail for his whereabouts after leaving Cheyenne."

"Thank you, brother."

"Has everything been quiet for Sky?"

"Too quiet. Makes me nervous that whoever's after her is busy planning something big." So fucking nervous that he didn't want to be apart from her.

He watched as she stood talking to both his mother and hers. Her smile was huge, and for a moment, he couldn't take his eyes off her.

"You need anything from me or Holden, even if it's just extra eyes on your street, you let us know," Jesse said quietly.

"Thanks. I might take you up on that. Everything going well with you and Aspen?"

An immediate softness entered Jesse's eyes as he looked at her across the lawn. "I love her so damn much. I didn't even know it was possible to love a person like this until I met her. And the knowledge that she's safe and her ex is gone means I can sleep at night."

Yeah, her ex had been a huge problem.

"I'm glad she's okay."

"You and me both."

"Okay, everyone," his mother called. "Food's ready."

Becket crossed straight over to Sky and slipped an arm around her waist. *This* was how close he needed to be to her to feel okay.

She leaned into him with a sigh.

They moved to the table, and over the next couple of hours, both their families ate and laughed and smiled. It felt good to be surrounded by everyone he loved. Even Roger cracked a couple grins. Maybe the old man was finally warming up to them as a couple.

And fuck, it was good to see Sky relaxed. She'd been on edge all week. She hadn't said it aloud, but he'd felt it.

He wanted to take that burden from her, but he couldn't.

She threw her head back and laughed at his brother's rendition of sixteen-year-old Becket.

He scoffed. "You make me sound like an arrogant prick."

"You kind of were," Jesse said.

"*Are*," Clara corrected with a laugh.

Holden sat next to Clara in a clean shirt he'd found in his car. "Hey. You guys are supposed to be talking him up in front of the in-laws."

"Not in-laws yet," Roger said firmly.

The laughter died and a heavy pause followed.

Esther gave an awkward laugh. "Well, this has been just lovely, Pam. Let me start clearing up."

Becket shook his head and rose. "No. You're a guest. Sit. Relax." Sky started to get up, but he stopped her. "You too."

He kissed the top of her head and took a pile of plates to the kitchen. He'd just set them into the sink when the back door opened. He expected to see someone from his family. They'd all been raised to clean if they hadn't cooked.

It wasn't.

Roger Williams stepped into the room, his eyes fixed on Becket, not even a hint of a smile on his face. He set the leftover tray of meat onto the island. "Becket, I was wondering if we could have a quick word."

"Sure." He'd answer anything. There was no part of him that would be scared away by this man. He cared about Sky. Hell, he was falling in love with her.

Roger crossed his arms. "As you know, faith is important to me. You not being part of my church is something I was really struggling with."

"Was?"

The older man cleared his throat. "It appears I'm fighting a losing battle, and at the end of the day, I love my daughter. All I've ever wanted is for her to be happy and taken care of. I thought I knew best...but she's made it pretty clear that I don't. Will you make her happy and take care of her?"

"I will spend the rest of my life protecting and caring for your daughter, sir. If she lets me." And he damn well meant it.

Roger's frown deepened, and he seemed to think about that for a long moment before finally nodding. "Good."

The door opened behind Roger. Sky glanced between them nervously. "Hey. Is everything okay in here?"

Roger held out a hand and Becket shook it—a silent understanding, hopefully that this tension between them was over.

Roger turned toward his daughter. He placed a kiss on her head. "Everything's fine, Skylar. I'll see you both outside."

When he was gone, Sky gave Becket a questioning look. "Were you just shaking hands with my father?"

Becket stepped forward and gripped her hips. "I think my charm and wit have finally won him over."

She lifted an eyebrow. "Really?"

"You sound surprised."

"No…well, yes. But not because you're not charming or witty. I just thought he'd never come around."

He lowered his mouth to hover over hers. "You worry too much."

"I think I worry just the right amount, considering everything we have going on."

"Let me worry for the both of us."

"Becket—"

He cut off her words with his lips. And it only took half a second for her to soften and sink into the kiss.

CHAPTER 30

*B*ecket stared at his computer screen. He was supposed to be writing up this morning's incident report for a car fire due to an overheated engine, but he could barely concentrate on that. It made him think about all the incidents with Sky. Not just the fires, but also the engine and brakes issues she'd had in Cheyenne. Someone must have done those things to her car, and that someone had to have a good knowledge of engines.

The boyfriend was still the most likely suspect because, as far as they knew, he was the person with the greatest motive.

But why couldn't Jesse find him? Especially if he was here? In a town the size of Amber Ridge, someone should have seen him by now.

And if it *wasn't* the boyfriend…then who? Tony? But there'd been no sign of him either, and her parents swore he'd left town.

His hands balled into fists. He lifted his cell and sent a text, needing to hear from Sky.

Becket: Hey, are you okay?

The three dots popped up right away.

Sky: I'm great. Bella and I are just snacking while we wait for Rosemary to pick her up.

Becket: Snacking on what?

Sky: Me—liver strips, Bella—chocolate.

Sky: Kidding, other way around :D

Becket: Are you allowed to joke about a dog snacking on chocolate? Doesn't the stuff kill them?

Sky: The only thing not allowed is actually giving Bella chocolate. I can joke about whatever I want.

Becket: I don't know, I heard it was like a sin or something.

Sky: Well, if that's the case and I go to hell, at least you'll have company.

He laughed out loud.

Becket: Why am I going to hell? I'm a firefighter. I save people.

Sky: Because you hate dogs and Seinfeld.

Becket: We've been through this. I don't hate dogs and Seinfeld just isn't for me.

Sky: Seinfeld's for everyone. And you cannot dislike dogs and get into heaven. Butchering trees and fighting with neighbors is also frowned upon.

Becket: Lucky I made up for those things then. Is the door to the daycare locked?

Sky: Yep. I'm locked in and safe.

Becket: Good. Stay safe.

Sky: You too.

He shook his head and was just turning back to the computer when his desk phone rang. He lifted it to his ear. "Becket speaking."

"Beck, it's Teddy. I'm going to be late to work, sorry."

There was a lot of background noise. People and movement. Maybe even…a radio? "Where are you?"

"The sheriff's station."

Becket straightened. "What's wrong?"

"It's a long story. You know how I've been dating Kristina?"

"Yeah."

"I stayed at her place last night. She's always stayed at mine, so it was the first time. And I found some stuff. Okay, not just some stuff. A *lot* of stuff."

"What kind of stuff?"

"The stolen kind."

Becket shot to his feet. "Kristina's the town thief?"

"It looks like it. I called the sheriff's station and they came down. I felt like shit doing it behind her back, but it was the right thing to do. They took her in."

Becket frowned. "Kristina's new in town, right?"

"That's another thing…she says she's only been here a few months, but I think she got here earlier. I saw a note from her landlord alluding to as much."

"Where'd she come from?"

"Um…I don't know. She might have said somewhere in Wyoming."

Becket grabbed his keys and left his office. "You said she's at the station?"

"Yeah, they just brought her in. Why?"

"I have to go."

He stopped in the break room. "Irene, can you finish the report on my laptop?"

"Sure." She frowned. "Everything okay?"

"I don't know. I need to check on something."

She nodded. "Go."

He jogged out of the station to his car.

On the way to the sheriff's office, he tried his brother's phone. No answer. *Dammit.*

He pressed his foot to the floor. When he finally got there, he stepped inside at the exact moment his brother walked out of his office.

Jesse frowned. "Beck…what are you doing here?"

"It could be her."

"What could be who?"

"The person who's been messing with Sky. It could be Kristina."

His brother urged him down the hall and lowered his voice. "Why do you say that?"

"Because she arrived in Amber Ridge when these things started happening. She got a job at Sky's doggy daycare, possibly to get close to Sky. And now she's been identified as the town thief, which means she was the one who broke into Sky's house."

"We haven't questioned her yet."

"Are you doing that now?"

"Yes, but—"

"I want to be there."

"Becket—"

"If situations were reversed and this involved Aspen, you would want the same access to the key witness. I'm not asking to be in the room. I know that's not allowed. Just to watch you interview her."

Jesse's jaw tightened. "Fine. Follow me." He led Becket into a small room. "You *watch*…that's all."

The door closed behind Jesse, and Becket looked through a window to see Kristina sitting at a table, head in her hands.

Jesse walked into the interrogation room, box in hand, and Kristina's head shot up. Her face was red and tear-stained, her eyes sad and scared.

Jesse sat at the table opposite her and hit the record button. "Kristina Cutter?"

"Yes." Her voice was low and defeated.

"You've already been read your rights and you've refused counsel. Now I'm going to ask you a series of questions and they'll be recorded. Do you understand?"

"I understand."

Jesse pulled a diamond necklace from the box. "This necklace matches the description of one stolen from Rose Harper's home exactly six weeks ago. This morning, it was found in your spare bedroom. How did it get there?"

Kristina's chest rose and fell with a deep breath. She looked at the necklace, then back at Jesse. "I don't know."

Becket's hands fisted. If she wasn't going to cooperate even when the evidence was right fucking there, this would take a long time.

Jesse pulled out a gold men's ring. "This ring was stolen from Giuseppe Bruno's home. We found it in that same bedroom. How did it get there?"

Her breathing rate increased. "I don't know."

Becket's feet twitched to march in there and force the truth out of her.

Jesse leaned forward. "Every time you lie, you make this worse for yourself. We've already got all the evidence we need, and once we have a DNA match, that's it. Don't make this harder than it has to be."

Her eyes flared with fear.

He pulled out a light blue bag. "This was stolen from Amelia Lambert's home. Why was it in your house?"

Her mouth opened.

"Don't lie to me," he cut in before she could speak.

Three long seconds passed.

"I took it," she finally whispered. "I stole all of it."

"Why?" he asked.

She lifted a shoulder, tears brimming in her eyes. "Because it's what I do. My real name is Josie Palone. I move to small towns, take what I can, and leave."

"Do you befriend people and rob them?"

"No! I didn't realize that was Sky's house that night. I was in her neighbor's house, saw the broken fence and took advantage of the situation. Then she got home and fell down the stairs and…I had to choose. Help her or run." Tears fell down her cheeks. "I chose to run. I'm sorry."

"Did you have anything to do with the other things that have happened to Sky?"

She frowned. "You mean when her car went over the bridge? No. I was working that day."

Becket frowned. She was? It could easily be checked, so there was no reason to lie.

"What about the day Sky was almost hit outside the doggy daycare, and Becket was sideswiped?"

Kristina was already shaking her head before Jesse had finished speaking. "I was with Teddy. He can confirm that. I was at his place."

Jesse didn't say anything, just watched her closely, waiting to see if she cracked.

"I'm serious." Her voice became more high-pitched. "That wasn't me! I break into houses and take stuff, but I never hurt anyone."

Shit. She was telling the truth. It wasn't her.

Jesse leaned forward. "Did you follow her here from Wyoming?"

"What? I *did* come from Wyoming. The last city I was in was Jackson. But I only met Sky when I got here. I get a job in every town I go to, and she was hiring."

Becket watched her closely. Her eyes. The tone of her voice. She sounded like she was telling the truth. But if she was, that meant someone else was messing with Sky.

"You know we'll find out if you're lying," Jesse pressed.

She lifted her hands. "I'm not. I swear!"

At the ringing of Jesse's phone, he glanced at the screen before rising and answering. He frowned and looked at Becket through the glass, tilting his head toward the door.

Becket met him in the hall. "Who is it?"

"One of the deputies letting me know the boyfriend called the station."

"Why the hell would he call the station?"

"Let's find out."

They returned to Jesse's office and he answered the call, putting it on speaker. "Sheriff Hayes speaking."

"Uh, hi, this is Mateo Flores. My old chief called…said you've been trying to get in contact with me?"

"Yes. I was wondering if you could tell me where you've been the last few months."

"In Merida, Mexico, visiting family and figuring my life out after losing my girlfriend." There was a small pause. "Why? What the hell's this about?"

"Can anyone verify this?"

"Yeah, my entire family. Do I need a lawyer?"

Becket's hands fisted. If it wasn't him either, that just left Tony, didn't it?

"Did Eloise have anyone else she was particularly close to?" Becket asked, receiving a glare from Jesse for speaking. He didn't damn well care. "Her parents? Friends?"

"No. She was an introvert, didn't have many friends. And she didn't get along with her parents. She moved out when she was sixteen."

"Who'd she move in with?" Jesse asked.

"Her grandmother. *They* were close."

Becket frowned. "Just her grandmother? No grandfather?"

"Nah, her grandfather was a mechanic who died at work ten years ago."

Becket's muscles locked…a mechanic. Which meant the grandmother could know something about cars.

"How did her grandmother react after Eloise died?" Becket asked, even though he had a feeling he knew the answer.

"She was gutted. Eloise was like a daughter to her. Other than her dog, Eloise was basically her only family. Eloise was with her grandmother when she got the call asking her to go in for that shift. I think she struggled with the fact that Eloise wasn't even supposed to work that day."

Becket's chest began to burn. "What was her name?"

"Rosemary...Rosemary Symes."

* * *

SKY SMILED as Bella licked her face. A lot of people were so critical of Chinese Cresteds. Dolly had even laughed when she'd learned Bella's name, which was Italian for beautiful. And Mr. Bruno had walked in that first time and gasped at the sight of her.

"People are just mean," Sky said, giving Bella another liver strip. "You're beautiful in your own Bella way."

The dog made a little sound, almost like she understood Sky's words and was in agreement.

The playroom was quiet since every other dog had been picked up. Which was unusual. Rosemary never ran late. Dolly had offered to stay, but Sky knew she played bridge on Wednesdays, so she'd refused to let her miss it. Besides, Becket would still be at work, so all she had waiting for her was an empty house.

Maybe she'd get Thai on the way home. Today had been tiring, with a lot of high-energy dogs, and she did not feel like cooking.

The bell for the front door rang through the daycare.

"There's your mama," Sky said as she rose.

She attached Bella's lead to her collar and made her way to the front. Rosemary stood on the other side of the glass, waving.

Another perk of working here—everyone was always happy to pick up their dog at the end of the day. No grumpy interactions.

Sky unlatched the lock and opened the door. "Hey."

"Hello." Bella jumped on the older woman, and Rosemary laughed and crouched. "And hello to you, my darling. Have you missed me?"

Bella yapped before licking Rosemary's face.

Sky grinned. "I'd say that's a yes."

Rosemary rose and took the lead from Sky. "I'm so sorry I'm late. I ran a bit behind delivering meals."

Rosemary cooked meals and sold them to locals, particularly the elderly.

"You are absolutely fine. Although I'm sorry to tell you that Bella might not be too hungry for dinner after all the liver treats she ate."

The older woman chuckled. "That's why she loves coming here. One of the many reasons."

"Well, I hope you—"

"Oh, I actually made a meal for you too. I went a bit crazy on the tuna mornay, so I'd love to give you some."

"Oh, thank you. That's so nice of you."

"Not at all! Unfortunately, my legs are so sore from getting in and out of the delivery van all day. I was wondering if you could get it out?"

Sky didn't even know she had a delivery van. "Of course I can get it."

Her cell rang from where she'd left it next to her bag on the front desk. Assuming it was her mother, she'd return the call when she got back inside.

"Are you sure you don't want to keep the meal for yourself?" she asked. "Save it for later?"

"No, I have enough."

They stopped at a vehicle. Sky frowned. It was a white van like the one that had run her off the bridge.

She shook her head. There were tons of white vans in town.

Rosemary opened the passenger door first. Once Bella had jumped in, she closed the door and moved to the back.

"It's just at the right corner, in the container," Rosemary said, once the big doors were open.

Sky climbed in and went all the way to the back. The van didn't have much inside. A couple of built-in containers. Some sheets.

Something rustled behind her as she opened the container in the corner. It was empty.

She started to turn. "I don't—"

A sting of pain cut off her words *and* her breath. She looked down…only to see something sticking into her stomach, through her top. She yanked it out.

A dart. What the hell?

She looked up—and shock made her belly cramp. Rosemary still stood by the door, but now she had a large strange-looking gun in her hand. It was almost comical, seeing the older woman holding a weapon.

"What are you doing?" Sky asked, her words slurring as black dots danced in her vision.

"What needs to be done, dear."

The door started to close.

She started to lunge forward, but her knees gave way. She dropped to the floor of the van, panic weaving through her veins. The deep hum of the van's engine thrummed under her cheek. She tried to stay awake…to keep her eyes open and her mind clear. But the dark swirls in her head sucked her under, turning her world black.

CHAPTER 31

Becket drove as fast as the vehicle would go. Far faster than he was supposed to in town.

Sky was in danger. And she wasn't answering her phone.

He cursed and pressed the key on his steering wheel to call her again. Again, it rang out.

Fuck!

Sirens wailed behind him. He didn't care whether it was Jesse or his deputies. He'd run out of the station the second he'd heard Rosemary's name. His entire focus remained on getting to Sky before the older woman did anything.

They hadn't even considered her. Why? Because she was elderly? Because she seemed friendly? Or because they'd been so fixated on the boyfriend?

Later, he'd kick his own ass, but right now he needed to find Sky.

He stopped in front of the doggy daycare, grabbed his Glock and jumped out of his truck. He spotted her car in the lot and didn't know if that was good or bad.

Jesse pulled up just as Becket tried the handle.

Unlocked.

He rushed inside. "Sky?"

Nothing. Only eerie silence.

He moved around the daycare, checking every room, the yard, even the fucking cupboards.

She wasn't here. *Dammit!*

He was running back into the reception area when he collided with his brother.

"Beck—"

"She's not here, Jess. She's not fucking here!"

His brother's radio sounded. "Sheriff?"

"What is it?" Jesse asked, pulling the radio from his belt.

"We just arrived at Rosemary Symes's address but looks like no one's home."

"Break in," Becket growled.

"Uh, we need a warrant to—"

"Do it," Becket barked, cutting off the deputy's words.

Jesse scrubbed a hand over his face. "Just do it, Luke. I'll cop the consequences."

"Doing it now," the deputy said.

Becket turned and spotted Sky's phone on the counter. When he lifted it, his fingers squeezed it so hard that he almost crushed the thing. She was gone, and he had no way of reaching her.

He wanted to punch his fist through a wall. Anything to divert the pain inside him.

They had just finished one more sweep of the daycare when Jesse's radio squawked again. "House is empty, Sheriff."

Jesse cursed. "Thanks for checking, Luke."

Becket's heart started to thump loud and hard in his chest. "She's gone."

Jesse's phone rang this time, and he walked outside to answer it.

Helpless. Becket was fucking helpless and blind.

When Jesse came back inside, the look on his face was grim.

"Rosemary had a white van registered in her husband's name, only she doesn't have a husband."

So many damn things they should have seen.

Jesse stepped closer. "We've got an APB out on the van and Rosemary's car. *Someone* will find them."

They had to. There was no other choice.

He wouldn't lose her. He couldn't.

* * *

A COOL BREEZE brushed against Sky's face, bringing with it a familiar scent, making her scrunch her eyes tight.

She frowned on her next inhale. What *was* that smell? Gasoline…?

One more squeeze of her eyes before she forced them open. Everything was a dark, foggy blur.

She blinked. Once. Twice. On the third blink, things started coming into focus.

Trees. Tall trees surrounded her. And leaves blew in the high wind. She glanced down. Dirt. Why was she lying in dirt?

She tried to push herself up, but something stopped her. Was she bound? And why were her movements so slow and uncoordinated?

Her heart started to beat faster, panic crawling up her throat.

"I was wondering how long the sedative would keep you asleep."

Sky gasped and her head turned toward the voice to find Rosemary Symes. The older woman was holding a large container, pouring its contents on the trees and bushes nearby.

"I didn't want to give you too much," Rosemary continued. "Because I want you to be awake for this."

It all came back to her at once. The van. The dart in her stomach. The strange-looking gun.

"It's you." Her voice was breathless, but she wasn't sure if that was the drugs still in her system or the disbelief that this seventy-year-old woman was the person who'd been tormenting her. "You've been trying to kill me?"

"Not very successfully, it would seem, because here you are. This, though…*this* is something you can't run from. Well, you can. You just won't make it. And that boyfriend of yours can't save you this time."

A dog barked. Sky turned her head. She couldn't see the front of the van, but the back door was wide open. Had Rosemary just rolled her out? Was Bella still in the front?

Her vision started to blur again, but she blinked, forcing herself to focus on Rosemary. "Why?"

She smelled gasoline. Was that what Rosemary was pouring from the container?

"Because, Sky, Eloise was my grandchild. But she was really like a daughter to me. I had my own daughter young and made a lot of mistakes. And because of that, she couldn't care less about me. But Eloise…she was my whole world, and I loved her." She turned to look at Sky, tears in her eyes. "And because of *you*, she's dead."

"I didn't start that café fire, Rosemary."

"No. But you were supposed to be there. Not her. We were together when you called her, *begged* her to take your shift."

Sky tried to push up, but her head spun and she fell back down.

"I think about her every day." Rosemary stopped pouring the gasoline to swipe a tear from her cheek. "About how scared she must have been stuck in that room, with flames all around her. You changed your destiny that day. But I'm making things right. You'll feel the same fear and the same pain that my poor Eloise did. The sedative still in your system will make sure you're too slow to outrun this."

"Don't do this…please!"

"I have to. I'm seventy years old. I can't do much to make up for not protecting her that day, but avenging her death…that's something I *can* do."

Jesus. Sky was living a nightmare she couldn't wake up from. "You really think Eloise would want this? She wouldn't. I may not have known her for long but—"

Rosemary swung around. "No! You *didn't* know her for long. So you were probably glad that this almost-stranger died in your place, while I lost the only person I had left worth living for! No…I'm sorry, Sky." The older woman's chest rose and fell, as if she was trying to pull herself together. "I really am sorry. I actually started to like you. But it has to end like this."

Rosemary moved back to the van and set the container inside. She closed the doors and pulled something from her pocket.

Sky's breath caught…matches.

This time when she pushed up, she refused to let her body fall again. That's when she noticed that it wasn't just her wrist that were bound, it was her ankles too. "Rosemary—"

"There's nothing you can say that will change your fate, dear. What's happening to you now is simply you meeting the destiny that was always meant to be yours." She lit a match and threw it at a nearby tree.

Bright flames danced in front of her vision, making the air in Sky's lungs stick so completely that she couldn't breathe. She tried to rise to her feet, but her legs wouldn't support her.

No…this couldn't be happening.

Rosemary turned to look at her. "I guess, in a few years, I'll see you on the other side."

"Rosemary, please!"

But the old woman ignored her. There was no anger in her movements, just resigned sadness.

A door clicked open.

Suddenly, Rosemary gasped. *"Bella, no, get back here!"*

Half a second later, Bella was beside Sky, licking her face and whimpering.

Oh, God! The sweet dog was too close to those flames.

"Bella, you have to go," Sky rushed out.

Rosemary rushed over to the animal and tried to lift her—then yelped when Bella bit her hand. She dropped the Chinese Crested.

Bella dug her head into Sky's neck and whimpered. She lowered her mouth and whispered, "Run, Bella! Go get help."

It was ridiculous to ask a dog for help. But when Bella looked up...Sky would swear she saw understanding in the animal's eyes.

Rosemary was just reaching for Bella a second time when the dog took off, sprinting away from them through the trees.

"Bella, *no!*" Rosemary yelled.

The flames grew, the heat already licking Sky's skin.

Rosemary looked at the flames, then back to where Bella had run.

"Please," Sky begged, muscles protesting as she once again tried to stand.

Rosemary scowled at her. "This was always how it was supposed to be." Then the older woman returned to her van, climbed in, and drove off through the forest, leaving Sky alone with the flames.

Shit!

Sky reached for the rope around her ankle, madly trying to undo the knot. Rosemary had driven the van into the forest on some kind of narrow trail. It had to connect with a road. All she had to do was outrun that fire until she found it.

Quickly, she worked the bindings on her ankles.

Come on, come on, come on.

It felt like it took hours, when in reality it was probably minutes. But finally, she got her ankles untied and again tried to push to her feet—and again immediately fell down, the world around her swirling.

The fire grew louder, drowning out the sound of the wind.

She forced herself back up with the help of her still-bound wrists, this time locking her knees, refusing to let herself fall.

She moved one foot forward, then the other. It was slow, but any distance between her and the flames was better than none. Each step was a small chance at survival.

CHAPTER 32

"You need to calm down, Beck."

"How?" Becket growled at his brother, the anger and panic and fear choking him. "How do I calm down when I don't know where she is? Rosemary has made her intentions pretty fucking clear."

"She's seventy years old and there's an APB out for both her van and her car. She won't get far."

Becket leaned his head back. He'd wanted to drive but his brother had refused to let him.

He couldn't *breathe*. It was too fucking much. If he lost Sky, he'd never recover.

His phone rang, and he pulled it out to see it was the fire station. He wanted to let it go to voicemail, but he was chief. If they were calling, it was important.

He answered it, almost barking into the phone. "What is it?"

"One of the helicopters that has been doing routine checks in the mountains has reported smoke," Irene said. "It's not far from the highway, but it's a lot. Makes me think an accelerant was used."

"The arsonist." Becket scowled. Just what he fucking needed.

"That's what we're thinking. I'm going to call a few other stations for backup."

He frowned, a thought hitting him so hard in the gut that it almost cut the air right out of him. "The arsonist…"

"Yeah, that's what you said."

He looked at his brother. "It's connected."

Jesse frowned. "What?"

"The fires only started a few months ago. Eloise died in a fire. What if she wants the same fate for Sky?"

"Chief, I don't—"

"She was practicing," Becket said, cutting Irene off. "She was testing different accelerants. Seeing which fire spread the fastest. How long it took crews to respond. She doesn't want Sky to be able to outrun it."

Jesse cursed.

"I think—"

"Irene." Becket cut her off a second time. "Grab my stuff. I'll track your location and meet the engine. I'm coming with you."

"Okay. Sure. See you soon."

He hung up and opened the app on his phone that showed the location of his engines. It didn't take them long to meet up on the road. Once they did, Jesse and the lead engine stopped. Becket jumped out of his brother's car, pulling on his jacket and helmet before climbing in with his crew. Moose drove, while Teddy and Irene sat in the back.

Jesse followed the engine, everyone's lights and sirens on.

Becket glanced at Irene. "You've called for a retardant drop?"

"I have." She frowned at him. "What's going on?"

"Sky was kidnapped."

Moose gasped. "What the hell do you mean, she was kidnapped?"

"Someone took her. And I think that same person set this fire, so she'll be close."

"Jesus Christ," Teddy cursed.

"Faster," Irene urged Moose.

They were speeding down the highway when, up ahead, a dog ran onto the road.

Becket frowned and leaned forward. "That's Rosemary's dog…Bella."

"Who?" Teddy asked.

Moose was slowing to swerve around Bella when Becket shook his head. "Stop!" He jumped out and ran up to the dog. "Hey, Bells."

Bella whimpered, biting his pant leg and trying to drag him into the tree line.

"You know where she is?" Becket asked.

She whined and tugged again.

"Just a sec, girl."

He ran back to the engine and grabbed his pack, the little dog right on his heels.

Teddy rolled down the back window. "Becket, what the hell are you doing?"

"Sky's in there."

"The engine won't fit here," Moose shouted.

"So find somewhere it *will* fit. I'm going in."

"Wait!" Teddy jumped out and grabbed his pack. "You're not going alone."

Becket shook his head. "It's too dangerous."

"Fuck that. If you're going, I'm going."

Becket didn't have time to argue. He looked down at the dog. "Take me to her, Bells."

Bella took off, and they followed her, moving fast toward the smoke.

* * *

THE TREES BLURRED AROUND SKY, the smoke thick in the air.

The fire was moving quickly, and every minute that passed had it spreading faster, not just behind her but all around her.

She didn't even know where she was going. Every muscle in her body was tired and her lungs burned. All she wanted to do was stop and rest, but she couldn't. The flames would swallow her.

Her chest ached from coughing and her knees trembled. She stumbled forward, almost falling.

Where was the road? Or people, or any form of help whatsoever? Would she reach it in time?

Yes. She would make it. She had to.

She hadn't even told Becket she loved him yet, and the thought of him never hearing those words hurt. A physical ache that spiraled through her limbs, competing with the other pains.

Her feet stumbled against the dirt as she ran, skirting around trees, tripping over roots.

Her next breath was more of a wheeze. She tried to leap over another tree root when her foot caught and she fell. Her bound wrists stopped her from fully catching herself, and she hit her head hard on a tree.

Pain crashed through her skull, making a deep fog set in.

She groaned and rolled. When she touched her forehead, a sticky wetness coated her fingers.

Blood.

For a moment, she didn't get up. Her limbs were too heavy and her chest too tight to move. She just wanted to *breathe*, but there was too much smoke. The heat of the flames was too intense.

Get up, Sky. You need to get up! The words were a shout in her head.

She tried to push up, but her arms collapsed.

Come on! You're stronger than this.

The fog threatened to pull her under. But she didn't let it. If she didn't get up, she'd die. And she *was not* dying in this forest.

She shoved herself up again, this time forcing her limbs to hold her. The world spun, a mixture of smoke and flames dancing in front of her eyes. Nausea crawled through her belly, and for a second, she thought she was going to be sick, but she swallowed the queasiness. When she was finally on her feet, she swayed and grabbed a tree.

One step at a time, Sky.

She was whispering the words in her head when she heard something. A noise that she barely registered over the roar of the fire.

She frowned, almost convincing herself it was in her head. That she couldn't possibly have heard his voice.

Then it came again…a shout that competed with the flames.

Becket's voice.

Was he really here?

A part of her rebelled against the idea of him being here, because it wasn't safe. But the other part, the part that barely had the energy to walk, let alone run, let hope bloom inside her.

"Becket?" She tried to yell but her voice was cut off by coughing.

She forced her feet forward, grabbing another tree, then another again, barely keeping herself upright.

"Becket?" she yelled again.

She wasn't loud enough. So weak that she couldn't even yell at full volume.

Suddenly, a second voice sounded, this one less familiar but also male. Was someone with him? Maybe someone from his crew, here to fight the fire.

She took a few more steps, a new determination inside her. A determination to reach Becket. To see his face.

"Sky!" Becket's voice was louder this time.

He was calling for her. He knew she was here.

How?

God, it didn't matter.

She forced her feet to move faster. Black dots danced in her vision, but she blinked them away.

Suddenly, something appeared in front of her. Something small and fast.

"Bella!" Sky gasped.

The small dog closed the distance between them, and Sky dropped to her knees, cuddling her to her chest. "You came back."

Bella licked her face, and Sky looked up to see another figure in the distance...Becket.

CHAPTER 33

This fire was out of control and it was spreading fast.

Becket's feet pounded the earth. Bella had led them straight to the center of it, and the blaze surrounded them. But he didn't stop. He pushed his body faster to keep up with the dog, praying she would lead them to Sky.

"The flames are getting thicker, Beck," Teddy shouted through his mask.

"You can return to the road."

"No. I'm staying with you. You shouldn't be alone."

Bella sped up, and Becket did too.

He pulled the radio from his belt. "Copter 403, this is Chief Hayes from Station 8. How long until the retardant drop?"

A deep voice sounded over the radio. "Station 8, this is Copter 403. We're looking at a couple of minutes."

Dammit.

Suddenly, Bella sprinted into a small gap between two trees. Everything around those trees was alight.

Becket cursed, barely feeling the weight of the pack on his shoulders as he yelled Sky's name and ran between the trees.

Then he heard it.

His heart fucking stopped.

Sky.

He forced himself to move faster.

"Becket! Dammit, I can't keep up," Teddy called.

Becket rounded another tree—then he saw her.

Sky. She was on the ground, blood running down the side of her head, fire raging around her and Bella tucked into her chest.

Alive. Sky was alive.

His knees trembled with relief and he nearly hit the ground.

He dropped in front of her and tugged off his mask. "Are you okay?"

Her eyes were glazed, her pupils too dilated. And there was a wound on her temple.

"I think I have a concussion," she breathed.

"Can you move?"

"Yes, but not fast."

He slipped his mask over her face and grabbed her arm. She'd just made it to her feet when Teddy showed up behind them.

"Thank God!" Teddy gasped.

Sky swayed, her knees almost buckling. Fuck. She wasn't okay.

Teddy took Bella from Sky. "Let's go. We need to move fast."

Becket anchored an arm around her waist and they moved through the trees, trying to avoid the flames that were now everywhere. But every couple of steps, Sky stumbled. And the fire continued to roar behind them, completely unforgiving.

They were moving too slowly.

"I'm going to carry you," he shouted before swinging her up into his arms.

Now he could move faster, running beside Teddy as fast as he could back toward the road.

And the flames grew hotter and taller, behind him, beside him, thick smoke everywhere, making breathing fucking hard.

Teddy pulled out his radio. "Is the drop close?"

"Almost there."

Fuck, they should have been here by now.

A tree suddenly fell several yards in front of them, flames covering it from root to tip.

They were completely trapped. The flames were moving in on all sides, growing closer by the second.

Becket looked at Teddy. They both knew the drop wouldn't come in time.

"We need to deploy fire shelters!" Becket shouted.

Gently, he set Sky onto the ground and took the shelter from his pack. He shook it out quickly and placed his feet inside.

The flames continued to close in on them, and Sky's eyelids began to flutter.

Teddy disappeared beneath his shelter with Bella, while Becket dropped down on top of Sky, tucking the floor panels of the shelter beneath her, the material completely covering their bodies.

"Stay awake for me, honey," he whispered.

He slipped his arms through the hold-down straps and gritted his teeth as the fire blazed over them.

A minute, maybe two, passed before he felt something heavy hitting the shelter.

The retardant drop.

Thank fuck!

Still, Becket didn't move. He remained over Sky's body, holding the shelter down for long minutes, until the forest around them quieted and he was sure they were safe.

Finally, he lifted the shelter to see Teddy doing the same. Becket looked back down at Sky…but she wasn't moving.

He quickly turned her over. "Sky?"

Nothing. *Fuck.* He felt her pulse. Faint but there, and she was breathing. But he needed to get her to an ambulance, and he needed to get her there fast.

He pushed to his feet. "We need to go," Becket shouted. *"Now!"*

* * *

WARMTH SEEPED into Sky's hand. It was a familiar warmth. One she wanted to tug closer. Wrap around her entire body.

But God, her limbs felt heavy and weak.

Her eyes were too heavy to open, so she tried to lift her hand, but it seemed impossible too. Why did moving feel so hard right now? And what was that high-pitched beeping? It pricked at her ears, so loud, the beats at regular intervals.

The warmth on her hand moved, squeezing.

She scrunched her eyes in concentration and forced her thumb to move. Swipe across the back of the hand that held hers.

A sharp intake of air sounded, then a voice.

"Sky?"

Becket.

The beats of her heart stumbled over one another, a new urgency to wake up burned inside her.

Finally, she forced her eyes open. At first, everything was a blur. She shut them for another second, then tried again. That's when he came into focus.

"Beck—" Her lungs spasmed into a round of painful coughing. When she tried to sit up and cover her mouth, she was met with an oxygen mask and a firm hand on her shoulder.

"Whoa, easy, honey." Gently, he urged her to remain still. "You need to rest. You inhaled a lot of smoke."

Smoke. The single word made it all come back to her. Rosemary. Bella. The fire.

She grabbed at her mask.

"Sky—" Becket warned.

She shook off his hand and removed it. "It was Rosemary!" Her voice was croaky and barely sounded like her own.

Anger glinted in his eyes. "I know. We got in contact with Mateo Flores, and he told us that Rosemary was Eloise's grandmother."

"Did you catch her?"

"Jesse's team is looking, but I haven't spoken to him since I got here." Fury shadowed his words.

"Are *you* okay? God—are Teddy and Bella okay? You guys ran into a forest fire for me."

His fingers tightened around her hand. "Everyone's fine. After we got under the shelters, the retardant drop arrived. My crew's still in the mountains working with other stations, making sure the fire's completely out, and I should be getting a notification soon that they're done."

The air rushed from her lungs, which made more coughs rack her chest.

A deep growl rumbled from Becket, and he reached for a glass of water and put the straw to her lips.

Cool liquid coated her throat. God, water had never tasted so good.

When he set the glass back down, she whispered, "Thank you for saving me."

"I was almost too late."

"But you weren't. You got there exactly when I needed you. Thank you."

"You should really be thanking Bella. If it hadn't been for her leading us straight to you…"

He didn't finish his sentence, but he didn't need to. If Bella hadn't done what she did, Becket wouldn't have found her in time.

She squeezed his hand. "Thank God for Bella."

A knock sounded at the door, and they both looked up to see Jesse poking his head in. "Hey. Is now an okay time?"

Sky nodded before once again trying to push up into a sitting position. Becket helped her, even though his pulsing jaw told her that he wasn't happy about it.

"I checked in with your crew—the fire's out," Jesse said.

Becket nodded. "Good."

Jesse's gaze shifted to Sky. "And we picked up Rosemary."

Relief hit her hard in the chest. "Thank God! Where?"

"She was driving down the highway, looking for Bella. She had no idea there was already a warrant out for her arrest."

"Good." Becket's voice was deep and full of rage. It was probably lucky *he* hadn't caught her first.

"Where's Bella?" Sky asked, needing to know that she was okay.

"We called your receptionist, Dolly, who took her to the vet and is looking after her until we figure out what—"

"I'll take her." The words were out of her mouth before she'd finished processing them. But they felt right. How could she *not* take Bella? "She saved my life. Taking her in is the least I can do."

"The least *we* can do."

She swung her gaze to Becket. He wanted to adopt Bella with her? The man hated dogs.

"I'll make it happen," Jesse said, not questioning Becket. "When you're ready, I'll need to get your statement, but that can—"

"No, I want to do it now," she cut in.

Another deep growl from Becket. "Sky. You need to rest."

"No, I need to get this over with." She wanted all of this behind her. She knew there'd be some recovery, both mentally and physically, but the sooner she gave her statement, the sooner that recovery could begin.

She started at the daycare, including every detail she could recall, from the dart in her stomach to Bella running into the woods. She even detailed Rosemary's demeanor, how she never raised her voice or seemed anything beyond mildly angry...just sad, mostly. Like she was genuinely doing what she thought she needed to do for her granddaughter.

"She really seemed to believe that killing me in the same way Eloise had died would bring her some kind of peace," Sky finished, not missing the rigid muscles in Becket's neck.

"Thank you," Jesse said quietly, snapping his notepad closed and hitting the "stop recording" button on his phone. "All of this will be used to make sure she's never a free woman again."

That was good. There was no way she'd feel safe if the elderly woman ever got out of prison, especially when she inevitably found out Sky had survived.

Jesse looked at Becket. "Would you like me to stay?"

Becket shook his head. "Go home to Aspen. Thank you for your backup today."

"Always."

He left the room, and Sky turned back to Becket, studying his hard features and the lines beside his eyes.

"Are you sure you're okay?" she asked gently.

"You almost died today, Sky. I won't be okay for a long time."

Her belly rolled. She *had* almost died. And Becket could easily have died trying to save her.

She gestured to his clothes. "When did you shower?"

The small lift of the corners of his lips almost made her feel better...almost. "Clara brought me some clothes and forced me to shower and change. She said I stunk."

"Good. I'm glad you have family looking after you."

"Speaking of family...I haven't called your mom and dad yet. I haven't been able to think about anything but waiting for you to wake up."

Oh, God, her parents. They needed to know, but at the same time, she didn't have the energy right now. "Let's just leave it for another hour."

He nodded, but his eyes were back to that dark, almost black shade. "How are you feeling?"

She looked down at his hand and traced a vein. "I never would have thought it was her. Even if evidence had been shoved in my face, I don't think I would have believed it."

"Me neither, Peaches. She surprised us both."

"She's locked up now though."

"Thank God."

"No, thank *you*." Sky smiled softly. "And thank Bella."

His lips twitched. "And Bella...who apparently we're adopting."

"Are you sure you want to adopt her with me? You don't even like dogs."

"I like Bella. Plus, you and me come as a team. So if she's yours, she's mine too."

Team. The word did funny things to her chest. "I'm glad you're on my team."

"You have no idea." Something almost primal passed through his eyes. Then he lowered his head and kissed her.

CHAPTER 34

Something wet ran over Becket's face. And what the fuck was that smell?

He opened his eyes to look straight into an open-mouthed Bella. Her face was right there, and she was breathing directly into his mouth. "You know there's this thing called personal space, Bella?"

Instead of running away, the mutt licked him again.

Fucking hell.

He rolled onto his back and scrubbed his eyes. Never would he have thought a dog would be living in his house, yet here he was. "You're lucky you saved Sky's life, or you'd be sitting in a very nice pound right now, eating dry dog biscuits."

If those words annoyed Bella, she didn't show it. In fact, she grabbed the bed sheets with her teeth and yanked them down.

"Hey. I'll get up when I'm good and ready."

She made a small grumbling noise before running to the end of the bed and walking down the steps Sky had asked Holden to build.

He frowned, finally focusing on the other side of the bed.

Sky. She wasn't there. She never started her day before him. And why hadn't he woken up when she'd gotten up?

Bella whimpered from the door.

"Yeah, yeah, I'm coming." He reached for his phone on the side table.

Eight thirty? Fuck, he never slept in this late. Maybe his lack of sleep over the last few weeks, since Sky's attack, was finally catching up with him.

He pushed up and ran his fingers through his hair.

He hadn't slept basically at all for the entire first week. Memories of Sky in the middle of that blazing fire had haunted his dreams. How many times had Sky woken to find him just lying there, eyes wide open? Hell, how many times had he finally fallen asleep, only to wake from a nightmare, needing to check that she was still beside him?

Too many times.

But day by day, he was coming out of it. Accepting that, while she *had* almost died, she was still here. She was alive. Safe. And Rosemary Symes would likely never be a free woman again.

Bella made another grumble.

"I'm getting up."

Her ears perked and she ran out the door.

He followed, pulling on some track pants on the way out.

He stopped dead in the living room at the sight of Sky in the kitchen, AirPods in her ears and only wearing his shirt, which almost hit her knees. She was dancing. Her hips moving in sexy sways that made his dick twitch. Pans sat on the stove and ingredients were everywhere. The room was a mess, but she was all he could see.

He loved her. He loved her so much that he *ached* for her.

His feet started moving before his brain could catch up. He wrapped his arms around her waist from behind.

She gasped, pulling the earbuds out and turning. A slow smile curved her lips as she sank into him. "Hey."

"Good morning, Peaches."

A cute frown cut into her brows. "Do you remember when I hated that nickname?"

She used to scowl at him every time he used it. God, he'd been an ass. "How do you feel now?"

"It's grown on me."

"Really?"

"Mm-hmm." She slipped her hands behind his neck. "A bit like how Bella's grown on *you*."

Bella clearly heard, because she gave a little bark from her bed in the living room.

Becket chuckled. "I think I'm growing on her too."

"It seems to be a common trend." She grinned before turning in his arms and tugging his head down to kiss him. A long, slow kiss that wasn't nearly enough for Becket.

He lifted his head and scanned the counter. Even though it was a mess, there was a stack of pancakes on a plate, bacon in one pan and scrambled eggs in another.

"Making breakfast?" he asked unnecessarily, looking back at her.

"Yeah, I wanted it to be special."

He drew her closer. "Really? Any special occasion I'm forgetting?"

"No. I just have something to tell you." Pink tinged her cheeks.

She tried to turn back to the counter, but he gently gripped her waist, not letting her move. "Tell me now."

Her eyes flared. Then she blinked and shook her head. "No. I made pancakes and bacon, and I'm going to make your coffee just the way you like it." She pushed at his chest. "Now go and play with Bella while I cook."

He shot a look over his shoulder to find Bella lolling on her back, tongue out.

Sky started to turn away.

"I love you."

She gasped and swung back. "What did you say?"

He stepped closer, once again gripping her hips, tugging her into him. "I said…I love you."

He couldn't hold it in any longer. He needed her to hear it. For her to know exactly what she meant to him. How he hadn't already blurted it out, he had no idea.

Emotion flared in her eyes, tears shining through. "One more time."

"I'll say it a million times. I love you. I love being close to you. I love fighting with you more than I love getting along with anyone else. Even when we were just neighbors who pretended to hate each other, the glimpses I got of you were the best parts of my day."

Her lips parted, her chest moving faster, tears shining in her eyes.

Then she whacked him.

"Ow!" He rubbed his shoulder. "What was that for?"

"I was supposed to say it first! I got up early and made this big breakfast. I was going to set the table all nice. You saved my life, so I wanted to make my declaration of love special and be the first to say the words!"

His lips twitched. He shouldn't be surprised she was mad. That was how this had all started. "You think I saved *you*? You saved *me*, Peaches. You added color to my life. I didn't realize I was living in gray shades until you came along. You made my life better."

* * *

SKY CLOSED HER EYES, a single tear rolling down her cheek. He loved her. The words felt big and important and good. So damn good. They wrapped around her heart, squeezing.

Then she opened her eyes and said the words that had been locked inside her for far too long.

"I love you too." Her words were a whisper, barely crossing the distance between them.

His arms tightened around her, emotion shadowing his features. "You do?"

"I love you so much, Becket. And not just because you've saved my life more times than I can count. I love you because you have become my entire world. Even when our relationship wasn't real, it felt like it was."

"It was always real to me."

She slipped her fingers around his neck again. "Thank God I didn't murder you when you butchered my tree."

His lips twitched. "Thank. God."

She drew his head down and kissed the man she loved. This, right here, was home. It was comfort and familiarity and safety.

His tongue ran over the seam of her lips. She opened and he slipped inside, tangling their tongues together.

This man was everything she hadn't realized she needed. He'd crashed into her life, changing everything and making it better.

His hands lowered to her butt, and she yelped as he lifted her and deposited her onto the counter. His mouth started to move down her cheek, then neck. His hands had just started sliding up her thighs when a knock sounded at the door.

"Ignore it," Becket growled.

He nipped her neck. She gasped, and the air in her lungs started to come out in short puffs as his fingers slid up her legs.

The knock came again. Then a chirpy female voice. "Beck? Sky? I know you're home. Your cars are out front. Open the door."

He growled a second time. "I'm going to kill her."

"You won't kill your sister. Then your mother would kill *you*." She pushed at his chest. "You let her in, and I'll throw on some clothes. Tell her she's welcome to stay for breakfast."

"No, she is not. I didn't plan to do much eating."

"Becket Hayes. I cooked you a big breakfast. We *will* be

eating." She leaned forward. "Besides, we have an entire lifetime to make love on the dining room table…just not this morning."

He groaned, and she pecked his lips before hopping off the counter.

Bella followed her into the bedroom, but she didn't miss Becket's angry muttering as he headed to the front door.

She waited for Bella to make it inside before closing the door. The dog had been following her around a lot, but she'd also taken quite an interest in Becket. He pretended he didn't like it, but she knew he kind of did. He was warming to Bella, even if he tried to hide it. She'd known all along this whole hating-dogs thing wouldn't last. Who could hate dogs? It was like hating ice cream. Impossible.

She gave Bella a little belly rub before taking a quick shower.

The last couple weeks had been a blur. She'd taken time off work, and fortunately, Dolly and Pearl had taken care of everything. She still couldn't believe Kristina had been the town thief. The woman had seemed so friendly and genuine, when in reality she'd broken into Sky's home and left her unconscious at the bottom of the stairs.

A shiver shook her at the thought as she threw on yoga pants and a T-shirt.

She'd been wearing yoga pants and T-shirts for weeks because she'd basically been a couch potato while she recovered. Becket had made everything easier though, barely leaving her alone. Her parents had also come over a few times, her mother more than her father.

Like she'd conjured him up with her thoughts, her phone rang, her father's name flashing on the screen.

She answered the call. "Hey, Dad."

"Hi, darling, I just wanted to check in on how you're doing before I head into the church for service."

"I'm good." She perched on the bed, and Bella immediately ran up the steps and sat on her lap. "My breathing gets better every day, and I feel ready to go back to work tomorrow."

"Good. That's good."

She frowned. "Is everything okay?"

"Yes. I just…I've been thinking lately, and I don't really share this kind of thing with you, but I realize I should. I want you to know that I'm proud of you."

Her frown deepened. He'd never said that before. Not with words, anyway. "I know you are."

"Not just for opening your own business but for having your own mind. I thought I knew what was best for you with Tony, but I was wrong. And you were smart to speak up for yourself. Becket's the right man for you."

A burst of warmth punched into her chest. Becket had told her what her father had said to him the day of the barbecue at his mother's house, but her dad had never mentioned anything to Sky. "He *is* the right man for me. Thank you for seeing that."

"He's going to take care of you."

"He's already taking good care of me."

"I can see that." There was a small pause. "I love you, darling. I'm sorry I don't tell you enough."

Tears stung her eyes. "I love you too, Daddy."

"Your mother and I will see you tomorrow night for dinner?"

"I'm making mushroom risotto."

"And I have it on good authority your mother's bringing brownies and potato salad."

"Can't wait."

After a few more pleasantries, Sky hung up, blinking the tears away. She loved her dad, but he wasn't the most forthcoming with his emotions. What happened to her had obviously scared him. It had scared everyone, including her.

Bella nudged her leg, and Sky chuckled. "Yes, I love you too."

She should really be thanking her father. If it hadn't been for his meddling, she never would have grabbed Becket at that fundraiser, and they might not be where they were right now.

When she went back out to the dining room, Clara was hitting Becket on the shoulder. "Becket James. Did you try to take bacon from a woman's fingers? Don't you know how dangerous that is?"

"James?" Sky asked.

Clara looked up at her and grinned. "Yeah, his middle name is James. We only middle-name him when he does something really bad though."

Becket just shook his head.

Clara popped the last bit of bacon into her mouth before lifting a dish. "I brought pesto pasta."

"Clara, you need to stop doing stuff for us. It's been weeks." She had brought over so many meals and given Sky so many free at-home acupuncture sessions. It was wonderful, but Sky was starting to feel guilty.

"I do *not* have to stop. I want to take care of both of you. Even my annoying big brother." She reached up and punched Becket's chest, and he threw an arm around her neck and jokingly ruffled her hair.

They were like this every time Clara came over, and Sky loved it.

Someone else knocked at the door.

"I guess I'll get it," Sky said with a laugh. She opened it to see Holden on the other side.

He grinned at her. "Hey, Sky."

"Hey. Here for Becket?"

"Yeah, we're going for a run this morning."

Becket cursed from the kitchen. "Shit, I forgot."

Holden lifted a brow as he entered the house. "Should I be offended?"

"Nope. But how about breakfast to make it up to you? Clara's already invited herself to stay, so what's one more?"

"Sounds good." Holden crossed into the kitchen. "Hey, Clara." He bumped her shoulder.

Clara's cheeks turned a pretty pink. "Hey."

God, Sky loved watching those two together. If there were ever two people who were destined to date, it was them.

"I'm just going to grab a quick shower," Becket said, pressing a kiss to her head as he passed her.

This time, *her* cheeks heated.

Over the next twenty minutes, Clara and Holden helped her set the table. Every time Holden spoke to the woman, or heck, even brushed past her, she seemed to get a little more shy.

When everything was ready, Sky glanced down the hall. "I'll go check on Becket."

She stepped into his bedroom—well, hers too, with how much time she spent here—just as Becket was pulling a shirt from his drawer.

Man, oh, man, he looked good in just jeans. Would she ever get to the point where looking away from him didn't feel like the hardest thing ever?

Probably not.

"Keep looking at me like that, and we won't make it back out there," Becket said, voice low and husky as he pulled on his shirt. Then he stepped close and curled his arms around her.

"Like what?" she asked innocently.

"Like you want to resume what we started in the kitchen."

Her lower belly rippled. "I'm just looking at the man I love."

A long exhale escaped his chest. "I'll never tire of hearing you say those words."

She rose to her toes, her mouth so close to his that she could feel his breath. Then she whispered, "I love you, Becket Hayes."

"I love you too, Sky Williams." Then he kissed her, and it made every moment leading up to this, every fight and lick of danger, worth it.

CHAPTER 35

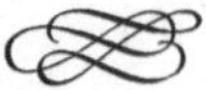

*H*olden Forbes caught the small side glance from Clara.

She did that a lot. Little glances she thought he didn't notice. Looks from beneath her lashes.

They'd been alone in the kitchen for about thirty seconds, and she hadn't said a word, just put her head down as she made coffee.

He should be used to it. He'd been best friends with Jesse for close to eight years and had known Clara for seven of them. She'd been like this since the day they'd met...but only with him. Around everyone else, she was fun and fearless. A completely different person.

And yeah, he wasn't stupid. He knew she had feelings for him. The idea of loving his best friend's little sister shouldn't scare him as much as it did. But he'd felt the weight of losing a loved one before, and he was definitely scared as hell to feel *that* again.

He cleared his throat. "How've you been, Clara?"

Her brows shot up. "Me? I've, um, been...yeah, I've been good. Busy stabbing people with my needles and making their lives better. I've been gardening a lot. Getting sunlight on my skin wherever possible. I started running—"

"Running?"

She frowned, looking him straight in the eye for the first time. "Yeah. Why do you say it like that?"

"How far do you run?"

"I don't know. The streets around my house. Why?"

"You're in remission from cancer and have chronic fatigue."

Her back straightened, pink tinging her cheeks, but he was pretty sure this time it was anger. "I know that."

"Are you allowed to run?"

She took a small step back. "Allowed?"

Shit. Get the proper fucking words out, Holden. "Has your doctor signed off on you running?"

By the narrowing of her eyes, it seemed he couldn't say *anything* right. "Not that it's any of your business, but it's been over five years, and I'm still cancer-free. I can run if I want."

Cancer...he'd just said it himself, but out of *her* mouth, it somehow felt heavier. He fucking hated cancer. He'd watched his mother suffer with it for years, until finally, she couldn't fight anymore. It had taken over his entire life, and when she was finally gone, he'd had no one. No family. No friends to take him in. He'd just been bounced around foster homes for two years until he could finally enlist.

The military had been his salvation. Where he'd finally found his purpose and place in a new world after the old one had been ripped away from him.

He inched closer to her. "It *is* my business because I care about you."

She was family. All of the Hayes' were. His found family.

Her eyes widened slightly, her chest rising on an inhale. But before she could respond, he heard a door opening down the hall, then Becket and Sky walked into the kitchen.

Clara immediately moved back, and while Sky and Clara

carried food to the table, Becket came to stand beside Holden. "Sorry about our run."

"It's fine. We can go anytime." His gaze flicked back to Clara before returning to Becket. He lowered his voice. "Did you know your sister started running?"

Becket's brows drew together. "Alone? She has chronic fatigue."

Holden's thought too.

"How are you and Sky doing after everything?" he asked, needing a change of subject.

Becket looked over at Sky. "She says she's fine, but her breathing isn't back to normal yet and she still has a cough."

"But she's getting better?"

"Slowly."

"Good. And what about you?"

"Not as good, man." The muscles in his arms bunched. "I can't stop remembering her in that fire. Surrounded by those flames. It was a close call. Too close."

"But you got her out."

"Just."

The way Becket looked at Sky made something tighten in Holden's chest. A part of him wanted that. But another part, the part that had felt the loss of those he loved most and the devastation that followed, didn't want to go anywhere near it.

He was about to turn to wash his hands when Clara lifted a mug of coffee…and swayed.

He lunged for her, catching her before she could hit the floor even as he took the coffee from her fingers. "Clara! Are you okay?"

She grabbed his biceps and blinked. "Yeah, I just…got a bit light-headed."

"Fuck, Clara. Is this from your running?" Becket growled from beside him.

Hurt cut through her features, and she looked at Holden like he'd betrayed her. She pushed at his chest, but he didn't release her right away. No way was he letting her fall.

"I *did* go for a run this morning," she started. "And I *am* a bit tired, but I'm also fine."

"If you're passing out, you're not fine," Holden gently pressed.

Her beautiful indigo eyes beamed up at him. For a moment, there was something soft in them. Then she blinked and stepped back, and he forced his hands to drop.

"Thank you both for your concern," she said, a new detachment to her voice. "But I'm okay."

A tense silence passed before Sky cleared her throat. "Why don't we all sit down for breakfast?"

Holden's jaw clenched as he watched Clara retreat from him. There were moments when he wanted to get closer to the woman. When he craved to touch her. Have her.

It would be so easy to love and rely on Clara. Exactly why it was safer to keep his distance.

Order book three, Holden and Clara's story, UNTOUCHED, now!

ALSO BY NYSSA KATHRYN

PROJECT ARMA SERIES

Uncovering Project Arma

Luca

Eden

Asher

Mason

Wyatt

Bodie

Oliver

Kye

BLUE HALO SERIES

Logan

Jason

Blake

Flynn

Aidan

Tyler

Callum

Liam

MERCY RING

Jackson

Declan

Cole

Ryker

BEAUTIFUL PIECES

Erik's Salvation

Erik's Redemption

Erik's Refuge

SHORT CHRISTMAS STORY

Hidden Shadows

RECKLESS SERIES

Reckless Hope

Reckless Trust

Reckless Fall

Reckless Faith

Reckless Love

AMBER RIDGE SERIES

(Series ongoing)

Unafraid

Unraveled

Untouched

JOIN my newsletter and be the first to find out about sales and new releases! CLICK HERE

ABOUT THE AUTHOR

Nyssa Kathryn is a romantic suspense author. She lives in South Australia with her daughter and hubby and takes every chance she can to be plotting and writing. Always an avid reader of romance novels, she considers alpha males and happily-ever-afters to be her jam.

Don't forget to follow Nyssa and never miss another release.

Facebook | Instagram | Amazon | Goodreads